CUT
OFF

DISCARD

DISCARD

Other books by Jamie Bastedo

FICTION

- *Nighthawk!*
- *On Thin Ice*
- *Sila's Revenge* (sequel to *On Thin Ice*)
- *Tracking Triple Seven*
- *Free as the Wind: Saving the Horses of Sable Island*
- *Reaching North: A Celebration of the Subarctic*

NON-FICTION

- *Falling for Snow: A Naturalist's Journey into the World of Winter*
- *Shield Country: Life and Times of the Oldest Piece of the Planet*
- *Trans Canada Trail: Official Guide to the Northwest Territories*
- *Northern Wild: Best of Contemporary Canadian Nature Writing* (edited by David Boyd)

CUT
OFF

JAMIE
BASTEDO

Red Deer Press

Published in Canada by Red Deer Press,
195 Allstate Parkway, Markham, Ontario L3R 4T8
Published in the United States by Red Deer Press, 311 Washington Street, Brighton,
Massachusetts 02135

www.reddeerpress.com

10 9 8 7 6 5 4 3 2 1

Red Deer Press acknowledges with thanks the Canada Council for the Arts,
and the Ontario Arts Council for their support of our publishing program. We
acknowledge the financial support of the Government of Canada through the
Canada Book Fund (CBF) for our publishing activities.

Library and Archives Canada Cataloguing in Publication
Bastedo, Jamie, author
    Cut off/ Jamie Bastedo.
ISBN 978-0-88995-511-0
Data available on file.

Publisher Cataloging-in-Publication Data (U.S.)
Bastedo, Jamie, author
    Cut off/ Jamie Bastedo.
ISBN 978-0-88995-511-0
Data available on file.

Cover and text design by Daniel Choi
Printed in Canada by Friesens Corporation

In memory of Doug Ritchie

Cada cual con su taburete
tiene un puesto y una mision.
(Each with their stool
has a place and a mission.)

*Humanity's greatest desire
is to belong and connect.*
– Jason Russell

*Be yourself.
Everyone else is already taken.*
– Oscar Wilde

CURRENTS

Looking back at seventeen, the memories pour through me like currents in a wild river:

The shadow of tapping shoes on a marble floor.
A rock bouncing off my zebrawood guitar.
A yellow iPhone slapping the surface of a pond.
The sound of crunching plastic, popping glass.
Blood pooling on a computer keyboard.
A long howl gushing out of the mountains.

I wrestle with each memory. I struggle to tame them in my words, in my music. I scout them like a scary set of rapids, searching for a safe way through.

Part I
XELA, GUATEMALA

All through my childhood Segovia's name hovered in the air,
the gentle god of the classical guitar.

– Glenn Kurtz, *Practicing*

ALIENS

I was born into a family of aliens, and not one of us was from the same planet.

My mom's name is Gabriela—Gabby to her buds and family. Her people are K'iche' volcano-dwellers from the mountains. Real live Mayans. Her people were here first. Before the Spanish came and wrecked everything. First people. Native people. *Indígenas*. My mom grew up dirt poor. But she got lucky. She got a job with a big mining company. She met my dad when he was in a good mood. He wanted to be seen with someone from her planet. She wanted to live on his.

My father's name is Edgar McCracken. A Scottish-born miner from Calgary. He came here to dig gold and take it back to Canada. He used to play a lot of classical guitar. He wanted to be famous—like, I mean, world famous. A guitar hero. I guess he thought he was pretty good. No one else did. Now he's a guitar zero.

Even my dog was an alien. Loba, the she-wolf. A

Belgian Malinois, the only one in town. A bully breed. Her great-great-grandparents were bred to rip the faces off attackers. Our so-called guard dog. Before we got Loba, she was a sniffer dog at the airport. But she flunked out. The narco cop who sold her to Dad later admitted she was *"demasiado dulce"*—too sweet.

Dad wanted to put Loba down. Called her useless, a freeloader, resented spending his money on her food.

As if we couldn't afford it.

My little sister Sofi is the red-haired Scottish lass of the family. We look so different, I'd say one of us was adopted if it weren't for our Mayan noses.

Then there's old Uncle Faustus, my grandmother's brother. He used to pick coffee in the mountains. That's where he lived most of the time—in his head, I mean. Walking those mountain trails. Humming those Mayan songs.

So there we were, all living on Planet Xela, in the western highlands of Guatemala.

I know what most people think when they hear that word. Guatemala. Drugs and guns. Crooks and corruption. Violence and poverty. Sure, all that happens in Guatemala. But there's other dark stuff no one's heard about.

Stuff only I can tell, *have* to tell, if I don't want my demons to come back.

PRACTICING

Mimita, my grandmother, was the first to see it. *Mi regalo.* My gift. After watching me fool around on a toy guitar at age four, she told everyone that I was a *niño prodigio*—a child prodigy. "Get a real guitar in his hands," she told my mother, "or his heart will break with longing. *¡Qué talento!*" What talent! "*Exactamente como su padre.*" Just like his father.

Mimita was also the one who named me.

Indio.

Native son. Wild child.

Nine years later, I was sitting in my magic spot, below the domed skylight of the practice room. The acoustics there were so sharp I could hear myself blink. Under the dome, it was impossible to hide a mistake.

I opened the case and took out my instrument, a classical guitar made just for me from Brazilian zebrawood and Canadian spruce. My dad always gave me the best guitars money could buy. He loved buying guitars. It was his only hobby. I won't say how much this one cost. It's kind of embarrassing. But I will say that its voice was incredible.

Some classical guitars shine in the low end, with boomy bass notes that drill into your chest and bust open your heart. Others have amazing mid-range tones that can mimic a singer's voice. Some guitars are famous for their sweet high-end tones that can jerk the tears out of your eyeballs.

This guitar had it all. I could get any kind of voice out of it I wanted. At least, when it was in tune.

I tapped a tuning fork against my knee and brought it to my ear, then plucked the low E string with my thumb. During the night, my guitar had wandered out of tune. It fought with the tuning fork, sending out a fast, whining vibration that got my ears buzzing. I tweaked the string's tuning peg until the whine slowed down, then dissolved as the two sounds melted into one.

I repeated this step with each string, smoothing any choppy sound waves with tiny twists of the pegs. Finally I strummed an open E chord with the back of my fingernails, Flamenco style. My guitar shivered with delight.

I shivered with it, itching to play.

That morning, I had to practice twenty right-hand finger exercises, the Hungarian gypsy scale, and a Russian tune I'd been working on for over a month, "Flight of the Bumblebee." It's a frantic piece that rides a non-stop roller coaster of sixteenth notes. Scares the pants off normal players.

Me? I was loving the ride. Climbing the notes up and up. Spiraling down in a funnel of crazy loops and dives. Then up again, higher each time, until the final streaking climb to the highest note on my guitar.

I'd pretty much nailed it but, as usual, Dad wasn't satisfied.

I caught him stealth-listening at the door again.

My roller coaster nosedived in the dirt.

Through the crack below the door, I could see the shadow of his tapping shoes on the shiny marble floor. I taunted him with random bursts of notes. I sped up. His shoes sped up. I stopped. They stopped. I held the silence, feeling it get heavier and heavier, until he barged in without a knock.

I hugged my guitar tighter. "Can't you just let me play, Dad?"

"Why are you stopping?" he asked. "I've got another concert for you and we don't have much time."

We? I thought. *Who's doing the practicing around here?*

He told me I was to perform "Flight of the Bumblebee" at the *Concierto de Navidad*, the annual free Christmas concert in Xela's Gran Teatro.

I stared at the galloping notes on my sheet music.

"All the usual Xela bigwigs will be there," he said.

Yup. All the bankers and beer-makers.

"Plus a plane-load of mine developers from around the world, coming to tour our gold mine."

I looked up at him for the first time. He'd been playing with his facial hair again. The latest was a skinny Latino moustache. "What's with the new 'stache?"

Dad touched it as if checking it was still there. "Oh, it might win a few votes in the villages near the mine. I paid for a busload of them to come to the concert."

He rubbed his hands together. I noticed his right-hand plucking nails were freshly trimmed. Nails that hadn't stroked guitar strings in years. "This concert will be good for business," he said.

I didn't know if he meant the gold business or guitar business.

In the guitar business, my father had been pushing me harder than ever.

"Every child prodigy needs a reliable stage dad," he once told me. "Someone on the *inside* to cultivate your talent, line up gigs, protect you from crowds."

Yeah, and steal my spotlight.

"Beethoven had a stage dad," he'd said. "Mozart, too. Even Michael Jackson. And look at them!"

Sure, look at them. Mozart burned out at thirty-five. Jackson drugged and dead at fifty. Beethoven dead in his mid-fifties from alcohol poisoning.

Like all their fathers, mine was strict as hell but had a nose for scrounging gigs. Since starting to play seriously at age seven, I'd performed for all kinds of audiences from here to Panama City. Talent shows, recitals, weddings, conferences. I'd even played a roving minstrel riding a donkey in an Easter parade.

I was "the Wonder Boy from Xela" who could play anything on guitar, or so the newspapers said.

My father drilled the basics into me when I was little. When other kids were out heading soccer balls or throwing food fights at school, I was being force-fed Mozart minuets and Bach preludes. But I ate it up as fast as Dad could dish it out. Then, when his gold mine took off, he had no time for lessons so he hired Guatemala's best classical guitar teacher, Magno González.

That's the way Dad told it, anyway. But I think he'd maxed out and had nothing more to teach me. I think he was scared by my talent. Not just scared. Jealous.

The better I played, the more nuts he got over my practicing and performing. Why? I think he wanted me to be the classical guitar god he never was.

Whatever.

The truth is, I loved performing, the feeling of power and control I felt nowhere else but on stage. Just bringing my hands into position over my guitar, before striking a note, could silence a crowd. And the applause! I couldn't get enough. Performing gave me an escape from the grind of practicing, guitar lessons, and home-schooling. From endless hours cut off from the world, behind the ten-foot walls and razor-wire that surrounded our property.

So I welcomed the Christmas gig. It would be no big deal. I'd played in the Gran Teatro before, Xela's fanciest concert hall. The catch for this gig was that it was the first time my father pulled out the Segovia card, a name that would haunt me for the rest of my childhood. Dad's hero, Andrés Segovia, the Spanish god of classical guitar who brought the instrument out of the closet and onto the world stage.

Dad had a plan for me. He wanted me to play "Flight of the Bumblebee" *in double time*. "You can do this, Indio," he said, standing over me with both hands clamped to my shoulders. "If you truly want to be the world's next Segovia, you have to!"

I turned my face away, grossed out by the smell of Scotch on his breath. "Who says I want to?"

The world's next Segovia? I couldn't tell if he was serious or it was only the booze talking.

I got my answer a few nights later when his mining buddies showed up for a nightcap.

COMMAND PERFORMANCE

It happened three days before the Christmas concert. I was sweating over a metronome, ramping up the tempo of "Flight of the Bumblebee" by ten-beat-per-minute jumps. I could feel the muscle memory building in my fingers. I pushed myself hard but never rushed. Every note had to be super clean before I let myself jump to the next level.

I was already way past the tune's original tempo of 170 beats per minute, the way Rimsky-Korsakov wrote it. I discovered I could play faster with a pick instead of my fingernails. My goal became not double time, not even triple time. I was gunning for *seven* times normal speed, about 1200 beats per minute, and I was almost there.

I hoped this little surprise might get Dad to ease up on my practice schedule, at least over Christmas.

I'd stayed up late to practice, just crossed the 1000 beats per minute mark, when Sofi stormed in with her fingers jammed in her ears. "Enough! Enough already! I can't sleep!"

She was wearing her Drama Queen pajamas and had a Scottish fire in her blue eyes—that look I knew too well from Dad. "Okay," I said. "You win."

I went straight to bed and conked out.

At 2:00 AM, I woke to someone else storming in.

Dad.

"Indio, wake up!" he shouted, yanking one of my legs off the bed.

"What? What?"

"I've arranged a special concert for you."

I had a crushing headache. The joints of my left fingers were sore and swollen from screaming up and down the fretboard.

"Come on, it'll be fun," he said. "Right now."

He grabbed my guitar off its stand. I hated the way he held it, like he was strangling it around the neck.

"Hey, watch my—"

"And just *who* do you think paid for this?" He looked at my gorgeous guitar like he was about to smash it.

Like he had that kind of power over me.

Which he did.

"Okay, okay, I'm coming. But who—?"

"Just come!" He steadied himself against the doorframe, trying to focus on me. "And keep those dumb pajamas on. They're perfect. You know, Wonder Boy!"

I ground my teeth at the sound of his laughter as he shuffled down the hall to his study. Where he stored all the guitars he never played and the booze he always drank.

They weren't cruel to me, Dad's mining buddies. They

didn't scowl every time I flubbed a note like Dad did. They didn't critique my playing after each tune like he did. Dad's mining buddies knew dick about classical music, even clapped when I finished tuning. After a few pieces, they ignored me, diving back into their drinks and dirty jokes. I became nothing more than a background musician at Dad's private cocktail party. But every time I tried to sneak away, Dad's arm shot out, pointing to my chair.

I sat down and played another piece. And another.

It wasn't till 4:30 AM, when Dad face-planted over his desk and everyone jumped up, that I ran out of the room crying.

FLIGHT OF THE BUMBLEBEE

Iclimbed the worn limestone steps of the Gran Teatro, counting them, *one-two-three, one-two-three*, like notes on a page of music. My cheeks stung in the chilly evening air, but the handle of my guitar case was all sweaty. I told myself to wash my hands again before walking on stage. Better check my nails while I'm at it.

A hundred pigeons exploded in front of us and ripped through the Greek columns lining the steps. One of them dropped a white bomb on Dad's pinstripe suit. His curse echoed off the cathedral gates way across the Parque Central. "SHIT!"

That's right, Dad, shit.

Sofi burst into giggles.

Mom's hand shot out to grab Dad's arm like he might've struck my little sister. With her other hand, she whipped out a hanky and wiped the mess off his lapel.

Dad glared at her like it was her fault.

People wearing tuxedos, fancy evening gowns, and traditional Mayan dress streamed by my spluttering father. I stopped to stare at them, my fans who had come to hear me play. Or maybe to see their kids on stage dressed up as reindeer.

Whatever.

All that mattered was my music.

"Try not to fart while I'm playing, okay?" I said to Sofi.

She gave me a lung-popping hug. "Go, Wonder Boy!"

Mom ran up the steps and kissed both cheeks. *"Vaya con Dios, niño."* Go with God, son.

Old Uncle Faustus twirled his cane.

Dad flicked me a wave, then drew a quick "s" in the air, his secret code for Segovia.

I turned my back on my family and walked away, head down, counting my footsteps to the stage door. *One-two-three, one-two-three ...*

My act followed a couple of off-key choirs and a Christmas play starring way too many angels. A stage manager with a beard halfway to the floor tapped me on the shoulder. I checked my nails one last time, took a deep breath, and walked onstage, hugging my guitar.

The applause I got when I stepped into the spotlight was almost embarrassing.

Just wait. I'll give you something to clap about.

I was surprised to find my fingers trembling as I set up my footstool. It took me forever to get comfortable on the wooden piano bench set smack at center stage. Somebody thought I needed a music stand, which almost crashed over when I pushed it aside.

Focus, Indio!

I finally looked up at the audience. I easily spotted my family in the front row. Sofi pumped both fists. Mom blew me a kiss. Uncle Faustus raised his hands in a victory salute. Dad was chatting up some bigwig beside him and pointing at me like a proud coach.

Another wave a few rows back. My guitar teacher. Magno had a pen and notepad balanced on his knee. Behind him I noticed a girl about my age, wearing an orange and black Mayan headband. She was staring at the Wonder Boy, a star-struck look on her face.

I felt perfectly prepared for this moment. Hundreds of hours of practicing had drilled each note deep into my fingers. All I had to do was get them moving.

My hands calmed down as I brought them into position. The hall fell silent. Everyone held their breath. Even Dad shut up.

I struck a low E, the opening note of my souped-up version of Beethoven's "Ode to Joy." The string slapped against the fretboard and I took off.

Next up was "Greensleeves," another Christmas crowd-pleaser I could play in my sleep. I followed this with "Capricho Arabe," a minor piece full of acrobatic slides and juicy harmonics.

My fingers behaved. I got lost in the music. I ate up the applause. I could have gone on like this for hours, until the stage manager raised a hand showing five fingers.

Five minutes. Okay. Plenty of time for my finale—if this

applause would ever stop.

I let my hands fall away from the guitar and gave them a shake. This hushed the crowd. I let the silence sink in until I could hardly stand it. The notes inside of me screamed for release.

I dove into "Flight of the Bumblebee," this time at its textbook speed of 170 beats per minute. I looked up after the last frantic note to see Magno nodding slowly, his notebook closed on his lap. Sofi rocked in her seat as she clapped. Everybody was all smiles.

Meanwhile, Dad had a video camera glued to his eye, its red light blinking at me. My stomach clenched. He'd never filmed any of my other concerts.

What's he up to now?

I glanced at the stage manager, who held up one finger.

I winked at him. *Don't worry, amigo, this won't take long.*

I pulled my metronome from my tuxedo jacket, clicked it to silent mode, and cranked the BPM control to 1400. I was on a roll. The crowd loved me. Why not go for a world record? I reached in my back pocket where I always kept my picks ... and froze.

No pick.

I checked all my other pockets, trying to hide a rising panic.

Nothing but a paper clip, candy wrapper, and 50-centavo coin.

Suddenly the spotlight felt like a flamethrower. Beads of sweat splashed onto my guitar strings.

I glanced at the audience and my eyes fell on Dad. Without lowering the camera, he drew another big "s" in the air.

I looked down at my right hand. *What the hell. I'll use my nails. Stand back, Segovia!*

In Spanish, I said, "It looks like I've run out of time so I'll make this quick. I will now play for you the same song, 'Flight of the Bumblebee,' at 1400 beats per minute, more than eight times faster than what you just heard."

A wave of gasps and nervous laughter swept through the audience.

"By the way, if I pull this off, it will break the world speed record on classical guitar."

Applause and cheers. From the back of the hall someone shouted, *"Arriba Indio! Higher! Higher!"*

I took one last look at my flashing metronome and set fire to the strings.

It was all over in seconds but the notes were there! I heard them all, clean as ever.

I dropped my hands from the guitar as the song's final notes echoed through the hall. My heart hammered against my ribs.

Silence.

Then ... a few claps from three balconies above me. The applause spread like a wave. It spilled over the railing, flooded the ground floor, and crashed onto the stage.

They love me.

A thousand people jumped to their feet. The whole theater shook to their applause and cheers.

All except Magno, who scribbled madly in his notebook,

and Dad, whose face was still hidden behind the blinking camera.

I stood and bowed low, noticing for the first time that my nails were in shreds. It would take weeks to get them back in playing shape.

Vale la pena. Worth all the pain.

WONDER BOY

"That was amazing," Mom said as our cook, Katrina, put a plate of scrambled eggs and fresh tortillas in front of me.

"It's not my first standing ovation," I said.

"And definitely *not* your last," Dad said as he walked in and sat down at the breakfast table, surprising us all.

I couldn't remember the last time he'd shared a meal with us.

Sofi squirmed in her seat. "Indio! Did you see the...?" Her words trailed off as she looked sideways at Dad.

"The what?" I asked.

"The video!" she exclaimed. "Dad let me watch it. You were still in bed."

It all came back to me. Dad glued to a camera for most of my act. That red blinking light.

I looked at Dad. "What did you do?"

"Not me," he said, holding up both hands. "What did *you* do? Just broke a little world speed record. That was certainly a nice Christmas present for me."

"With your video, I mean. What did you do with it?"

"*Our* video? I posted it, of course. It went viral overnight, for Christ's sake."

I looked at Sofi for some sign.

"It's cool, Indio," she said. "Can I have your autograph?"

"It'll cost you."

I looked at Mom. "Don't worry, Indio. The only danger is I'll lose my son to show biz."

The worry in her eyes told me she was serious.

Dad chuckled. "A good possibility at this rate. Especially after we beef up our practice schedule."

"*Our* practice schedule? I just finished a monster gig and you're already sending me back in there? To practice? *More?*"

Dad wiped a glob of salsa off his lips with the back of his hand. "That performance was peanuts compared to all the gigs this video will generate." He studied his Blackberry. "In just ... nine and a half hours, we got over *fifty thousand* hits." He leaned across the table and squished my hand under his. "Indio, listen to me, son. You now have fans from as far away as New Zealand, China, Vietnam! Who knows where you'll be performing next?"

"Yeah, but my fingernails are all—"

"Don't worry. You can still bang out the notes. They'll grow back before your next gig."

"Where, Dad?"

Dad leaned back with a big grin on his face. "Hollywood!"

"You mean—"

"Yes, son. Hollywood, California. A big recording company wants to sign you on. Imagine that, Indio!"

I glanced out the kitchen window at a jungle of potted plants Mom put there to hide the wall around our house. Hollywood. Music gods. Fame. *Freedom.*

I looked at Dad. "You could make this happen?"

He closed his eyes, bowing his head to me. "I'm at your service ... *Señor Segovia.*" He straightened up. "That is, *if* you keep practicing."

Mom came behind my chair and squeezed my shoulders. "Edgar, please. At least let the boy watch the video."

"Yeah, Dad. You said it was *our* video."

Dad pushed away from the table and stood over us, jangling coins in his pocket. "Okay, but make it quick."

He led us upstairs to his study where he locked away our family's only computer. I hadn't set foot in there since being held hostage for Dad's mining buddies. My whole body tightened when I entered the room.

We all squeezed around his desk, cluttered with maps and fat reports about his gold mine. He grabbed one open report, slammed it shut, and shoved it into a filing cabinet. As the drawer closed, I leaned over to catch the title: *Security Tactics for Depopulating Mine Site.* He shot flaming arrows at me. "Sorry—that's classified information."

He hunched over the keyboard as he punched in a long password. A freeze-frame of me on stage popped on the screen. At first I didn't recognize myself. This little man dressed in a tuxedo and frilly shirt, hugging a classical guitar.

"Hit play, Dad," I said.

Up jumped the title: *Guatemala's Wonder Boy—World's fastest classical guitar player.*

"Just in English?" I asked.

Dad shrugged. "That's where the money is."

Magno sometimes filmed me playing to help correct my posture or finger technique. Or he'd make audio recordings so I could check my tone and dynamics. But I'd never watched myself perform.

The sound wasn't great through Dad's little camera. And when it got to the flaming finish of "Bumblebee," my whole arm blurred. But like I thought onstage, all the notes were there. The feeling was there. And God, the speed.

It actually sounded pretty amazing.

The comments were even more amazing. Dad let me scroll down the first of many pages:

OMG Indio! I cried during your Capricho piece. I'm not ashamed of it. I actually cried.

Too amazing for words! Now I want to go to Guatemala, just to learn from you. Do you mind that I am five times your age?

one word of advice: keep a fire extinguisher handy when you play that bumblebee thing. that was SO HOT!!! :D

How I wish I could see you perform live. Please come to Zambia soon. You can stay at my house.

Love Kakanda. 😊

God bless you, Indio. It's hard to believe you are so young and have so much more music ahead of you. Please take care of yourself. You are a world treasure.

I looked at Mom. She gave me a little hug around the waist. I had to wipe my eyes to see the screen clearly. For the first time I could remember, maybe ever, I had this feeling that life is good. That besides my dog and my guitar, I could make some real friends, even if they might only be online. A new door had opened for me. A door to freedom.

I clicked on the *show more* button, a small act I may regret for the rest of my life.

My only question: how did such an amazing musical prodigy end up with such a sick name?

Indio.

What was Mimita thinking when she gave me that name? *Nacido del suelo*, she told me before she died. Born of the soil. *Niño salvaje*. Wild child. Or just plain, "Indian," whatever that was.

But Mimita, when you named me, did you know its other meanings?

Dirty savage. A fool.

And then this comment.

Sensational! The spirit of Segovia lives on in you!

I shook my head. *Jesus. They just had to mention Segovia.*

Dad broke into a crazy smile. He pointed a fat finger at the screen. "What did I tell you, Indio? Segovia! The next Segovia! Anyone can see it!"

I tried to grab the mouse, but he flicked my hand away and put the computer to sleep.

"Hey!"

"That's enough for now," he said. "You don't want this to go to your head."

"Yeah, but I just want to see the rest of the—"

"You'd be on the computer all day. I've got important work to do."

I stared at Dad's locked filing cabinet. "So, uh ... what does de ... depopulating mean?"

Dad scowled. "I told you it's none of your business." He pushed me away from his desk so hard I almost fell over Sofi.

Mom reached for my arm before I hit the floor. "*Jesucristo*, Edgar! What are you doing?"

Dad glared at the mess on his desk. "Uh ... sorry, Gabby. I didn't mean to—"

Sofi stepped in front of me like a human shield. "You did so!"

I loved how Sofi stood up to him. Better than I ever could.

Dad turned to me with his coach face back on. "Now, Señor Segovia, shouldn't we be practicing? It's going to take a lot more work to keep all your new fans happy."

THE SOURCE

A week later, Dad had me working on two new pieces for the Hollywood gig, Beethoven's "Pathétique" sonata and Tárrega's "Lagrima." Pathetic tears. Right up my alley.

After two solid hours of practicing, I got up to have a pee, eat a couple of Katrina's brownies, and bury my nose in Loba's furry neck.

Instead of opening a door, Dad's viral video of my Christmas gig had slammed it shut and locked it. Seriously. *Locked it.* The door to my practice room.

Mom had pleaded with Dad to drop his crazy lockdown plan to get me to practice more—"to help squeeze the Segovia out of you," he'd said. His solution? Hire someone to build a little bathroom inside the practice room and install a bar fridge for snacks. So I wouldn't shit myself or starve to death while practicing.

"And what if there's a fire or something when he's locked in there?" Mom asked him.

Dad said I could jump out the window into the swimming pool.

Very thoughtful, Dad.

I returned to my stool and set my guitar vertically on my lap. I wrapped my arms around her waist and breathed in her woodsy scent. I drooped my chin against her curved shoulder and pressed my cheek against her neck. I'd been doing this since I was little, hugging my guitar. Sometimes, if I closed my eyes, I got the feeling she was hugging back.

I heard the security gate rattle open. A car thumped over our cobblestone driveway. Muffled conversation in the kitchen. Footsteps echoed up the marble stairs. The thump of Loba's tail. A knock at the door.

"Come in," I said, "if you've got a sledge hammer."

Dad had programmed the electronic lock to open on Sundays at exactly 3:00 PM. Along with an amazing ear, my guitar teacher had a perfect sense of timing. The moment I saw the doorknob begin to turn, there was a soft click as the lock automatically disarmed.

"*Buenas tardes,*" my teacher said. Good afternoon.

"Hey, Magno."

That's the only Spanish I'd hear from Magno all day. He liked to teach in English. No surprise, since the guy trained at the Royal School of Music in London, England. He took off his New York Yankees ball cap, revealing the shiny top of his mango-shaped head. Not a stitch of hair except for a soul patch below his lower lip.

"Brownie?" I asked.

He opened his case and lifted out his two-hundred-year-old rosewood guitar. "What, and soil my darling? Let me earn it first."

He pulled up his chair, so close our knees almost touched. He looked at me, reading my mood. "I know you're under a bit of pressure these days."

"A bit? This Segovia thing is going to kill me."

Magno leaned back and closed his eyes. "Between you and me," he said slowly, "keep it the *Indio* thing."

"Hah. Tell that to Dad."

"Segovia didn't hit the stage until he was sixteen. Look at all you've done. Only thirteen."

"Yeah, no pressure. Dad's lined up gigs for me in Peru and Panama next month. A recording session in Hollywood the next."

Magno raised his eyebrows. "You see? Segovia's got nothing on you."

I used to love listening to Segovia's recordings, playing his music. Now, just the sound of his name made me sick. "Segovia got me into this mess. I *hate* him."

"Look, Indio, whoever you're trying to be, you won't go anywhere carrying all this tension. It's infecting your playing."

"What do you mean?"

Magno leaned forward, ready to dissect every note with his razor ears. I *so* knew that look. It didn't matter if it was Bach or the blues, Magno had a way of "deep listening," as he called it, like he heard past the guitar, past my fingers, past even the composers, to that place inside where they first found the music.

Magno called it "The Source."

I could tell it was going to be an intense afternoon.

"Play me the Capricho," he whispered.

I took a couple of deep yoga breaths, like Magno had taught me. I wanted to play notes that were perfect in every way. The right volume, clarity, timing, and tone. Just like he could.

Forget Segovia. I wanted to play like Magno.

I got the beat going in my head. *One-two-three, one-two-three.* I lightly plucked the first harmonic at the seventh fret. I was ten bars into the piece, just about to jump into the main theme, when Magno pinched the top of his nose and pointed a finger at my guitar.

"Stop. Right there. *That's* what I mean."

"What?"

"That tension. Look. You're white-knuckling the guitar, clutching it like it's trying to escape. You're breathing funny. Tension screws up everything."

He made me stand up, touch my toes, walk several times around the practice room. Loba got up and followed me, wagging her tail like we were going for a walk.

"Now, start again."

He was right. This time, all I was aware of was the tension, in my shoulders, my arms, my hands. A vice squeezed my brain.

I stopped halfway through. "Now every note sounds crappy."

"Your notes are there," Magno said. "Your technique is there. You just have to lighten up. Free the music."

"In this prison?"

Magno tapped his perfectly sculpted fingernails on the side of his guitar. "Don't think of this room as a cage, Indio. Think of it as a ... a *refuge*, a musician's dream, sheltered from the craziness of the world. You should thank your father for that fancy lock."

As much as Dad paid him, Magno couldn't hide the sarcasm in his voice. I knew he was talking bullshit. "Yeah, really."

Magno stroked his soul patch. He carefully pulled on each finger, one by one, then shook them out. "Come on. Play Capricho again for me. This time together. Keep an eye on my fingers, not yours."

He played quietly, the sound of his instrument teasing the notes out of mine. As I watched his fingers, I imagined he was in control of both guitars. I'd played this piece hundreds of times. That day, I felt Magno leading me somewhere I'd never been before. Somewhere too scary to go alone.

I concentrated harder on his fingers, forgetting that mine were moving. That they even existed. And then something strange happened, like a bolt of lightning opened my chest. What we were playing was *so* beautiful. But I couldn't tell where the music was coming from, his guitar or mine.

My heart started jumping. I got this freaky urge to scream.

"Just keep playing," Magno said softly.

I refocused on his fingers, so graceful, so natural, like they were made for only one purpose: to glide up and down the fretboard of a guitar. My heart settled down. I breathed into the music until ... it just felt good. I stopped worrying about how it sounded, about what Magno thought, or even what Dad might think. The music came alive under my fingers and I just let it go.

And with it, a few tears. Happy tears.

"That's it. Let it come, Indio. Find the music. Follow it to The Source."

The last D-minor chord ricocheted off the dome above us. We looked up at each other, smiling.

Then we both turned to the window.

Somebody was shouting outside the gate. No ... it was several voices, chanting something.

I stood up and took a step toward the window. Someone screamed and a fist-sized rock came crashing through the glass. I watched it spin in slow motion, straight for my guitar. I wrapped both arms around it—too late! The rock bounced off my guitar with an awful twang. I flinched like it had struck me in the face.

Loba jumped up, sniffed the rock, and snarled.

"What the hell?" Magno cried.

I looked down at an ugly dent in the flowered rosette surrounding the sound hole. "My guitar!"

Magno took the guitar out of my shaking hands and pulled me away from the window. "Don't worry. I know someone who can fix your—"

A shower of stones clanged against the metal gate. "My car!" He set my instrument in its case, like a doctor settling a wounded patient. "Keep back," he said, slapping on his ball cap. "Bullets could be next." Then he ran out to check on his precious Corvette, the only one in Xela.

Another volley of stones against the gate. The chanting rose.

"¡Sí a la vida! ¡No minería! ¡Sí a la vida! ¡No minería!" Yes to life! No to mining!

I grabbed my binoculars and placed myself in the only corner of the practice room where I could glimpse the outside world. Between the razor-wire at the end of the wall and the bullet-proof windows of the guardhouse was a v-shaped gap I could peek through to watch normal people doing normal things on the street and in the park across from us.

What I saw was not normal.

A bunch of village women dressed in traditional Mayan clothing marched in a circle in front of our gate. Men stood in a ring around them, arms locked together. Some people waved signs.

¡La mina no pasa! No to the mine!

¡Te duele la mina oro! The gold mine hurts you!

Dejar de robar! Stop stealing!

Everyone was shouting. Little kids ran around the mob, throwing rocks at our house.

Dad came running out of the house with his cell phone glued to his ear, yelling orders at Juan Carlos, his bodyguard. Juan Carlos nodded, whipped out his handgun, and fired three shots into the sky.

More stones. Angrier chanting.

I heard police sirens, a squeal of tires, and seconds later, loud bangs. Two smoky things rocketed into the mob. Everyone scattered with their hands over their faces.

Tear gas!

White smoke leaked through my smashed window. My eyes started stinging like crazy. Loba whimpered behind me, madly rubbing her eyes with both paws. Through the tears and smoke, I recognized someone wearing an orange and black headband. The Mayan girl at the Christmas concert. The one who seemed so blown away by my music.

Today her face was creased with rage.

Would you still clap and cheer for me if you knew I was caged in here? If you knew I was the mine owner's son?

XBS

Soon after I turned fourteen, I got to go to a real school. This was hardly your typical Guatemalan school. I mean like the one Mom talks about from her own past, with crumbling classrooms packed like sardine cans.

Instead, my parents sent me to a ritzy school for ritzy kids. The Xela British School or XBS. My social studies teacher told me that some British ambassador started it years ago, felt sorry for the poor Guatemalan rich kids. Thought they should all speak the Queen's English.

At first, Dad totally opposed the high school idea. "How are we supposed to make a Segovia out of the boy if he's out playing soccer or goofing off at school dances?" he asked Mom

Sounded good to me.

"How can we make sure Indio's safe out there?"

Truth is, I think he saw me as juicy bait for narco-kidnappers who would've happily traded me for his fortune.

Mom, on the other hand, saw school as good medicine

for what she called my *melancolía*, depression.

So, after a few rounds of shouting and table banging—of course, I was upstairs sweating over my guitar through all this—my parents reached a compromise. I could go to school two days a week, Mondays and Fridays. The rest of the week, it was two hours a day of home-schooling from my tutor, Luiz, followed by five hours of practice. On Saturday, Dad bumped it up to six hours—even higher than Segovia's daily max of five—followed on Sunday by a three-hour lesson with Magno.

If Dad was doing his stealth-listening thing at the door and I slacked off or took too many breaks, he would barge in with a wooden mining stake in hand and plunk down in Magno's chair. He'd sit there, watching my every move, as if he had something to teach me.

As if.

I had outstripped my father's guitar chops years ago and he knew it.

Hated it.

Sometimes, especially if he'd been drinking and I flubbed a couple notes, he'd whack me across the shins with his mining stake. If I lost the beat for a second or played a tempo Dad didn't like, he would stomp down on my tapping toe, once so hard it turned purple.

My father's dream of guitar glory had become my nightmare.

Before high school, I lived like a monk. A forgotten, beaten monk cut off from the world.

Now I had an escape hatch, at least a temporary one.

Even though it was only a twenty-minute walk from our house, Mom insisted that Juan Carlos drive me to and from school.

That rock through my window had changed Juan Carlos. The mine protests had been snuffed out by regular police patrols of our neighborhood and bigger guns for Dad's guards. But things were heating up in the villages near the mine, and it was making front-page news. All this made Juan Carlos extra twitchy.

Juan Carlos had been in my life forever. He was almost like a *tío*, an uncle. Mom told me that when they brought me home from the maternity ward, Juan Carlos arranged a police escort for me, sirens and all. It was like all those years he'd worked for my father were a waiting game for Something Big. And, after so many boring days raking Dad's tennis court, skimming leaves from the swimming pool, lifting weights in the garage, or picking Loba's crap off the lawn, he couldn't wait for it.

Juan Carlos had started wearing his Beretta handgun on his belt instead of hidden under his jacket in a holster. He told me that he'd shaved his head, ponytail and all, to get a cleaner shot if he needed to. "Right in the forehead," he said. He insisted we rehearse the *protocolo*—the battle plan—in case somebody started tailing us or tried to rip me out of the car. He'd suddenly whip out his handgun and shove me under the dashboard so I didn't get caught in the crossfire. Or he'd look in the rearview mirror, go all bug-eyed, and floor it like some narco scumbag was chasing us.

All this while driving me to school.

My biggest surprise when I first arrived at the school was that half the students came from somewhere else. I mean like, u.s.a., England, China. Even some real live Canadians, the only ones I'd ever seen besides my dad and his mining buddies.

Juan Carlos called them "expat brats." The kids of expatriates, foreigners who worked in Guatemala for a few years, made a pile of money, then took off. The rest were rich Guatemalan kids.

The trouble was, I didn't know where I fit in, with the expat brats or the *rico Guatemaltecos*. So I mostly kept my head down as I roamed the grassy campus from class to class. I blended in as best as I could in my blue tweed blazer and red tie.

Things were pretty crappy the first few weeks. Sports were huge at the Xela British School, but the only activities I'd ever done that faintly resembled sports were backflips into our swimming pool and kicking a soccer ball around the lawn with Sofi, Loba, and the guards.

They even played hockey at xbs, on one of Guatemala's few indoor ice rinks. Of course, everyone expected that I knew all there was to know about Canada's national sport. Nobody got that I was actually born here. The only ice I'd ever seen was in my father's Scotch glass.

What I really wanted to play was soccer. *Fútbol*. But the first time I tried out, I tripped over our own goalie and popped a ligament in my plucking thumb. This made practicing almost impossible and forced Dad to cancel all my gigs until it healed.

Did I ever pay for *that* in bruised shins!

Dad threatened to yank me out of school until I promised, "Okay, no more soccer!"

Academics did not go well either. Everyone else was light-years ahead of me, thanks to Luiz's freewheeling approach to home-schooling, and the fact that I had little space in my brain or my schedule for anything but guitar.

Things turned around when, instead of going to soccer practice, they let me loose in the computer lab.

I'll never forget that day.

I was alone in the lab with an hour to kill before Juan Carlos came for me. For the first time in my life, I was free to sit down at a keyboard and screen and do something that millions of kids my age did every day, as easy as breathing.

Go online.

I could taste the forbidden fruit my father had locked away from me for so many years, "in the best interest of practicing," of course. The joke was, as I waited for my computer to boot up, I noticed a familiar pick and shovel logo on its side from one of the school's sponsors, CanaMine, the Canadian mining company whose president was none other than Edgar McCracken.

My computer whirred to life. I clamped on headphones and brightened the screen to max. The Internet opened up and drew me in like a powerful magnet. I was free-falling through a wormhole into a whole new world.

The cyber world.

The forbidden fruit tasted good. *Very* good.

I discovered hilarious videos, pictures, and games. Cool

sites featuring movie trailers, science news, and live sports. Online shopping, teen chat groups, and blogs.

And the music! All the classic bands Magno had turned me on to over the years. My headphones shook to the songs of Pink Floyd, Nirvana, and Metallica. Coldplay, U2, and the Beatles. For the first time, I could watch bands playing riffs that Magno snuck into our lessons when we knew Dad wasn't listening at the door or was out at the mine. I dipped into a few classical guitar videos, but most of them were so amateur to me, it was painful to watch and I quickly moved on.

I surfed tourist videos of exotic lands. Africa, India, Australia. I visited Canada, as familiar to me as Pluto.

My head swam. My heart pounded. I lost myself in a flood of dazzling information, flashing images, and pulsing sounds.

Until somebody poked my shoulder and I almost jumped out of my chair.

"Excuse me, *chico*, but it ees time."

I turned to see Jorge, the school janitor.

"Everybody home esept you and me."

"What?" I said, slowly returning to the world of 3D people and things. "Oh, right." English was a struggle for Jorge but it was the law at XBS. For both students and staff, the penalty for speaking Spanish was no ice cream privileges for a week.

"Your ride ees here."

"*Gracias*, Jorge." I scooped up my backpack and ran for the door.

"Eh, wait! You ees the bumblebee boy, no?"

"The what?"

"*Abejorro*, bumblebee. I watch the movie of you playing at Christmas concert. That was, how you say, awwww-some!"

"Oh. That."

"You must play school concert. Band Night. Lots of fun games, good food, prizes, *y mucha música viva.*"

I'd seen the posters but ignored them. Playing guitar was the last thing I wanted to do at school. Hadn't I fought to come here to escape from all that? What would a music geek like me have to offer a bunch of super-achieving jocks and bookworms? Who could care less about my kind of music, anyway, let alone understand it?

"But I'm not in a band, Jorge."

He laughed, showing a serious lack of teeth. "You can be a one-man band." He opened his hands to the ceiling. "*¡Por favor*, Indio! Please."

There was something in Jorge's begging face that softened me up. So far I'd been most comfortable with the guards, cleaners, and kitchen staff at school. In my father's walled world, I'd never learned to make friends my age. Maybe I'd do better if I made a splash at the school concert.

Then this thought. Maybe I could start my own blog about my music and stuff and see where it took me. See if anyone out there might find me interesting.

"I'll think about it, Jorge. *Buenas noches.*"

My pack pounded against my back as I sprinted across campus, almost tripping into the swimming pool. I was propelled by a delicious new lightness, like a bird set free from its cage. In those stolen moments, running wild on the computer, I'd discovered another reality that promised everything that was missing in my life.

Connection, freedom, and friends.

FIRST BLOG

Looking for fame in all the wrong places: Musings of a caged guitarist

FINDING YOUR HAT

Hey guys. Have you heard the rumor that we're all plunked on this planet for a reason? I mean all 7,391,825,982 of us (last time I checked the human population clock, anyway. Here's the **link**).

Have you figured out your reason yet? Lucky you.

Still working on it? Don't worry. All is not lost.

"Wait! Who's at the keyboard?" you ask. Good question, since this is my very first blog. I'm basically a 14-year-old guy living in Guatemala. Living here, yes. Born here, in fact. But notice I didn't say, "I'm Guatemalan." That's something I'm still working on. More later.

It's one thing to spend your whole life figuring out what hat to wear. It's another thing when life hands you the whole outfit and says, "Here, put this on. This is who you are."

Don't ask me how it happens—fate, space aliens, or a fanatic parent—but it happens. (Trust me, I know. It happened to me.) Maybe you're handed a soccer uniform. Or salsa shoes. Or a white lab coat. You put it on and away you go down a sunny path. You know what to do with your life.

On the flip side, maybe you're fumbling around in a dark maze, bumping into brick walls. Your life is full of detours and dead ends. You're still looking for that special path only *you* can walk.

Well, in my case, life handed me a guitar. When I was just four years old, my father shoved a three-quarter-size classical guitar into my little hands. Lessons started soon after. You know, nylon strings, playing Bach and Beethoven, with one leg up on a funny little footstool. That's me.

Ever met a child prodigy? Well, now you have. Me. Or so my father keeps telling me.

Maybe you've heard of me: Guatemala's Wonder Boy. The Bumblebee Boy. World's fastest classical guitar player. "And just a kid!" shout the newspapers. *¿Muy glamoroso, no?* Very glamorous, right?

FAME: NOT ALL IT'S CRACKED UP TO BE

But I'll tell you a secret: that little guitar, and a bunch more since, burned up most of my childhood. Some days, stuck in my practice room, just me and my dog, listening to kids in the park or laughing in the street, I wish I was out there bumping into brick walls, still looking for my special path. Days when I'd happily trade the spotlit stage for a dark maze, looking, looking, while maybe having a life on the side.

Except at last Saturday's Band Night at xbs. "What's that?" you ask. The name of my band, of course: X-rays Beat Sunshine. Haven't heard of it? Where ya been? Actually ... no. I lie. It's the name of my school. xbs. The Xela British School. At first I was dead against going to Band Night, let alone playing. Why bother with a Mickey Mouse talent show when I can perform for a thousand people in fancy theaters across Latin America? When I've got a recording gig lined up in Hollywood, California?

But a secret fan twisted my arm and I went for it (*¡Gracias, Jorge!*).

And am I glad I did! It was like my first real picnic, like some big happy family out on the grass with tents and a stage. Okay, so the sound system crackled and spit. The flashing stage lamps were too fast and freaky. The tent leaked when it rained. But I didn't care. There was no tight-ass stage manager poking my ribs to get me the hell on and off stage. No stuffed shirts or fashion queens in the audience. No reporters shoving microphones in my face like I was some walking, talking freak show.

Just live music, laughter, and light.

TWO LESSONS

I learned two things at Band Night. First, no matter what life hands us, a sunny path or a dark maze, we can get lost and lonely either way. That was me for sure—before Band Night, I mean. Second thing I learned: the highest walls are inside us.

Fear's a biggie. Judgment, too. In my case I have to add snobbery. I'm a child prodigy, remember. After playing for you at Band Night, mixed in with your cheers and applause, I could almost hear the sound of those inner walls crashing down.

NO TURNING BACK

To my new friends at xBS, I felt your love that night and I'm firing hug bombs back at ya. I can't return to my empty practice room without taking you with me. Thank you, thank you!

To those on the other side of the planet who sadly had to miss the 20th annual xBS Band Night, I promise to post a video of my performance. It features a reggae version of Beethoven's "Moonlight Sonata" and a classical version of Chuck Berry's "Johnny B. Goode." That is, once I figure out how to post a video! No kidding, I've never done this. I'd barely touched a computer until I was fourteen. Forbidden, actually. Outlawed. Taboo.

That's part of my story. Please stay tuned.

You've read this far, so I'm guessing you might actually be interested in learning more about my music and life and stuff. Feel free to share my blog with your buds who might want to check it out: **www.CagedGuitarist.blogspot.com.**

But please remember, I'm a newbie teen blogonaut. How am I doing so far?

Yours inside the music, Indio ♫

CLASS DISCUSSION

One Monday a few weeks after Band Night, our hippie social studies teacher, Adam Upjohn, announced that the next Friday we would be going to visit a huge foreign-owned mine. "To help understand," as he said, "what Guatemala does and does *not* get out of such megaprojects."

I looked up from the back of the class. Adam was staring at me. "It happens to be a Canadian mine, Indio, the Eldorado gold mine. Would you happen to know anything about it?"

"Uh ... no sir," I said, which was more or less true, since Dad never talked about his work, other than to bitch about "the local natives throwing a wrench in the works." What instantly worried me was that my classmates would connect me with the mine and blackball me as a greedy racist pig.

Which would be kind of ironic since I'm half Mayan.

Then it occurred to me that once Dad found out about this field trip, he'd go ballistic and pull me out of school. Which would bring the guillotine down on my budding friendships. And my blog.

In the friend department, there was now a lot at stake.

My first blog caused quite a stir, both at school and in the far corners of cyberspace. Teens from around the world asked me how I'd possibly survived so long without going online. Don't you know that our generation was born with special gills to swim in the cyber sea?

Or how can a musical prodigy have a normal life? I've been chained to a cello since I was four. Any tips on smelling the flowers?

Or what's my real nationality? You grew up in Guatemala but say you're not Guatemalan, so ... what are you?

Others asked me heavy questions about fate versus free will, as if I was some kind of online shrink. My parents think I'm God's gift to cricket but I'd much rather play soccer. Help!

When I started blogging, I never thought much about answering a bunch of questions, let alone how much time that would take. I just wanted to connect with somebody, anybody. Once I figured out how to embed videos of me performing, the comments really started piling up. I spent most of my free hours at school answering them.

But God, it was worth it.

What the hell kind of music is that—truly badass classical funk? Whatever. Keep doin it. Sweet.

God has blessed you with the balls of an artist. Keep them rocking!

fuckin amazing. im blown away

Wonder Boy, we're so proud of you!

¿Cómo puedes ser tan bueno, tan pronto? ¿Empezar a practicar en el vientre de tu madre?

Good question. How did I get so good so fast? Practicing in my mother's womb? I didn't bother answering that one. I wanted to feed the mystique. Keep the focus on performing, not practicing, the thought of which made me nauseous.

People even asked for pix of me that they could use as screensavers or to pin up on their walls.

How ridiculous is that?

But of course I posted them.

A picture of me and my new tousled hairstyle, jamming with a couple of rockers backstage after Band Night.

A picture of me in my tuxedo, performing "Flight of the Bumblebee" at Xela's Gran Teatro, my right hand a total blur.

A picture of me balancing my guitar on one finger while standing on Nevado Huascarán, Peru's tallest mountain. Okay, so I faked some stuff. I was learning tons on the computer and loving it.

So there I was in class, wishing this field trip to my dad's gold mine would blow away, yet curious to see just how bad it was on the ground.

Adam, who refused to be addressed as "Mr." like all our British teachers, held up a bunch of news printouts from around the world and read out the headlines.

Latin Mining Boom: Who wins? Who loses?

Blood-stained Minerals

Guatemala's Eldorado Mine: All that Glitters is Not Gold

Hidden Hegemony: Canadian Mining in Latin America

Katie put up her hand. "What's a ... hegemony?" she asked. If you look carefully at the photo of me jamming, you'll see a girl with long chocolate hair and a square, serious face, drumming on my guitar case. She kept wiggling her legs in time with our music and I found it a little distracting. In a good way, I mean. That was Katie with the nightingale's voice. A banker's daughter from Toronto, Canada.

Adam stroked his 70's sideburns. "Hmm. Any takers?"

Tang from Hong Kong sat up straight and inhaled sharply. He had all the answers but seemed allergic to raising his hand.

"Yes, Tang?"

"Hegemony. The dominance or control of one group over another, sir."

"And who's controlling who in this context, do you think?"

Modesto flicked a hand at Adam. He's one of the *Guatemalteco* rockers I played with after school. We were even thinking of starting a band. "With all respect, sir," he said, "I would say it's the Canadians screwing the Guatemalans."

An outbreak of barely controlled laughter.

I caught Katie's eye and felt my cheeks flush.

Adam almost smiled. "Interesting. You think so, in spite of the mining dollars that help support this very school?"

Modesto laughed. "A few computers? Soccer trophies? That's token, sir. Optics. Window dressing."

"I see. Let's explore this topic further on Friday, shall we? Please prepare two interview questions before we set out for the mine."

Adam waved a couple of fingers at me as we piled out of class. "Indio, can I talk to you?"

"Uh ... sure. What's up?"

"This mine trip. You okay with it?"

"Well, yeah. Why wouldn't I be?"

Adam took off his glasses and wiped them on his psychedelic tie. "It's just that ... your father—"

"Does he know we're going?"

"I'm not sure. We have our own contacts. Villagers, not miners."

"Oh."

Adam put his glasses back on and studied me like one of his aquarium fish. "You could skip this field trip, you know. It's not like it will be on the Social Studies exam."

"No, I'll go. It's just that ..."

"Yes?"

"Well, maybe I could just be Joe Student for the day? Like, everyone doesn't need to know that I'm—"

"The mine owner's son? Certainly, Indio. I can respect that."

"Do you have to tell my parents where we're going?"

Adam gave me a sly look. "On paper this is simply a field

trip to some K'iche' villages in the highlands."

My mother's home turf. My father's mine. I'd never made the connection.

"I'm cool with that," I said.

"Tickety-boo, Indio." Adam gave me a firm British hand-shake. "Joe Student it is. We'll see you Friday."

ELDORADO MINE

I managed to tiptoe through the rest of the week without spilling the *frijoles* about Friday's field trip. I stuck to my practice schedule, even putting in extra hours. I tried my best to focus on Luiz's home-school ramblings. I kept my nose clean. Dad seemed oblivious to the fact that kids from the school he sponsored were going to snoop around his mine.

I passed a good chunk of those nights lying awake composing my next blog post or planning my next video. Of course, with no access to a home computer, I had to hold all this in my head, or get up ten times to scribble down ideas before they faded from my burned-out brain. I worried that the field trip might interfere with my regular twice-a-week posting. Already there were hundreds of teens around the world expecting it and I couldn't let them down.

I was still waffling about the trip the night before when I had a steamy dream about Katie. Her long chocolate hair on my chest, warm breath in my ear, locked legs, the whole bit.

That clinches it. I'm going.

I slept through my alarm Friday morning. It was only thanks to Juan Carlos's racecar chops that I made it to school just as our bus was pulling out. He cut in front of it and screeched to a stop like he'd just nabbed a small army of narcos. Even slapped a portable red strobe light on the car's roof for extra splash. Before I jumped out, I made him promise he wouldn't tell my parents about where we were going. He pulled out his Beretta handgun and made the sign of a cross over it. "On pain of death, *amigito.*"

I grabbed my sweet little three-quarter guitar out of the back seat and hopped on the bus to a round of hoots and applause.

Twenty songs and two hours later, our bus filled with disgusting blue smoke and ground to a halt on the shoulder of a narrow mountain road. We sat in the long grass eating our bag lunches, singing more tunes, and throwing rotten figs at passing trucks. I was just tucking into the Beatles' "While My Guitar Gently Weeps" when our replacement bus arrived from Xela.

We stopped at a village balanced on top of a steep ridge that fell away into nothingness. After a gut-busting four-hour journey, we were all feeling like caged monkeys, but Adam motioned for us to sit down as he let some local guy on.

We kept going.

Compared to some of the skinny *campesinos* we'd seen

out the window, the guy we picked up looked pretty well-off with his fancy leather jacket and professor glasses. But he had a serious bruise on his cheek and had to struggle to keep his balance under a pair of crutches.

Adam introduced him as Miguel, our guide. I never got what happened to him but, from what we heard later, it was easy to guess. Someone working for my dad's mine probably roughed him up.

We got our first glimpse of the mine as we drove through a patchy eucalyptus forest. Between gaps in the trees, I could make out a bunch of oil tanks, dirt piles, and scummy ponds.

"We drove four hours for *this*?" I asked Adam.

"Just wait," he said. "Remember, our focus is on the villagers."

We wound our way up another ridge. The forest suddenly disappeared and we stopped beside a bare-naked mountain. We poured out of the bus, took a big stretch, and stared at my father's mine.

Miguel told us that most of the gold was found deep beneath these mountains. Some had been poked full of tunnels and shafts that went down over a mile. Far below, long ore trucks were lining up, like wasps at a nest, waiting to enter a tunnel. Other mountains had simply been blown up, Miguel said, as he hopped on his crutches to the edge of a yawning hole that I couldn't get my head around.

Miguel explained that this was the main pit, now as deep as the mountain was once tall. I latched onto a bush with one hand and gazed down to the bottom at a tiny bug of a truck. Miguel was telling us about all the four-story-high dump trucks it took to haul away the mountain, when I realized I was looking at one.

"Whoah!"

He traced his fingers through the air, moving up from the base of the pit to where the mountaintop used to be. *"¿Muy grande, no?"* he said. *"Fue una montaña sagrada."*

There was a buzz from my classmates as they got how big that mountain once was.

I felt a warm bare arm next to mine.

Katie. "What's he saying?"

Her Spanish was pretty sketchy, having just arrived from Toronto a month earlier, so I was happy to serve as her personal translator. "It was a big mountain," I said. "A sacred mountain."

Our next stop was at the edge of a village that looked like it, too, could soon be eaten by the mine. Miguel led us through a pasture hopping with goats. Some local kids stopped kicking their homemade soccer ball, a scrunched-up blob of newspapers wound up in string. They stared at us. I was suddenly aware that our Reebok hi-tops and blue blazers must have looked pretty strange.

We gathered in front of a rundown adobe house like you'd find anywhere in rural Guatemala. We learned that what made this house special is that it's perched next door to Canada's Eldorado Mine. On the property line, in fact. Living in this house was a woman Miguel said you don't want to mess with, even if you are a multi-billion-dollar company. Diadora Itza, who he introduced as a *"verdadero luchador de libertad.*"

"A what?" asked Katie, who had glued herself to me.

"A true freedom fighter," I whispered. "*Activista*, shit disturber." Even though we were at the back of the mob, I purposely whispered so Katie had to move closer to hear me.

Diadora came out carrying a big plate of *champurradas*, a traditional sesame seed cookie. She was a slight woman who could've used a few cookies herself. She presented them to Adam, who gave her a big smile, grabbed two big ones, then passed them on. While we all towered over her, she sat down on a log beside Miguel and began to tell her story. As soon as she opened her mouth, I felt a warm tingle down my neck. She was speaking K'iche', my mother's native tongue.

With Miguel translating for her into Spanish, she explained that she had no big demands. Just the basics, like clean water and air. "*Sólo quiero vivir en paz con mis animales.*"

Katie elbowed me.

"Uh ... right. She just wants to live in peace with her animals."

"So what's the problem?"

"Listen."

Diadora's problem was the gold under her house. And her goat pasture. And the skimpy forest beside it that helped shield her from the machine noise and dust and flying rocks tossed up by the mine. She pointed to a big dent in her tin roof where a boulder had landed after an especially big explosion.

Katie pointed to several ugly pockmarks beside the door. "More rocks?" she said, looking at me.

"What?"

"Go ahead, ask her."

I did, in K'iche', kind of showing off.

Diadora got pretty worked up when she answered me. Even started crying.

"What, what?" Katie said.

"Not rocks," I said. "*Balas*. Bullets."

The company's problem was that Diadora refused to move. Worse, she organized protests against the mine. Against what some villagers felt was the end of their world. She told us that since the mine arrived, her village had seen more robberies, more prostitution, more drugs. In just five years, the number of bars in the area had gone up from nine to ninety.

Miguel shook his head. *"Más violencia también."*

"More violence, too," I said to Katie.

Diadora told of receiving a knock at the door late one evening. *"Dos hombres musculosos"* were waiting for her behind it. Two muscular men.

They said they were travelers.

She didn't believe them.

They asked for beds.

She refused.

They asked for coffee.

She gave them coffee.

They paid her with a bullet in the head.

Her neighbors found her lying in a pool of blood. They

got help.

When her neighbors went home, they found their houses sprayed with fresh bullet holes.

"It's a friggin' war zone!" Katie said. "Did she say who those guys were? Like, were they *Canadians*?"

"No," I said. "I mean ... I don't know. Does it really matter? It's all about the company."

My father's company.

Diadora pointed to her right temple. That's when I noticed a dark shadow there, a little pit, shaped like the ones they took gold out of. That's where the bullet went in. It tore through her right eyeball and grazed her nose, carving a notch that goes white when she frowns.

And this woman had a lot to frown about.

After three months in Guatemala City's best private hospital, paid for, strangely enough, by CanaMine, she returned home to find more trouble. *"Cuando regresó, descubrí que habían cortado mis pipas de agua."*

Katie looked at me in shock. "Her water pipes?"

I discovered that Katie understood more Spanish than she let on. My days as her personal translator were numbered. "Yeah," I said. "She came home to find somebody had cut them."

"Y habían cortado las gargantas de mis cabras."

"Goats?" Katie said. "What happened?"

"Slit their throats."

Diadora buried her face in her hands. I saw tears leaking through her fingers.

"¡Qué dolor," she cried. *"Qué dolor!"* What pain!

What happened next made a lot of my classmates go green.

Diadora suddenly lifted her head and started poking around her right eye. *"¡Mira!"* she said in Spanish. *"¡Esto es lo que la mina ha hecho a mí!"*

"Look!" I whispered to Katie. "This is what the mine did to—"

Something dropped into Diadora's other hand.

Katie covered her mouth like she was going to puke.

Diodora's glass eye sat unblinking in the palm of her hand. It glared back at us, at me, the mine owner's son.

If she only knew.

A girl about my age ran out of the house and put her arm around Diadora. There was something about her that stopped my breath. The tight orange and black kerchief around her head.

I pulled away from Katie, from the mob of students, wanting to hide. I stumbled over a root and landed flat on my ass, almost squashing a goat that galloped away, bleating like crazy.

Now all eyes were on me, including the Mayan girl's. Nervous laughter from my classmates. Even some clapping. I gave my best stage bow, trying to hide my face from the girl.

Then I remembered.

The last time we'd locked eyes was at my Christmas performance in the Gran Teatro. That was months ago. But the Wonder Boy's face had been in the papers a couple times since. Even once on TV. Would she know me?

The next time I'd seen her, she was protesting in front

of our house. But I'd been invisible, secretly watching her through binoculars behind ten-foot walls.

My guts relaxed. Whether she recognized me or not, I felt certain she couldn't know I was the mine owner's son.

The girl turned back to Diadora, addressing her as *abuelita*, granny. She helped her up and guided her toward the door.

A fire seemed to ignite in Diadora's good eye and she waved us all into her tiny house.

I had to duck to enter. It was so dark, I bumped into backpacks and shoulders and what felt like a bed. Katie grabbed my hand, I guess thinking I might do another ass plant. Somebody turned on a naked bulb and I found I was standing beside a stack of crudely painted signs. Protest signs I'd seen before.

¡Sí a la vida! ¡No minería! Yes to life! No to mining!

¡Unidos en defensa de Madre Tierra! United in defense of Mother Earth!

Diadora seemed to have recovered. Her eye was back in, anyhow. She was pointing excitedly at a big gash that snaked down the wall and across the floor. *"Tantas explosiones. Están destruyendo nuestros hogares."*

Katie looked at me, her dark eyes more serious than ever.

"So many explosions," I said. "They're wrecking our homes."

I was suddenly suffocating and started to squeeze through the bodies.

"You okay?" Adam said as he stepped aside.

"Just need some air." I was almost at the door when the

girl in the kerchief came up to me with a torn scrap of paper and a pencil. *"Su autógrafo, por favor."*

I was hardly feeling like the Wonder Boy at the moment. The Indio who signed autographs after concerts seemed a solar system away, if he ever existed. But this Mayan girl now showed me that same star-struck face I'd seen in the theater.

I forced a smile and asked her name in K'iche'.

"Eliza," she said.

While Diadora carried on about the evil mining company, I flattened Eliza's paper against the mud wall and wrote, *Believe in the music! Love, Indio.* When I dotted the last "i" in my name, the pencil torpedoed through the paper making a big ugly hole, like the bullet marks in Diadora's house. I pulled the paper away to see another gaping crack in the wall.

I wanted to scream.

Instead, I smoothed out the paper, handed it back to Eliza, and got the hell out of there.

I took two steps onto the grass when it dawned on me that I wrote her autograph in English. *Jesus!* I looked at my hands, wondering who was really inhabiting my body.

Then another thought. If I wanted to keep building my musical career, it was high time I changed my name. My last name, at least, to remove any possible connection with this foul place.

PARTY'S OVER

"Who was that girl back there?" Katie asked me as we walked back to the bus.

"Beats me. Some groupie, I guess."

"Way out here?"

"Hey, I have groupies in New Zealand. Even China."

We walked in clumsy silence until Katie stopped and slapped both legs with her hands. "Oh, my God!" She threw her backpack to the ground and started wrestling with it, trying to rip something off.

I leaned over her shoulder. She was attacking a Canadian flag. "Uh ... what are you doing?"

Katie looked up at me, her eyes bloodshot. "I'm so totally embarrassed to be Canadian!"

I said nothing. I was so totally embarrassed to be the mine owner's son. No, not embarrassed. Ready to throw up, actually.

"Well, aren't *you*?"

"Yeah ... I guess so. But I'm not really Canad—"

"Did you believe that eye thing? Those cracks in the wall?"

"Pretty sick, eh."

Katie got nowhere with her flag.

I went for my jackknife on the bus. I grabbed my guitar, too, thinking we could chill on the grass before climbing on board for the slog home. Maybe knock that shitty feeling from my guts.

My knife did the trick. Katie whipped the flag into a smoldering fire pit. One of Diodora's goats trotted over, plucked the flag out of the pit, downed it in one gulp, then let out a big belch.

Katie broke into a kind of crying laughter and folded herself into me. I carefully leaned my guitar against the back of the bus and rested my arms on her shoulders.

"Tighter," she whispered.

I let my arms drop to the small of her back and gave her the squeeze I'd been craving all day. No guitar could ever hug like that. "That goat's gonna have bad gas," I said. Then we were both laughing like fools.

Adam strolled by us without a look. "Let's go, you Canucks. Party's over."

The bus driver leaned on the horn and we dashed for the door.

Everybody was letting off steam after a heavy afternoon. Sounded like a soccer game. The bus lurched backwards, spilling packs and water bottles off the overhead racks. I reached out to protect my guitar in the seat beside me ... and my stomach did a flip.

"*¡Para, para!*" I shouted to the driver. "Stop!"

But he didn't hear me. He didn't stop.

I jumped out of my seat.

Too late.

I heard a sickening crunch.

My childhood, such as it was, pretty much ended that day with the death of my first guitar. And my discovery of the disgusting truth about my father's mine.

THE SADDEST SONG

The day after our mine tour, I was back in my practice room with my zebrawood guitar cradled between my thighs. The morning sun shone like a spotlight on the flowered rosette surrounding its sound hole. I ran a finger over the scar made by the protester's rock months ago. The scar that, in the end, no luthier could fix.

It reminded me of the bullet wound on Diadora's temple.

As much as I loved that guitar, my sweet little three-quarter model would always be my favorite. The one that now lay ground into the dirt behind Diadora's mud hut.

Our house was quiet that morning. Loba snored beside me on her sheepskin rug. Through my window I could hear old Andres, our gardener, raking sweetgum leaves off the lawn. The random thump of Juan Carlos lifting weights in the garage. Distant thunder ricocheting off the mountains that protect Xela.

It was one of those rare moments when I didn't have to practice or rehearse or do anything, really, but hang out with my guitar. After our visit to the mine, I felt more like I was clinging to it for dear life.

Magno was on tour that week, doing his own concerts "to help feed my Corvette," he'd told me. So no lesson the next day. Dad was away all weekend, "kicking butts at the mine." So no fear of him stealth-listening down the hall. Mom was out shopping for more shoes or whatever. Uncle Faustus had Sofi covered.

The practice room door was wide open, letting in a cool breeze that got my sheet music dancing on the stand.

I could have played anything I wanted. Some Hendrix or BB King, or maybe some of the Beatles tunes I'd arranged for classical guitar, the ones my classmates screamed for on the bus.

Instead I sat there, with my hands in ready position, wondering what would come.

I closed my eyes and waited.

Magno called this process "spontaneous musical combustion." You don't choose the music. It pops up by itself. You don't play the music. It plays you. You have to calm down, he told me, turn off your brain, forget trying to please anyone. "Not me," he said. "Not your father. Not even yourself." Eventually your fingers twitch, you feel a mild burning sensation, then ... out it comes.

This was a fun exercise we'd use to break up our three-hour lessons.

What erupted that morning was the saddest song I knew.

Albinoni's "Adagio in G Minor." Magno told me this piece was famous for showing up in the darkest moments of the saddest movies ever. Like *Phantom of the Opera*, for starters.

The Adagio poured out of my fingers like a slowly building thunderstorm.

I played it through once. Just three and a half minutes but it felt like forever. My ears rode the last notes out the window and into the gray sky. I played it again, falling deeper into the music. I played it again, feeling it massage a lonely spot inside that I knew only music could touch. I played it over and over, feeling my hair and skin and flesh strip away, until all that was left was the pain.

Getting Inside the Music

MUSIC AS MIRROR

My guitar teacher is a bit of a philosopher. He'll say stuff like, "*Music imitates life, only more so.*" I don't exactly get what he means, but somehow it makes more sense when I grab my guitar and play something that shakes me from the inside out. Another time he told me that, "*It's pointless to ask what a piece of music means.*" That really got me scratching my head, but I think he's saying that music is about expressing feelings that words can't touch.

You can see I learn more in my guitar lessons than just scales and stuff!

I've learned, for instance, that if you *really* listen, music can take you to some pretty cool places inside yourself. Sometimes scary places, too. In my music history book, I triple-starred this quote by the German poet Heinrich Mueller, who takes this idea to the limit:

"Listen well enough and music will show you everything you are."

TRY THIS EXPERIMENT

So, are you ready to experiment with this? To really listen and see what you discover? Try this one on for size: Albinoni's "Adagio in G Minor" (here's the **link**). I made this recording for you in the stairwell of my house where I can get some cool churchy acoustics. There was a storm in Xela when I recorded this, so if you turn your volume up, you'll hear tree branches knocking against the window. Also, my dog scratching at the door, begging to be with me. Sorry! I can control many things but not the weather or my dog!

A small warning: buckle up; this could be a rough ride. And do let me know what you discover. By the way, this piece will be on my first CD that will be available in late summer. I hope you will listen to me then, too.

Yours inside the music, Indio ♫

That piece struck a chord, so to speak. My followers, whose numbers had just broken 1,000, shared a ton of pretty personal stuff.

i was reading some emails while listening to your masterpiece and suddenly i couldn't finish the line i was on! my eyes just stopped dead and then—guess what! —they started gushing. i haven't cried like that since i was a brat. what are you doing to me indio? sounds weird but I wanna THANK YOU for that sad sad song.

Dear young maestro, you are right. There are no words for the feelings this music touches. When I listened deeply like you said, something flew out of me, like a dark bird.

incredible song! my two little nephews were running around, shouting, breaking heads, then i hit play and, you won't believe it, they sat down in complete silence and just listened to you. i had to run for some kleenex. well played!!

Thank you for sharing such a beautiful sadness.

So perfect! How did I feel? So jealous!

The pile of comments kept me busy online for hours after school, until Juan Carlos came storming into the computer lab, pretending to reach for his gun.

EARTHQUAKE

T he earthquake struck the day old Andres and Juan Carlos were decorating our ten-foot wall with Christmas lights. Andres held the ladder while feeding strings of lights up to Juan Carlos, who draped them along the top of the wall. Those guys normally stayed out of each other's faces. Couldn't stand each other, actually. But Mom insisted they get the damn lights up *prontisimo*.

She'd invited a bunch of her family over to celebrate *Las Posadas*, the traditional welcoming of the pregnant Mother Mary into Bethlehem. Her sister Dora was full-on pregnant, so Mom thought it would be especially good to get together that year. She'd even arranged for a donkey for Dora to ride on up to our gate.

Beyond Uncle Faustus, who'd lived with us forever, *Las Posadas* was the only time of year I ever got to see anybody resembling family. As far as I knew, the closest relatives on Dad's side were sheepherders in Scotland.

It was after dark by the time Andres and Juan Carlos

argued their way to the last string of lights. I'd been watching the show from my practice room and had to laugh when I saw the lights looking extra cheery, reflected in the coils of razor wire.

The first tremor hit while Juan Carlos was climbing down the ladder for the last time. He must have thought Andres was fooling around and started yelling at him—until he noticed Andres running for his life. I grabbed the windowsill with both hands as another tremor hit and the marble floor beneath me turned to Jell-O.

"Jump!" I shouted out the window.

Juan Carlos leapt from the ladder and hit the ground running just as the wall above him cracked open and spilled a bunch of razor wire over the edge, Christmas lights and all.

That wasn't all that came crashing down that night, according to the next day's front-page headline: *Contamination from Canadian mine disaster angers villagers*. I was about to read the article when Dad grabbed the paper off the kitchen table, spilling the special Christmas hot chocolate Katrina had made for me.

"Shouldn't we be practicing?" Dad said as he watched Katrina clean up the mess.

I stared at the newspaper crushed under his armpit. "So what's up at the mine?"

"Oh ... just a technical hitch caused by the quake. Need to plug a few leaks."

"Will you shut it down?"

"Hell, no. Business as usual, you know. Keep pouring those gold bricks. Wouldn't want the workers to miss a day of pay, would you?"

"Or maybe ... an eyeball?" I said.

That just kind of slipped out.

I hadn't planned to confront Dad about what I'd heard out there. About company thugs roughing up villagers who got in the way. Maybe slitting their goats' throats. Or the villagers' throats. I was scared he'd take it out on me somehow—more practicing, less school, more bruised shins.

But it was too late now. There it was, sitting on the kitchen table between us.

Diadora's glass eye.

Dad slowly took the morning paper out from under his armpit and rolled it into a tight tube. Loba ran to the glass door and scratched madly to get out. Sofi kicked it open and Loba bolted across the grass. Dad looked at the rolled-up paper like he was deciding what to do with it.

"Ever heard of Diadora Itza?" I asked him.

Mom went over and started rubbing Dad's back. His shoulders dropped about a foot. His face softened. Only Mom could do that to him. She called it the Mayan touch.

Dad looked up at me, smiling. "Never heard of her."

"Itza," Mom said. "K'iche' name. One of us."

"You mean ... she could be *related*?" I said.

Mom shrugged. "Maybe. Our people—*your* people, Indio—they cover the mountains like trees." From behind Dad's back, she flashed me a hurt look, like she was feeling the villagers' pain. "Who is she, this Diadora?"

Dad was getting dark again. He stared at me in a way I did not like.

"Just some villager," I said. "Got into trouble with the mine, I guess."

Dad slowly put the newspaper down and folded his hands on the table. "Who told you this, Indio?"

"Oh ... somebody mentioned her at school, that's all. In Social Studies class. It's nothing, Dad." It hit me that what I just spilled might get my favorite teacher, Adam Upjohn, fired.

"Good." Dad crammed the newspaper into his jacket and stood up. "Now, I'd really love to hear some of that new Bach prelude before I go."

"To the mine?" Mom asked.

Dad frowned. "Yes. A little tremor and the villagers don't show up for work."

"It's Vivaldi," I said.

Dad was half out the door. "What?"

"The prelude. It's by Vivaldi, not Bach."

"Yeah. That one. Would you play it for me when I get back?"

"Sure, Dad."

MATH CLASS

It was business as usual for home-schooling that afternoon. If I learned anything in that math class, it was that not even a major earthquake could shake up the schedule my father set in stone for me.

It's not that my teacher Luiz was a dolt. One look at his Roman nose and bushy beard and you might have said he was brilliant. But it's a wonder I even knew my times tables.

Luiz sat in Magno's chair as if he belonged there. It would always be Magno's chair but I tried not to let it bug me. Even though Luiz once home-schooled *El Presidente's* kids, he secretly called himself an *anarquista*—an anarchist—and was always happy to share his political views with me. Actually, that's about all he shared.

Not with Dad, of course. What gave Luiz a foot in Dad's door wasn't his politics or teaching skills. Luiz had presidential connections. That's all that mattered to Dad. Beyond enforcing the schedule, Dad showed zero interest in my home-schooling. For him, it was all about guitar.

So what happened in class, stayed in class.

Luiz started this class by scribbling some numbers on a whiteboard. Numbers I'd seen many times before. I said nothing, filing my guitar nails behind his back. It was Luiz's usual breakdown of Guatemala's class structure. I doubt if he shared this with the President's kids.

Los ricos (the very rich) 2%
Clase media (middle class) 28%
Pobreza (the poor) 50%
Extrema pobreza (the very poor) 20%

Luiz spun around and looked steadily at my left ear. I knew there was something wrong with his eyes but, after all these years, it was too late to ask. "Now, listen Indio, if you do the math, assuming Guatemala has, say, 16 million people and a growth rate of 2.5 per cent, how many years will it be until the next revolution?"

I gave Luiz a blank face. I never knew if he was kidding or just a little crazy, but I crunched some numbers that seemed to satisfy him.

More whiteboard scribbles, this time on the ups and downs of Guatemala's economy, which, Luiz explained, was basically controlled by five *rico* families. "How do the rich get richer?" he asked.

I shrugged. "I dunno, by—"

"Jumping into bed with multinational companies! Exactly, Indio. Very good."

"You mean companies like ... CanaMine."

Luiz glanced at the closed door of the practice room. He quickly wiped the evidence off the whiteboard. "Sorry, Indio, math class is over. Time for Shakespeare."

"No, wait, Luiz, tell me, what happened out at the mine yesterday? Some kind of *disaster*?"

From Luiz I learned that the earthquake's epicenter was located "not far from the mine's soft underbelly." About the time Juan Carlos was running from a downpour of razor wire and Christmas lights, an earth dam at the Eldorado mine popped open and vomited a million swimming pools of toxic tailings into *Río Madre Noble*, the Noble Mother river that, Luiz explained, is "*super sagrado*"—super sacred—for the local Mayan villagers. "Not to mention it's their only source of drinking water," he said, "their source of life."

Luiz glanced at the door again, then leaned toward me. "They won't take this lying down," he said. "You don't have to be a political scientist like me to know there's going to be big trouble."

"You think so, Luiz?"

He tugged hard on his beard. "Indio, I know so."

PROTEST

The trouble arrived the next day, just like Luiz said. I was in the practice room, slogging through a new Villa-Lobos étude, when something made me freeze.

It started with a low growl. I looked up from my guitar to see Loba with her front paws on the windowsill. The fur on her back formed a ridge of tension. I tucked my guitar in its case and locked it. I joined Loba at the window, smelling chaos in the wind. I felt another tremor, this time in my stomach.

The quake had torn a v-shaped crack in the outside wall. Andres had tried to plug the gap with chicken wire.

A kid on a tricycle could've crashed through it.

The ladder still lay where it fell two nights ago, like a corpse half-hidden in the grass.

Loba's growl swelled into a deep bark. I scratched her ears, tried to smooth out her back. "It's okay, girl," I said, knowing it wasn't. Together we strained our ears, sniffed the dusty air.

Distant shouting. Chanting.

After a year of fragile peace, they were back.

A lot more of them.

Getting closer. Fast.

I heard a door slam and someone crunching across the chips of broken cement that littered our driveway. Juan Carlos, wearing his camo flak jacket and handgun already drawn.

Two of Dad's outer guards, now dressed up like soldiers, paced back and forth. Their shotguns were pointed at the ground.

For the moment, at least.

The villagers arrived like a swarm of angry bees.

Women and children raised cardboard crosses above their heads with the words *Madre Noble* painted in dripping red letters.

The men raised fists.

Loba whimpered and I realized I had been gripping her neck too tight.

Something green and shiny sailed over the wall.

Splintering glass.

I stared at a wet splotch on the driveway, waiting for flames.

Molotov cocktail, the homemade bomb of choice for riots like this. Luiz once told me how to make one. Pretty simple. A bottle full of gasoline. A rag wick. Just add a lit match and toss at your enemy.

Another bottle sailed over the wall. And another.

Smash! Smash!

No flames.

One crashed on the edge of the swimming pool and squirted brown guck into the turquoise water.

More smashing bottles. More muddy stains.

Then I got it. *The blood of Madre Noble.*

Contaminated water from the villagers' source of life.

Two worlds merged in our swimming pool. *Rico* and *pobreza.*

Angry bees.

Juan Carlos shouted something into his walkie-talkie.

Two shotgun blasts. I didn't know where. Into the sky?

Angrier bees.

I ran across the room for my binoculars.

There she was again. Eliza. Her once star-struck face now screwed up in fury.

Shaking her fist right at me.

The sun was in her face. She couldn't possibly have seen me. Or could she?

Shaking her fist at what could be her distant cousin.

Me.

More shotgun blasts.

The bottles flew.

Approaching sirens.

Screech of truck tires.

The stomp of army boots.

Juan Carlos jammed a shoulder against one side of the crack and leveled his gun with both hands.

At what? At who?

I cringed at the sound of gunfire, this time much closer.

A cross fell to the street, and with it, the young mother who'd held it a split second ago, the top of her skull blown clean off.

Part II
CALGARY, ALBERTA
EIGHT MONTHS LATER

Technology is a queer thing.
It brings you great gifts with one hand,
and it stabs you in the back with the other.

–C.P. Snow

"Why can't you just stop?" non-addicts will often ask.
When you ask us to stop gaming or to give up online social networking,
you might as well ask that we stop living.

–Kevin Roberts, *Cyber Junkie*

SWAPPING PLANETS

It was weird moving to a new planet. Very weird.

Soon after the shooting, Dad ran from Guatemala, figuring he might be next. We rocketed from Planet Xela to Planet Calgary at lightning speed.

Calgary. Alberta. Canada. Where I heard that real guys wear cowboy boots, have sunburned necks, worship hockey, and bathe in oil sands.

Calgary. My dad's town. We were on his turf now.

I was an alien all over again.

Dad knew that a lot of Guatemala's *pobreza* hated his guts. His enemies grew as news spread about the crappy construction of the tailings dam that popped, wrecking their river. News about how local people had lost their land, their water, and in some cases, their lives. The press pored more gas on the fire when it broke the story that ninety-nine percent of the profits from my father's gold mine went straight to Canadian banks.

The Guatemalan government called for a temporary

shutdown of the mine while it investigated the disaster.

The villagers wanted it closed forever.

Village leaders organized community-wide votes. They kept the question simple: *"Mina sí or Mina no."* Villagers came out in hordes, marking their ballots with a thumbprint. Ten out of ten villages voted *¡NO!* to the Eldorado Mine.

The protests got bigger, noisier, closer to the source of the villagers' anger.

That would be my dad.

Our house became what Luiz called "the protest epicenter of Guatemala."

So, days after that Mayan mother's brains spilled onto our street—Juan Carlos blamed the army—after more tear gas, police sirens, and shouts for vengeance, my father fled the country. Before somebody sent a bullet into our house instead of rocks.

Right after landing in Calgary, at a safe distance of, like, 4,000 miles, what did my father do? Turned around and sued the Guatemalan government for, as he put it, "fucking with his mine."

So it was goodbye, Guatemala.

No more need for ten-foot walls, razor-wire, or shotgun-toting guards. No need to live in a padded prison where my father was Chief Warden and could boss me around with a wave of his Scotch glass. And no more bullshit about me being the reincarnated Segovia. The Wonder Boy was dead, thanks to the press smearing my name with Dad's blood-soaked mine.

Even Katie tarred me with the same brush. She axed our budding romance with four words. The last words I ever got from her, emailed the day after the shooting.

WHAT HAVE YOU DONE?????

Like it was me that pulled the trigger.

Dad might still have fantasized that his boy prodigy would one day be world famous, but you'd never know it. He'd been too busy fighting fires and suing everybody to find me a classical guitar teacher. And I wasn't about to start.

Touching my guitar made me physically sick.

So now it was hello to a hilltop mansion, jumbo shopping malls, and fulltime high school.

That's where my new troubles took off.

That's where I was a zero. Maybe even a negative number.

FALLING

I can't pinpoint the moment when I started falling. Maybe it was when I first went online in Calgary and discovered all the stinging comments tacked onto my blog.

How can you sit there in your ivory tower and play your pretty music when your dad is out there raping the land and murdering its people???

You quote some German egghead who says that "music will show you everything you are." My earnest wish is that you find the music that shows you what a total shit you are. Stop messing with the third world!

go back home you cannibalizing canucks!

The Xela me would have carefully trimmed out any nasty comments, which in those days were few and far between. Smacked in the head by pages of hate mail, the Calgary me closed Mom's laptop, ran for the bathroom, and threw up.

Or maybe I started falling after my first visit to a mega-mall. I was alone in a clothing store a week before school started, trying to figure out what Canadian guys my age were supposed to wear. I felt flames at my back and looked up at the mirror in front of me. The man at the cashier was sizing me up, a scrawny teenage Latino male, rifling through his carefully folded jeans. When I left the store empty-handed, he followed me out the door. He watched me shuffle down the hall and get on an elevator. He didn't take his eyes off me until the elevator door closed. A lone woman on the elevator clutched her purse tighter and held her breath until she could get off at the next floor. Then, as I crossed the street outside the mall, I heard locks clicking shut as I passed in front of cars stopped for the light.

Or maybe it started the Saturday night I was holed up in my basement bedroom, lying in the dark, bored out of my mind. I'd already slept most of the day but was still dead tired.

Dead tired.

Dead.

I felt a sickening urge to cry.

I forced myself to sit up, to stand, to walk, to look out the window at the night sky. I gazed up at stars I'd never seen before. A dim melody pricked the edge of my brain. My fingers twitched. My back tensed. Albinoni's "Adagio in G Minor" limped to life then stole center stage.

I knocked my head against the wall. I made loud humming noises, grunted, clapped my hands. I did a belly flop onto my bed, crammed a pillow against each ear, and sobbed.

However my new troubles started, going to high school only made them ten times worse.

ROLL CALL

First day of classes. Mom had trouble finding the school and the buzzer was already ringing by the time she dropped me off. I ran through what looked like the main doors. Before I could figure out where I was supposed to go, speakers above me started blaring the national anthem of my latest country.

O Canada! Our home and native land!

Random bodies caught in the corridor stopped suddenly as if trapped in a UFO tractor beam. I was standing across from the principal's office. Our eyes locked and he gave me a dirty look that glued my feet to the floor. Above his desk, an old queen draped in white fur frowned at me.

God keep our land, glorious and free!

My shoulders hunched under the weight of all this newness.

Later, I was sitting at the back of a Grade 11 English class. The teacher, Ms. Mackenzie, was at the front reading names from a computer screen.

"Jeremy Williams?"

Jeremy put up his hand. He was a tall guy with long blond hair rolled into a bun.

"Carol Miller?"

Carol raised both thumbs without looking up. She wore black lipstick. Tattooed spiders crawled up her arms.

"Brian Moore?"

He was a chubby guy with straight brown hair, his back pocket bulging with golf tees.

"Morris Kritch?"

Morris propped up his gelled hair and flashed a movie-star smile for all to see. "Yoh."

The teacher paused. She leaned closer to the computer screen and her forehead wrinkled.

I sat up straight. Something shiny dropped onto my desk. A drop of sweat.

This must be it.

Seconds, minutes, years passed as Ms. Mackenzie mouthed a name several times before saying it.

"In-DEE-oh McCracken?"

I twisted my palm toward the ceiling as if asking a question. The whole class turned around, even spider girl. My black hair turned into feathers, my Mayan nose a beak.

Ms. Mackenzie took off her reading glasses and studied me. "That's an interesting name. Where's that from?"

My heart was about to burst through my chest. "Actually, it's ... it's *Ian*," I said. The feathers and beak fell away.

"Oh, really," Ms. Mackenzie said as she put her glasses back on.

"Yes. Really. Call me Ian."

LUNCH BREAK

L unch. My favorite period of the day—not.

I hung outside the cafeteria door. Once enough students had streamed in, I could see the safe spots. After a week at school, I was still eating alone except for Danilo, a twenty-something Filipino dishwasher who liked to practice his Spanish on me. Making friends with kitchen and cleaning staff was one of my specialties, a throwback to my Xela days. I was glad for the few minutes Danilo had for me during his breaks. But honestly, the cafeteria was the last place I wanted to be caught speaking Spanish.

"*Hasta mañana, amigo,*" Danilo said, looking at his watch and beating it to the kitchen.

"Yeah, see you tomorrow."

I turned back to my squashed tuna sandwich, addressing it like it was worthy of great attention.

I caught what snippets of conversation I could, determined to build my bank of Canadianisms.

"... and like, she's reaching for a book on the top shelf and

I can see half her gonch!"

"... you mean your mom gives you a jam buster like that *every* lunch?"

"... so we ditched our mountain bikes and built this, like, humungous inukshuk at the end of the trail ..."

Then this.

"Hey, Pedro!"

Some guy behind me.

"Pe-*dree*-to, hey!"

My tuna sandwich suddenly became even more fascinating.

I recognized the smooth voice of Morris Kritch. I gulped down the last of my sandwich. The crust stuck halfway down.

A crumpled paper bag ricocheted off my head.

"What are ya—deaf?"

I slowly turned around. Morris and a couple of his hockey buddies sat one table away. He had a questioning look on his face. His buddies eyed me like cats casually studying their prey. One of them was twirling a hockey puck on the table.

"Uh ... it's actually Ian," I said, gagging on the bread crust. *Why the hell did I pick that? My father's middle name!*

"Oh, right," Morris said, nodding politely. "Ian ... Ian." He said this like he was exploring a new taste. Something sour, disgusting. He grabbed the puck and started tossing it from hand to hand. "So, Pedro ... I mean, Ian ... how's about trading a burrito for this hockey puck."

I looked around for any teachers in case he decided to

wing the puck at my head, too. Just the principal, Mr. Grimsby. His back was to me as he chatted up a fashion plate running for student president.

"No, thanks," I said. "I don't play hockey."

"So what *do* you play?"

"Uh ... football. I mean soccer. What *you* call soccer. We call it football. *Fútbol.*"

It didn't even occur to me to tell him I played guitar.

Morris stopped tossing the puck. His eyes narrowed slightly. "Who's *we*?"

Jesus, now I've done it.

That's when the hiccups started, the violent kind that get your whole chest heaving. My throat closed around the crust.

Morris's eyebrows went up a notch. "Sorry ... am I making you jumpy?"

His buddies laughed.

I hopped to my feet and opened my mouth but nothing came out. I clutched my throat.

"So, I guess that's no burritos for my hungry friends?" Morris asked as laughter rippled out to other tables.

"Sorry," I managed to gasp, while desperately looking for a water fountain. "We don't eat burritos."

"Then ... what *are* you?"

But I couldn't answer Morris. I was already bolting for the kitchen and Danilo's sink.

Danilo got it right away and grabbed a sudsy coffee cup. He blasted a shot of water into it which I downed in one life-saving gulp.

"What happened, *amigo*?" he asked.

I just shrugged.

Even though Danilo was standing right beside me with a comforting hand on my back, I could not have felt more alone if the cafeteria were empty.

SIXTEENTH BIRTHDAY

"It's just a small thing," my mother said.

I cracked one eye open as she placed a slim white box on my bedside table. I saw the Apple logo on it. I rolled over and closed my eyes.

"*Felis cumpleaños, Indio.*"

"Huh?"

"Happy birthday, Indio." Mom leaned over and kissed me on the cheek.

I grimaced and pulled the covers over my head.

"This will help you stay connected."

"With who?" I mumbled.

"With us ... when you go out."

"Go where?"

"You know, *out.*" Mom started ripping off the tinfoil I'd carefully plastered over every window. "Out of this cave, for starters."

I flipped the covers down and squinted into blinding sunshine. A dusting of snow covered the crabapple tree in our backyard.

How could it be winter?

Loba jumped up and licked my face.

"It's a new day, Indio. You're sixteen. You can't go on living like this."

"Who says?"

Mom crunched the tinfoil into a tight ball. "*I* say!"

I pushed Loba away and covered my head again. "You sound like Dad."

"Indio, please. You haven't been to school for weeks. Your principal called us. He said something about a suspension unless we get a doctor's note saying you're sick."

"So get one."

"You're not sick!"

"I'm sick of school."

"You hardly gave it a chance."

"Didn't take long. I'm a fast learner."

"You're falling way behind, Indio. This *is* Grade 11, you know."

"Okay. So let's go back to home schooling. Get a tutor or something."

"For every subject? Do you know what that would cost?"

"As if we can't afford it."

"You know how expensive it is to live in Canada. And Dad's mine is—"

"In deep shit, yeah. So why not fly Luiz up here? He'd be a lot cheaper and he could moonlight as your live-in maid."

Mom half-laughed. "Somehow I can't see Luiz in an apron."

"I'm not going back there."

"To Xela?"

"To school."

Mom's lips went tight. She looked almost as wrecked as me. "At least open your present. Your principal told me about a new homework app you could download. Might help you catch up while you recover from—"

"From *what*? I'm not sick, remember?"

"From your *melancolía*."

"Who's depressed?"

Mom nodded. "Oh. It's normal to always be cranky?"

"I'm *not* cranky!"

She looked at me stone-faced, then started counting my crimes on her fingers. "To sleep all day? To have these crying fits? To lose interest in doing *anything*? Look where you were going with your guitar and you threw it all away!"

"Dad alert. Dad alert."

"No, Indio. This is your mother talking. I was *so* proud of you. But you don't practice anymore. You don't perform. You don't even blog about your music, let alone play it."

I squeezed my eyes shut. My head was a brick, my body a rotten log. My heart thumped to the beat of Chopin's "Funeral March."

Dum, dum, da-dum ...

I heard Mom dragging her feet toward the door, the sound of frustration and worry in every step. And something else.

Fear.

The shuffling stopped. I could feel her eyes on me. "Come on, Indio. You should at least get out of bed on your birthday ... please."

Faster, lighter steps on the stairs. Then, right beside my ear, the shriek of air escaping from the stretched lips of a balloon. "Yeah, come on, Indio!" Sofi yelled. "I made a decadent chocolate cake for you. Get up, ya lump!"

CRAWLING

My climb back to life started with one short email. I found it by accident while poking around the homework app on my new iPhone. The first thing I did when I went online was obliterate every comment on my blog page. Good or bad, love letters or hate mail, read or unread, it didn't matter. I took a deep breath and hit *Delete all*.

The cloud of poison comments dissolved from the screen like tear gas vaporizing into the sky.

I was about to do the same to thousands of stale emails when I spotted a two-word subject line that froze my thumbs.

Miss you.

It was from my Israeli girlfriend Shoshana.
I clicked on it.

Indio, where are you? I miss your magic music.

Shoshana had been a loyal follower since my early blogging days in Xela. Like me, she was born with a thing for music. Like me, she had a father who breathed fire down her back to get her to practice. Unlike me, she played the *oud*. Think stretched-out lute with no frets. Shoshana called it the guitar's great-great grandmother. It has a strange, prehistoric voice that, as she said, "can stir up desert gales and the cries of whales."

We used to trade tunes back and forth. I'd send her a Bach cantata for her to "oudify." She'd send me her arrangement of Taylor Swift's latest hit played on her four-hundred-year-old oud.

We had a good thing going, like we were a culture of two, sharing a secret language.

Her email included an MP3 called "Crawling Out of the Dark," her own composition.

This I could not delete.

I hit *play* and my small dark world caved in around me.

Shoshana's music cracked me open and a bunch of buried memories came leaking out.

The sharp click of a locked door.

The sting of mining stakes against my shins.

A lifeless eye dropping into an open palm.

The sickening crunch of a dying guitar.

A young mother falling to the ground in a fine red spray.

The mournful voice of Shoshana's oud left me sobbing. But not the random kind of sobbing that ambushed me at night. It was hot and healing, like it burned the poison out of me. *Buena medicina* Mom would call it. Good medicine.

Shoshana's music got me off my ass and crawling at least, out of the dark.

I felt connected again. And wanted more.

A month later, I was still at home in my basement room. A copy of my doctor's note was pinned to my bulletin board. I looked at it now and then and smiled. Maybe it was the drugs smiling. There it was in ink, my official diagnosis: *Clinical depression.*

I was on drugs, all right. Prozac in the morning, Ativan at night. But they couldn't touch the highs I was getting from being back online.

This feeling's got to be illegal. Could even get me arrested.

BLACKBIRD

The Internet became another instrument. Mom's laptop and my new iPhone were the strings. The hottest apps and websites were the songs. I learned, I practiced, I played. My new improved blog became the stage.

I lost hundreds of musical followers after the Xela shooting. But I gradually rebuilt my fan base by feeding them the rare gems I'd discovered, digging deep into the online guitar world. Interviews with master guitar players, videos of amazing performances, the best teaching sites, coolest recording apps, and tons more.

What was missing, of course, was me playing guitar. That's what got me connected in the first place. It didn't take long for my followers to speak up:

> great stuff Indio. i especially like the "guitar candy" app. never woulda found it on my own. u r making me a star! but where's your amazing chops? gotta have your inspiration!

Glad you're back online. Looking forward to your next coolisimo concierto ;)

OMG I thought you had died. Time to strut your stuff again, Wonder Boy!

Soon after you disappeared I had a dream you played Led Zeppelin's "Babe I'm Gonna Leave You" on your classical guitar. Please make my dream come true! And please, please don't ever leave me again! ♥♥♥

My fans were screaming for me. But there was just one problem. My guitar and I were not getting along.

Over those months since we'd moved to Canada, the closest I'd come to playing my guitar was in my dreams. A melody would pop into my head, invade my arms, and wake up my fingers. My guitar was back on my lap, my hands in ready position. The melody called me, teased me, seduced me. I chased it with my fingers, like those magic moments playing with Magno, note by note, in perfect unison.

I'd wake up with this weird ache in my chest and wonder, could I start again? Could I be that guitarist with "talent to burn," as Magno used to say? Could I buckle down and practice, but this time on *my* terms, not my father's?

Once, after such a dream, I actually took out my guitar, just to feel it in my hands. It felt awful. The strings were dead, the wood cold and stiff. I couldn't even tune it. I played a few chords. I tried the first notes of my dream melody. I looked at my hands in disgust. I could still hear the melody in my head. I could see myself on stage performing it. I could hear the applause explode after the last ringing note.

But my guitar chops were gone. And just over my shoulder was my father, pouring hot coals down my back. Even though he was a million miles away, busy with his Guatemalan lawsuit or down in Colombia drumming up another mine, he was watching me. I could feel the heat.

Still, my fans were screaming for me.

I wouldn't let Dad wreck this chance.

Okay, Indio, I said to myself. Start over. Go back to basics. Back to the first tune Magno ever taught me. "Blackbird" by the Beatles.

At first, even this simple ditty was a stretch. But eventually it came back. And with it, some ideas on how to use the cool apps I'd found while staying home, alone in my room, supposedly recovering from my *melancolía*.

A warm Chinook wind had punched the seasons back to summer overnight. That's Calgary for you. I decided to film the whole thing outside. I propped my iPhone on the lid of Dad's barbecue and hit *Record*. Loba and I walked into the frame and sat down on the grass under the big crabapple tree. She gently swatted the guitar strings a few times with her paw, as if begging me to play—a little trick I taught her. I nodded to her, then played "Blackbird" exactly like Paul McCartney.

I got lucky with the black bird part when a raven showed up the next day. I caught him on camera, hopping back and forth across our fence.

With all the raw footage now in the can, I was back on the

laptop, playing.

The Chinook had blasted all the snow off the crabapple tree but, with the right app, it was easy enough to put it back on. I draped some digital icicles and Christmas lights on the tree. Next came the job of getting the raven to hop all over me and my guitar while I played. This was no sweat with a special app I'd found for video splicing. Using another app called "Cheshire," like the disappearing cat in *Alice in Wonderland*, I made my body fade away, leaving only the guitar, my fingers, and the hopping raven. I couldn't help fooling around with the music itself, adding concert hall acoustics, a funky bass track, and a whispering wind. I ended it with some hilarious raven calls recorded at the bottom of the Grand Canyon. Just as the music ended, my body returned. Loba licked my face. I blew a kiss at the camera. All the icicles melted and the Christmas lights exploded into spring flowers.

It took me two days to polish my first high-tech music video to the level I was happy with. It felt a lot like getting a guitar piece ready for the stage. I watched it one last time, had a good belly laugh, then hit *Publish*.

"What were you laughing at?" Sofi asked when I went upstairs to snarf down half a hot dog.

"Come and see," I said crashing back downstairs.

Sofi watched the video open-mouthed. "That's pretty cool, Indio. How the heck did you—?"

I held up both hands. "Sorry, that's classified information."

Minutes after publishing, the comments came pouring in

from all over the world. I clapped my hands and gave Sofi a bear hug that lifted her off the floor. "I'm back!"

We plan to show your music video at my little sister's funeral. She had cancer. She loved ravens. The flowers at the end made us all cry but also gave us hope. Thank you!

Truly amazing, Indio! The raven is my Animal Spirit Guide. They follow me everywhere all the time—like your beautiful dog follows you!

Sweet! Why the hell does this video have less than 1,000,000 views??? Please, everybody, share this widely!!!

Mends my soul. So grateful for this. Tear ducts still working ok.

AWESOME video. You are my guitar avatar! ;-P

BEIN' IAN

The Blackbird video lifted me high enough to go back to school, even though I was still on low-dose meds. They helped me ride the bumps, like walking into class super-late after blogging all night, or enduring another math class that made my home-school days with Luiz look thrilling.

Then there was Morris, who liked to trip me up in gym class or corner me in the hallway. Like one Monday morning I'll never forget.

"Hey, Pedro!" Morris said, stepping in front of me as I tried to swerve around him. "Where ya been?"

I stood up as tall as I could, still a head shorter than Morris. "It's *Ian*, okay?"

Morris was so close I could smell the gel in his hair and the weed on his breath. "I heard you got AIDS," he said loudly.

"Who told you that?"

Morris waved a hand at a line of chic chicks standing by their lockers. "Like, everybody."

"It wasn't AIDS."

He scrunched up his face. "But it must've been something awful. You hooked off for so long." He looked around, nodding at the girls. "Something *awful*," he repeated.

The girls nodded to each other.

I fingered the meds in my pocket, craving another hit. "It was nothing special."

"Not special for *you*," Morris said, backing away. "So it's true, then."

"What's true?"

"That it's easier for your kind to catch those sorts of diseases?"

"What do you mean, my *kind*?"

Morris shrugged. "I don't know. You tell me."

The buzzer went off above my head. A mob of students pushed past us, knocking me into Morris's barrel chest. "Uh … sorry, Morris," I mumbled.

He stepped aside, almost politely. "What, for existing?"

I dove into the mob and ducked into class, sweating.

As I closed the door behind me, I realized I was standing in front of the wrong class.

That was not a good day.

It got better when I opened this text.

morris is a jealous muscle-headed twerp! ignore him.

It was from Monica, the fashion plate running for president.

How did she get my number? Why would she write me?

After the initial high, I figured she was just after my vote.

Things got much better when Morris started missing school, even more than me. Some said he'd dropped out. But then I'd see him talking to stoners in the stairwell. Or I'd spot his orange Mustang cruising by the school, belching hip-hop music loud enough to shake the pavement. He'd pull up by a group of smokers behind the arena; down would go his power window, and in went a wad of cash—and he wasn't selling pencils.

But that was none of my business. As long as Morris was out of my face, school was tolerable.

I showed up for most classes, kept my ears open and nose to the ground. I tried to fit in when I could. When I couldn't, I became invisible.

My real life was online.

Since no one at school knew me as Indio—I reserved that name for my global guitar audience—I decided to experiment with a second blog, a random, quirky teen forum, featuring the coolest apps I could find, the funniest jokes, goofiest pictures, freshest gossip, and hottest links. The sky was the limit.

The catch was I included only Canadian content. I figured this would be a good way to learn how to be a Canadian, while convincing my local followers, and myself, too, I guess, that I actually was one.

I named my new blog **BEIN'canadIAN.blogspot.ca.**

What do Canadian Schools really teach us?

1. Absolute truth comes from the weather.
2. Intelligence is the ability to remember and re-peat donut names.
3. Accurate memory & repetition are required to find your way home in a blizzard.
4. Non-compliance is punished, especially when running a dog team.
5. Conforming is rewarded, especially when ending sentences, eh?

Click **here** for more tools on organizing student-led revolts, Canadian style.

ILYG, Bein' Ian 🍁

In spite of such lame beginnings, the BEIN'canadIAN blog took off. I built a second base of followers, totally separate from the thousands following some Guatemalan guy named Indio, the caged guitarist.

At school, people who used to ignore me, even some of Morris's followers, would stop me in the hallway to talk about my blog, trade apps, and suggest new stuff to put on it. My list of contacts in Calgary alone grew to over a thousand. They kept me busy flipping texts back and forth, easily two hundred or more on a normal school day.

But thanks to our principal, Mr. Grimsby, the next Friday would definitely not be a normal school day.

THE CONCERT

"I'm sorry, Ian, but today is Friday."

Mr. Grimsby was on the school stage with me, flipping his palm open.

I thwacked my iPhone to my chest. "So?"

"You know the routine. The last Friday of every month all devices stay home ... *or else*."

"Or else what?"

"I confiscate them."

I started to sweat under the stage lights. I looked out at a sea of expectant faces. Not classmates, not anyone I'd see walking down my street.

Indio's guitar fans. I recognized them from their profile pictures. I saw Paula from Argentina, Rashid from Pakistan. And there, my Israeli girlfriend, Shoshana, the oud player!

They'd come from all over the world to hear me play.

My throat tightened.

Mr. Grimsby hovered over me. "Hand it over, Ian."

I crammed my phone under my butt. "It's off, don't worry!"

I reached for the guitar and rested it over my left thigh. It felt weird. I looked down. I was hugging Dad's darling Ramirez.

I always got nervous before performing. Now it felt like God was listening.

I poised my fingers over the strings ... and spotted Dad in front of the stage. He was dressed like an usher, complete with pillbox hat and gold-striped pants. Ridiculous. He didn't freak over me touching his guitar. He was too busy pacing the floor, staring at his watch.

The school gym morphed into a fancy theater. All my friends now wore tuxedos and long dresses. Staring at me, holding their breath.

I gritted my teeth.

Nothing came. Not one note.

I heard whispering from the audience. Grumbling. Laughing.

I looked up at my virtual friends, now so real before me. All heads down, all thumbs flying. Everyone texting like crazy.

What were they saying about me?

Like robots, they suddenly lifted their phones and pointed them at me.

My jaw relaxed. I knew what was coming. They'd hit the candle app and wave their phones around for me like in big rock concerts.

But no.

A blinding flash from a thousand cell phones. Taking pictures of me, choked and sweating, looking like an idiot.

All heads down again, posting photos of the world's greatest guitar zero.

My phone jumped to life under my butt.

Mr. Grimsby's nose and cheeks puffed red. "Hand it over, Ian. Now!"

"No, wait!"

I yanked out my phone. Where was that video of me playing guitar on top of a speeding train? They'd see. I'd post that and they'd see I could—

Mr. Grimsby snatched my phone away.

It felt like losing an arm.

"Hey, back off!" I yelled. "Student assault! Help! Police!"

Loba blasted out of the crowd and galloped across the stage. She leapt at Grimsby's chest and knocked him flat.

"Good dog, Loba!"

My phone skittered across the stage and over the edge. I lunged after it. Dad's guitar flew off my lap and crashed to the floor, shattering into matchsticks.

Forget the guitar. Get the phone.

I slipped in something warm and wet.

The principal's blood.

People jumped from their seats, screaming, stampeding for the exits.

I turned to see Loba ripping something pink and straggly out of Grimsby's neck.

Forget Grimsby. Get the phone.

"Loba, phone! Fetch!"

Loba flew past me in a spray of blood and jumped off the stage.

Dad pulled out a mining stake and started clubbing people, shoving them out the door.

Forget the audience. I can text them later. Get the phone.

Loba, nose to the floor, bounded through a jungle of thrashing legs. She clamped down on something yellow, then lifted her head to show me, her tail wagging.

"Yesss! Good girl, Loba!"

I jumped off the stage but, before I got to Loba, Dad had pushed her out the door and slammed it shut behind him.

I kicked at the door. "Dad, what are you doing? I need that!"

I pounded the walls. They'd turned into sunbaked adobe. Like Diadora's hut. I looked up to see razor wire lining the top.

Forget the wire. I'm going over. Get the phone.

I backed up and took a running leap, raking my hands and chest through the razor wire.

I landed in something soft, like a bed, but my fingers were all torn up.

Forget playing guitar. How will I ever text again?

I heard the sound of heavy traffic. Loba was running toward me across a busy highway with my yellow phone in her mouth ...

"*¡Dios mío!* Would you turn that damn thing off!"

I slowly moved my fingers and felt the soothing imprint of my iPhone in my hands.

Good dog, Loba.

"Turn it off for once, Indio. You're doing it again."

"Huh?" I cracked one eye open and made out Mom's silhouette against the hall nightlight, hands on hips.

"You're sleep-texting again!"

"What?"

"I heard you shouting for Loba. I come in and you're lying there with your arms up, thumbing your phone." Mom threw up her hands. "No wonder you're so zonked at school."

I jerked the phone to my face and checked sent messages.

Hry evrbod# che out mo= lat3st gitrar vidwo

What have I done? Sent gibberish with no weblink or attachment to 10,147 followers.

I scrunched my eyes and fists. "Aaagh!"

Mom came at me like a five-foot freight train. "Here, give me that!" She tried to grab my phone, but I rolled over and pinned it under my chest. I flashed back to Grimsby's torn throat. "Why is everybody trying to steal my phone?"

"Everybody?"

"I mean … I … I *need* this!"

"Not tomorrow, you don't. It's Friday. Remember? Device-free Friday? You won't die if you go without it for a few hours."

"Oh, no?"

"What *will* kill you, Indio, is not sleeping. Not eating. Not moving. That thing has hijacked your brain!"

"You gave it to me."

"Yes, but I never thought that ... oh, just give it to me, would you?"

"But it's not Friday yet."

"Technically, it is."

"What about homework? We have a big math assignment and I might need to call—"

"At 3:30 in the morning? Come on, Indio."

"Well ... what about my friends? I sent this crazy stupid message. Just let me tell them that I didn't—"

"Your so-called *friends* won't care. Now give me that thing and you can use your hands-free Friday to make some real friends."

I took one last look at the screen. Already, in less than two minutes, 458 replies. I slowly stretched my arm out to Mom. "Take it, then. But don't you lose it."

I felt like I was sticking my head in a guillotine.

Mom pried my iPhone from my hand and tucked it in her nightgown. "Don't worry, Loba can always find it. Now, just for once, you can sleep unplugged."

I buried my face in my pillow. My arm slipped off the bed and I heard a familiar drumbeat on the floor. My fingers found my best friend's pointy ears. The thumping stopped.

I suddenly lifted my head, wondering if I'd trained Loba well enough to sneak into Mom and Dad's room and steal back my phone.

SABOTAGE

It didn't take me long to find ways to hack through the school's website-blocking programs. And the principal's restrictions on cell phone use in class were a joke. Thumbing text messages under my desk while pretending to listen was now as easy as playing an open C scale on guitar with my eyes closed.

But when it came to the next month's device-free Friday, Mr. Grimsby had new weapons to shoot down our God-given right to stay connected 24-7.

That is, until I posted this blog the night before.

Sabotaging Our E-Rights

My esteemed fellow students of Edgemont Heights, you've probably heard the news by now. (For those of you from other schools who are reading this, listen up. You won't believe what's happening to us. And you definitely don't want it to happen to you.) The news about this month's Device-free Friday.

Just in case you were too busy texting and missed the PA announcements, the Principal's speech at Assembly, the posters wallpapering our hallways, and, ironically, the flashing notices on our school's whiz-bang website—just in case you missed all this propaganda, here's the news: you are about to be stripped of your personal rights and freedoms to the cyber world in which we teenagers live and breathe.

How will this devious plot be hatched? Through the installation of two fiendish forms of technology. In the digital world they call it ATT—Anti Terrorist Technology.

First, our principal has installed a METAL DETECTOR at the main door so you can't bring your phone to school even if it's off. You know, like they use at airports to stop terrorists from blowing up planes or knifing pilots or flying into office towers.

Any of your friends into that? Didn't think so.

And if that weren't bad enough, he plans to install a CELL PHONE JAMMER in our school to block all calls, texts, and Internet access if you manage to slip through his metal detector with your cell phone (Did I just encourage that?). Cell phone jamming devices were originally developed for cops and the military to block communications by criminals and terrorists—like you and me. Got any plans to trigger explosives? Organize an assassination? Take a few hostages? Or maybe conduct a little corporate espionage? Not during school hours, I'm afraid. At least not once our principal turns that thing on.

Click this **link** for more dirt on jamming, and I'm not talking here about your Saturday night garage band.

WHAT'S AT STAKE?

Is it just me or does this seem like overkill? Technically speaking, our school is launching a "denial of service" attack. Deny us any chance of using our cell phones—and what's supposed to happen? We will magically become more attentive? More respectful? Better behaved? More socially well-adjusted? All that stuff we heard from the principal's podium?

Can this technology fix our "fixation with technology," as Grimbsy says?

I kinda doubt it.

After all, do we really have a problem here to fix?

We are the most connected generation in history. We have a planet-full of information at our fingertips. We depend on our cell phones to keep in touch with our friends, to entertain ourselves, to check in with our parents, to keep us safe, to build family and community and global harmony, etc., etc., and to avoid germ-laced payphones. Oh, yeah, and to access the state-of-the-art homework app developed and paid for by our own school fees!

So what gives?

Ultimately, this techno-muzzling plan represents a blatant denial of every Canadian's right to freedom of expression—"to freely exchange information, thoughts, ideas, beliefs, and opinions through any media of communication, including the Internet." I'm not spouting off the top of my head here. I'm quoting from the Canadian Charter of Rights and Freedoms.

No one can deny us that freedom, least of all Mr. Grimsby. His plan basically throws a finger at Canada's constitution.

Are you going to take this lying down?

JUST ONE MORE LITTLE THING: IT'S ILLEGAL!

I have more news for you. Not only is installing a cell phone jammer in our school unconstitutional, it's ILLEGAL. I discovered that a high school principal way over in Gander, Newfoundland, tried to pull the same stunt on his students. He ordered the device online from China, where—

guess what—jammers are legal. But here's the thing. The dad of one of his students happened to be a criminal lawyer, who politely told the principal that civilian use of such devices in Canada is illegal, and that he could go to jail if he installed it. The principal's original idea backfired. Now the right to use cell phones in his school has become a hot student rights issue with no solution in sight.

Click **here** to find that story. You can file it in the *whoops-forgot-about-that-law-thing* department.

So, I ask you now, just *who* is the criminal?

FIGHT FOR YOUR E-RIGHTS!

I found plenty of schools online that have reasonable cell phone controls without resorting to Anti-Terrorist Technology. But first, let Grimsby prove to us there's a problem, show it to us under a microscope. If it's true, then it should be up to us to draft the guidelines for their use and, on the flip side, the penalties for violating them (click **here** for good examples). This could go a lot further in reigning in his power, while gaining him a little respect, rather than sabotaging our e-rights and freedoms by installing an illegal device that could land him in jail for five years.

Hmm. On second thought ... five years, eh? We should all be out of high school by then ... LOL!

But before all that warm, fuzzy collaborative

stuff can happen, we have to fix our real technology problem—by kicking its butt the hell out of our school!

ILYG, Bein' Ian 🍁

JAMMED

With my iPhone stashed somewhere in my mother's laundry basket or her shoe collection, or God knows where—even Loba couldn't find it—I had no choice but to stop at a drugstore on the way to school and pick up a cheapie flip phone. As I walked up the steps to the school's main door, I hid it behind my biology textbook and checked reception. The number of bars dropped with each step until they hit zero. The message I dreaded seeing popped up on the screen:

No service available.

I discovered what it felt like to be jammed. To be forcibly unplugged. To be brutally, maliciously, illegally stripped of one's identity and meaning in life.

Okay, that might be going too far but, I'll tell you, it did feel like shit.

I decided to fight this tooth and claw.

I soon discovered I was not alone.

A line of students half a block long was marching two-by-two straight for me. Many carried signs.

Take your jammer and stick it!

We are not terrorists!

Save our right to bear cell phones!

Lock away our principal, not our phones!

As the crowd got closer, they started chanting. "No A-T-T for you and me! No A-T-T for you and me!"

I got this stupid smile on my face that I couldn't wipe off.

They read my blog!

The shouts got angrier, the chanting louder. I saw raised fists, felt the vibration of many feet pounding up the steps toward me. The hair on the back of my neck went all bristly. I remembered protesters, mud bombs, and blood. I wanted to run, to hide, to escape from the mob before I got caught in the crossfire.

Then I felt cheery slaps on my back. My esteemed fellow students were shaking my hand. Monica, the would-be president, even kissed my cheek. "What's wrong, Ian?" she asked. "You look a bit green."

"I'm okay, really."

"We *need* you in there, Ian," Monica said, pausing as the

line of chanting marchers parted around us.

"Go ahead," I said, catching her vanilla scent. "I'll catch up."

I waited for the rest of the marchers to pass, then wrapped my cheapie cell phone in a plastic bag. I carefully slipped it inside my ham and cheese sandwich, dropped the whole thing in my lunch bag, and marched up the steps into battle.

REVOLT

Getting my cell phone through Grimsby's metal detector was a snap. He was standing beside it like some airport security guard, telling us to empty our pockets of coins, keys, and mobile devices and dump them in plastic trays. Mr. Priddle, our gym teacher, carried the trays around the machine and handed everything back, except for devices. He was a big guy whose arms were thicker than my thighs. "You can collect these in the principal's office at the end of the day," Priddle said, scooping up handfuls of phones and stashing them in a locked silver briefcase like they were confiscated handguns.

When it came to my turn, Grimsby looked at me as if I'd let off a stink bomb in the staff room, which, in a way, I had. I knew that he and many teachers had been stalking my BEIN'canadIAN blog since I first launched it. I'd publicly accused him of a criminal act and everyone in the school knew it.

Hundreds of students were milling around the main

foyer, still chanting, "No A-T-T for you and me!"

"Well, good morning, Mr. McCracken," Grimsby said, towering over me with his arms folded. "Anything to donate to our cause today?"

I placed my lunch bag on top of the metal detector, where I hoped its sensors couldn't touch it. "No, sir. I'm clean."

"Oh, what a surprise. We've reformed, have we?"

"Yesss, sir." I walked through the detector with my pack on.

Beep! Beep! Beep!

I was thinking I'd blown it with the machine's sensors, when Grimsby seized my pack and unzipped it before I could get it off my back. "Aha! We'll just see who's reformed."

He pulled out my biology text, a dictionary of Canadianisms, and a package of steel guitar strings that must have been there since my Xela days. He sniffed and squeezed the package. "I didn't know you played guitar."

"A little."

Grimsby held the package up to a light, then, finding no hidden devices, crammed everything back into my pack, almost knocking me over.

"There he is!" some girl shouted.

I turned to see Monica. She was running over to me, bringing a parade of her groupies with her. She pulled me away from Grimsby and brought her hot lips close to my ear.

That's when I noticed how many students were looking at me, including Morris Kritch. He and his hockey buddies were leaning against the trophy cabinet.

"It's getting crazy," Monica said. "Everyone's really pissed off, ready to break something! To string someone up! The march went okay, but this ..." She stared at the chanting students. "This could go bad, really bad. Then we'll *never* get our phones back."

Her face was so close to mine I could feel the heat from her flushed cheeks.

"What do we do now, Ian?"

Monica's scent, Morris's stares, the swirling, shouting students all got my head spinning. But I'd seen this kind of mob chaos before. We needed to put a lid on it before any shit happened. Before we lost our bargaining power.

I plunked down on the floor. "Sit down!" I said, tugging Monica's hand.

"What? Right here?"

"Yup. With a crowd like this, the best way to stand up for our rights is to stage a sit-down strike."

She suddenly sat down, almost on top of me. "Of course!" All of her groupies were next.

"This'll cool 'em down," I told her. "We can start talking with the enemy. You seem chummy with Grimsby. Why don't you lead the charge?"

"Sounds good. But ... what do I say?"

I wondered what kind of school president Monica would make. Maybe I could be her campaign manager. She definitely had my vote. "Don't worry, I've got some ideas."

"Whatever you say." Monica motioned for everyone to sit

down. "Come on, people," she shouted. "We're on strike! You want to protect your right to bear cell phones?"

A huge "YEAH!"

"Well then, we're gonna sit it out till they're guaranteed!"

Hoots, shouts, cheering. The foyer was instantly carpeted with wall-to-wall students. All except for Morris and his buddies, who ducked out of sight.

I felt a hefty tap on my shoulder. I looked up at Mr. Priddle, holding my lunch bag between two fingers.

Damn! Busted!

"You forget something?" he said, handing it over.

"Oh, yeah," I said, breathing easier. "Thanks."

The sit-down strike dragged on and on. By lunchtime, Grimsby agreed to turn off the jammer, but still dug in his heels on our cell phone freedoms. With one hand discreetly tucked in my lunch bag, I was back online. I fired off a bunch of blind texts to local media, inviting them to witness cyber-democracy in action.

Grimsby was visibly shaken when the TV crews and reporters showed up. His position softened dramatically. After several more rounds of negotiation, we ended up with some pretty decent cell phone guidelines, co-signed by Monica and our much-humbled principal.

Monica and I took turns reading them out loud into a microphone, to bursts of cheering and applause. Back home I fired a brief blog to the world, declaring our student-led revolt a smashing success. The comments started pouring in seconds later.

Thanks for saving our cyberbutts!

i still say that guy should go to jail for even thinking of jamming us. give him 10 years hard labor.

As a teacher, I have to walk that fuzzy line between limiting students' phone use while not infringing on their personal freedom. Your success raises the bar for other schools to follow. Congratulations from Australia!

The score: Ian McCracken 1, Oliver Grimsby 0. Well played!

my phone has my whole life in it. i would simply die without it. you're my hero!!!

CYBER ATTACK

The next Monday, Grimsby greeted me on the front steps with an icy smile.

"Good morning, sir," I said cheerfully.

More ice. Enough to get a small glacier moving.

His expression was so priceless, I whipped out my iPhone and took his picture before he could say a word. After a friendly nod, I entered the foyer, already posting his picture on my blog site. The caption:

Grumpy Grimsby saved from jail sentence!

In Grimsby's eyes, I had become public enemy number one. But what could he do to me? Canadian law had been upheld. The student body had spoken. Democracy had prevailed. I was untouchable. And thanks to our new "PUMP" guidelines—*Positive Use of Mobile Phones*—I and eleven hundred other students could stay connected pretty much whenever and however we pleased.

Now I could walk our school hallways with my head high and hands clean. In the cafeteria, students I'd never seen before pulled chairs up to my table to celebrate the previous day's battle and talk about where we should go from here.

Something had clicked between Monica and me. She made me feel ten feet tall. Her bubbly laugh gave me goose bumps. I wanted to stage another revolution with her, or maybe just ask her out to a movie or something.

But my status as a local hero got killed soon after.

The first shot was one stupid comment on my BEIN'cana-dIAN blog.

Lay off laying on Monica, or else.

It was fired by a faceless source with the name *Knock-out123*.

Those seven words soured my entire next day at school.

Monica kept stopping me in the hall, asking for help in her election campaign—building her platform, designing her logo, writing her theme song.

This was exactly what I'd hoped for.

But every time Monica and I talked, I felt eyes burning my back. Somebody named *Knockout123* was watching me, threatening me.

Or else what?

My poison pen pal.

Day after day, he fired comments into my blog, faster than I could delete them.

She deserves so much better than you!

Hey faggot, what's it like having no friends?

You want to help Monica be president? Then get the hell away from her NOW!

I'm giving you one last chance to leave her alone before the truth comes out.

All these comments wore me down. I shrank inside. I couldn't sleep.

What truth?

That old *melancolía* crept back inside me. The high I'd felt after conquering Grimsby was long gone. Even Monica seemed to be pulling away, probably because now when we talked, I was barely there. My eyes would always dart around, looking for my torturer.

Then came the photo, hacked into my BEIN'canadIAN blog.

It was a picture of me playing guitar in our Xela home. *Las Posadas* candle lanterns burned all around me. Two little boys, my Aunt Dora's kids, sat on each knee, looking up at me. Slapped across the photo, in flashing neon orange, were the words:

PEDRO THE PEDOPHILE

No one on earth called me Pedro. No one, that is, but Morris Kritch.

Mr. Knockout123.

After the first bomb went off in my head, I thought, *Wait*

a minute! Where did he get that photo?

I'd been ultra-careful about keeping my two blogs separate. They protected different worlds, different identities. Totally incompatible. My Ian followers knew nothing of Indio, the Guatemalan guitar star. My Indio followers knew nothing of Ian, the true blue Canadian kid who pushed the latest teen gossip and gadgets.

My fingers froze over the keyboard. Had Morris hacked *both* blogs?

I hit enter and my heart stopped.

Morris had posted the exact photo, pedophile text and all, on my guitar blog.

I collapsed over the keyboard, my guts spilling out from a deadly double hit.

LISTENING

It took two weeks and a lot of meds to get me out of bed and back at the keyboard. My doctor called it a relapse. Mom told me my *melancolía* always hid just below the surface, ready to burrow into any *grietas en el alma*—cracks in my soul.

Morris's dirty little post shook up my soul, all right. Cracked it open and poured me into the gutter.

"Nobody home in here," said a hollow voice in my darkest moments. "Nothing to live for."

The correct term for this place is "Pit of Despair."

It was Loba who saved me. She never left my bedside, always had a face lick for me when I rolled over, thumped her tail with the slightest wiggle of my toes. Things turned the corner when I found myself humming to her. That really got her tail going.

At the bottom of that awful pit, I tasted a trickle of something sweet.

A wisp of a melody.

It wasn't much of a tune, not anything I'd played before, but it had a simple charm, like Bach's "Air on the G String" or Pachelbel's "Canon," only fresher, not wrecked by too much elevator airtime. I hummed and hummed this new melody, clinging to it like a drowning sailor grabbing a lifeline.

Let it come, Indio. Find the music ...

At first I couldn't recognize the voice in my head.

Find the music. Follow it to the source ...

The source. The source ...

Below all the bullshit and pain.

Now I knew.

It was Magno calling.

Lying there in my dungeon bedroom, with the tin foil back on the windows, I let the melody come. It opened up and took me in. Got my fingers twitching.

I sprang out of bed, gave Loba a massive hug, and ran for my guitar case. Even in the dim light, I could see a layer of dust on it.

I pulled out my long-abandoned friend, grabbed a textbook for a footstool, and started playing like mad, trying to capture the melody before it evaporated.

My first composition on Canadian soil.

I discovered a quiet, soothing melody in waltz time, perfectly suited to classical guitar. The name of the piece hit me between the eyes when Loba came over for a nuzzle.

Loba's Lullaby.

I heard heavy stomping on the stairs. Cowboy boots.

I didn't stop. I didn't look up.

"What are you doing?" Dad asked.

I ignored him.

"I mean ... it's great that you're up."

Dad's voice had softened, like he was almost happy to see me alive. "It's ... uh ... great that you're playing again."

I hadn't seen my father for weeks. But I didn't lift my head. I didn't stop.

I wouldn't play his games anymore. I refused to let him wreck this moment.

"Nice piece," he said, taking a couple more steps toward me. "What's it called?"

"Shitstorm," I said. "Now would you just let me *play*, Dad?"

"Sure, son ... sure."

My father actually shut up. He sat down in my big leather chair. I glanced up for a second and watched him watching me. His head rested on the back of the chair. His hands were loosely folded on his lap.

I played on.

He just sat there, listening to my music.

Like he used to when I was a little kid. Those were our best times.

Before things soured between us.

I played on.

Sofi came pounding down the stairs. "See?" she said to Dad. "I *told* you he was faking. How come he gets to miss so much school?"

Dad chuckled and patted the fat arm of the chair for her to sit on.

Instead, Sofi leaned against the doorframe and folded her arms, listening to my music.

I played on.

LOBA'S LULLABY

A week later, I was reviewing my latest and greatest music video one last time. It had to be perfect. I wanted to honor every ounce of creative power I knew it had.

The power that probably saved my life.

The success of my "Blackbird" video showed me how important it was to mix good music with good effects. I also needed a good storyline. Even though "Loba's Lullaby" had a round feel to it, I wanted it to go places, to take the viewer on a journey.

A journey with Loba.

First stop, believe it or not, was my bathroom. It had the best acoustics in the house.

Loba's Lullaby began like a billion other amateur videos out there, looking rough and wobbly, totally unplanned. Just me and Loba chilling on the braided rug that Sofi made me out of old T-shirts. I sat cross-legged with my guitar on my lap. Loba sat beside me, wagging her tail. Prompted by my wink, she did her begging routine, gently swatting the strings with one paw to get me to play.

I plucked the opening chord, a spacey c7b9, and we took off.

Literally.

We were on a magic carpet ride across Canada.

The bathtub and toilet behind me dissolved into blue sky, with Loba and me sailing through it on Sofi's rainbow rug. In the blink of an eye, we were tailing a snowboarder down British Columbia's Whistler Mountain, landing on the spinning top of the Calgary Tower, then riding a tundra buggy beside a polar bear near Churchill, Manitoba. Next, we leap-frogged through the clouds to Toronto's Wonderland and zipped down the country's biggest roller coaster. Then we spilled over Niagara Falls, blasted down Quebec City's giant toboggan run, and hovered above the wild horses of Nova Scotia's Sable Island. Last stop was the deck of an ice-breaker busting its way to the North Pole. By the time we made it back to my bathroom, Loba's head was in my lap with her eyes closed. I strummed the last spiraling notes and we faded to black.

Since Morris had hacked both of my blogs, Ian's and Indio's, I decided to post the video on each. My hope was that it would blow Morris's pedophile bullshit out of the water while rebuilding my fan base. I could deal with the fallout over my real name later.

My last tweaks to the video included a dedication to my dog.

For Loba, my guardian angel.

I took a deep breath, loaded the finished video onto my blogs, and hit *Publish*.

Little did I know how that would backfire.

DROWNING

Sure, I felt good about *Loba's Lullaby*. But this, *this*, I never saw coming. Within two days, my music video had raked in over seven hundred thousand views. In three days, it broke a million, in a week, twelve million. My global fan base exploded.

I never did get through all the comments.

I screamed out loud when you went over the falls! So funny! 😊

I can't wait to learn your piece and play it to my girlfriend. Now I just need to get the girlfriend!

omg! im gonna die of a cuteness attack! Please love your dog and hug her all the time!

I'm a cat person, but this video is fuckin' awesome!

The comments went on and on and on. The questions, too.

Can you send me the sheet music?

What apps did you use?

Did you really go to all those places?

Plus the inevitable comments from people who had nothing better to do but shit on me.

When you learn to play REAL music like heavy metal you MIGHT get my attention.

your dog is obviously on drugs. shame on you!!

fake fake fake. even your music is fake. don't waste my time you fake.

Reading, answering, defending all this took forever. It was like another roller coaster ride—only this one was real. I'd never felt such highs. Then another hate bomb and down I'd go. Up, down, up, down. I didn't go to school. I didn't sleep for four days. I think I ate one Mars bar the whole time. I don't remember drinking anything.

All I remember is my glowing screen and the sea of comments washing over me. I kept pushing and pushing, trying to deal with the endless flood of online attention.

Of course, Mom was pulling her hair out.

She actually tried to yank me into bed once, but I bounced right back to the keyboard. She begged me to see a doctor but I refused. "I'll be fine," I yelled, "once I get through all these comments."

At one point, I had to pee real bad and, for some reason, ran outside and relieved myself under the crabapple tree. I stood there a long time, my dick hanging out, staring bleary-eyed at the Calgary skyline.

How many people down there saw my video?

I just stood there, burnt out, brain dead, until I heard my neighbor's window slam and saw a woman inside pointing at me, talking excitedly on her phone.

Minutes later, I heard a car door slam, Mom's worried voice, heavy footsteps coming downstairs. I zipped up and dove into bed. I buried myself under the blankets. I groaned like I was dying—which maybe I was. Mom slowly opened my door. I poked my head out enough to see the red hatband of a Calgary cop.

More groans.

"Well, at least he's in bed now," Mom said. "He won't cause any harm, officer."

NOSE HILL WALK

In the end, it took Mom slamming my laptop shut and scooping it off my desk to get me out of my chair.

"Hey! What are you doing?"

She tucked the computer behind her back. "Time for a break, Indio. You haven't walked Loba for days. You've been totally ignoring her."

I looked at Loba on her sheepskin rug. Her tail thumped, her eyes brightened, she waited for my command. My stomach sank when I realized she'd probably been lying there the whole time, the star of my viral video, my guardian angel. I hadn't patted her once since I'd posted it.

Mom thrust Loba's pink leash into my hands. "Please, Indio. It'll be good medicine for both of you."

"*Buena medicina*, eh?" I said.

"*Sí, Indio. Cuídate*," she said. "Take care out there. You're not yourself."

"Myself? What's that?"

Loba got up, grabbed the leash in her teeth, and started

pulling me toward the door.

"Okay, but just for few minutes. I really gotta—"

"Walk the dog. Right. Now, get out of this jail cell."

I slurped down a few mouthfuls of stale ginger ale and threw on my jean jacket.

"Take an umbrella, Indio. It looks threatening out there."

Umbrellas were big in Guatemala. Even teenagers piled under them in a good rain. "Naw," I said. "This is Canada, remember?" I automatically grabbed my iPhone on the way out.

"Oh, no you don't," Mom said, reaching for it. "You're a wreck. You need a total break *offline*."

"Yeah, but ... just in case I need to call you or something."

"Where are you planning to take her?"

"Dunno. Nose Hill, maybe."

Mom pointed a finger at me. "You promise me you'll cross at the lights?"

"Yeah, yeah."

I fell more than walked down the grassy hill that led to Shaganappi Trail. My head felt like concrete, my legs like lead. Somehow we made it to the bottom, safely crossed the six-lane intersection, and picked up the gravel path that winds to the top of Nose Hill.

I took off Loba's leash and she sprinted up the trail.

There was a little pond partway up where Loba always liked to sniff around. It was surrounded by a scruffy forest full of interesting smells, in a park that was mostly grass and wind. Loba zeroed in on something furry at the edge of the pond. Something dead. She clamped down on it and dropped it at my feet with great pride.

A jackrabbit skewered clean through by some kid's arrow. "Gross, Loba!" I said. She backed away with lowered ears. I stared at the rabbit like it had fallen from outer space. Its cotton-bob tail and ridiculously long ears made me laugh out loud.

The next minute, I was sobbing into my hands.

Maybe Mom's right. I am a wreck.

I whipped out my iPhone and took a photo of the dead rabbit for my blog. I wasn't sure why. Maybe I thought that once I posted it, this strange creature from another world would become more real for me. Or maybe I could seek vengeance on the bastard kid who killed it.

I went online and was about to post the photo, when I noticed that my video had scored another five hundred comments in less than an hour.

"NO MORE COMMENTS!" I screamed, flinging my iPhone high into the air. It spun in a steep arc, slapped the surface of the pond, and sank out of sight. "NO!" I screamed again, and ran up the hill as fast as my half-dead legs could carry me.

A minute later, Loba was bounding along beside me with my yellow iPhone in her mouth.

She offered this, too, at my feet, her tail almost flying off.

I stared at the phone with a mix of joy and nausea. "Good dog, Loba," I finally said. Without checking it, I jammed it in my pocket and kept running. I didn't stop until I almost crashed into a young father pushing his son on a bike with training wheels.

"Ian!" the dad said. "Where ya been? You okay?"

I worked hard to focus on his face and realized it was my dishwasher friend from school. "Oh, hi, Danilo. Yeah, I'm ... I'm fine. Just a little busy."

"Cool video, man!" He noticed Loba. "Is that her? The famous Loba?"

She came over and licked Danilo's hand.

"There's your answer," I said.

"You busy working on another video, man? That was *so* cool. How did you do that part where—"

"Uh ... maybe later, okay? I just need a—"

"A break, right. I get it. You artist types."

Danilo's son was rocking his bike. "C'mon, dad, let's go."

"I didn't know you had a kid," I said. "Does he like to play with bows and arrows?"

Danilo looked at me funny, like I was drunk or something. "Sorry, what?"

"Forget it."

They continued down the hill. Both father and son waved back at me. "*Hasta prontisimo*, man," Danilo yelled. "See ya soon!"

"Yeah, maybe."

Father and son. Outside playing together.

What a concept.

By the time we made it to the top of Nose Hill, the wind had picked up and the temperature had dropped by, like, ten degrees. Crazy Calgary weather. I plunked down on a bench, thinking: what a nice place this would be to sleep for a week—when I was assaulted by a screaming monkey ringtone.

Damned if my iPhone still worked.

I pulled it out and checked missed calls and text messages. There were over two thousand of them. I let out a massive sigh, realizing I hadn't checked anything but my blogs since I started to make the video three weeks ago.

Two hours later, I was still sitting on the bench going through my messages, when a crack of thunder exploded over downtown Calgary. I lifted my head and saw a wall of black clouds rolling off the mountains. I buttoned up my jean jacket and dove back into my messages.

Just two hundred more to go and I'll ... Wait a minute. Where's Loba?

Another screaming monkey. Incoming from Mom.

"Yup," I said.

"Where have you been, Indio?"

I stood up and scanned the trails in all directions. "Nose Hill, like I said."

"Did you hear that thunder? You should get off the hill right away. Remember that woman who was hit by lightning up there?"

"What woman?" I saw a flash of fur darting through the grass and started running toward it.

"About twenty years ago, I think. Whatever. You need to come home."

"Okay, okay," I said, stopping in my tracks when I saw it was a coyote.

"Right now, Indio."

"Yeah, yeah. Be right there."

I spun around and around, looking frantically for Loba.

"Indio, what's wrong?"

"I'm okay. Loba just took off after something."

"You've *lost* Loba?" Mom cried.

"No, no, she's just ... I'm coming home. Bye."

I shoved the phone in my pocket and ran. "Loba!"

I ran over to another clump of trees. "Loba!"

Down to the pond where she found the rabbit. "Loba! Loba!"

Next to the fence along the road where my shouts were drowned out by rush-hour traffic. "LOBA!"

Back up to the bench ... where I found her proudly sitting beside a Calgary Flames ball cap that I'd lost up there months ago.

I buried my nose in her fur. I smothered her with hugs. I was crying again. "Good dog, Loba! That's my sniffer dog. Where did you find that? Good dog, good dog."

Another crack of thunder, closer. The first drops of rain.

"Let's go," I said to Loba, slapping on my ball cap. I started down the trail, leaning over my phone, dealing with more messages. All of them about the video. Good, bad, ugly. Reading, responding, deleting.

The rain came down in buckets. Cars streamed past me, sending up angel wings of spray. I was almost at the intersection when I opened a text from Monica, now the school president.

RUOK? sorry to hear your blog got hacked. fng evil stuff 😣! luv your video!! didn't no u played guitar.

would luv to learn some time. u r HOT! can I have your autograph 😵?? news flash: grumpy grimsby tinkering with our phone guidelines. trying to water down while u r away. we need u here Ian. miss u! xoxo

I glanced up at the traffic light as it turned green. I was back on my manic channel, levitating across the intersection, held aloft by Monica's words. *Hugs and kisses! Wow!* I started thumbing her a quick response when I heard a train-sized horn behind me and a screech of brakes. I looked back just in time to see a dog rolling sideways under a big red Coke truck.

"LOBA!"

I ran back across the intersection against a red light.

"LOBA!"

Cars started honking at me from all sides, among them, an orange Mustang with a cell phone sticking out the driver's window, pointed right at me.

DR. POZNIAK

The smell of dog pee and floor cleaner had me reeling in my chair. Mom sat beside me, her fingers wrapped in mine like she was holding me up. The way I felt, she probably was.

A vet technician walked into the waiting room, all smiles. "Good news," she said. "Loba is going to be fine."

I felt Mom's fingers relax. "*Gracias a Dios*," she said. "Thank God."

"She's one lucky dog," said the technician. "And tough! Rolling under a Coke truck like that? But no broken bones. Just a dislocated hip. We'll need to put her under to—"

I jumped out of my chair. "Put her under! You mean, like—"

"No, no. Just an anesthetic so we can pop her leg bone back into her hip."

"Didn't you already give her anesthetic?" Mom asked.

"That was just a mild sedative to keep her calm for the x-ray. And some pain killer."

"Is she in a lot of pain?" Mom asked.

"Likely not. Just a precaution."

"Isn't that kind of overkill?" I said.

"Routine procedure," the technician said, as she moved down the hall. "Would you like to see her before we fix her up?"

I ran down the hall after her and pushed open the operating room door. Loba looked pretty stoned but was able to lift her head and wiggle her tail on the stainless steel operating table.

The bearded vet, Dr. Pozniak, was filling a syringe beside her.

More drugs.

I took Loba's head in my hands and gave her a final nuzzle. "I'm sorry," I whispered. "I'm so sorry, girl. You'll be okay. I promise."

The vet gripped a loose fold of her neck and stuck in the needle. "This won't take long," he said in a thick European accent, "but we'd like to keep her overnight for observation, if that's all right with you."

"Yeah, sure," I said. "Whatever it takes."

"You can pick her up tomorrow at ..." Pozniak looked at his watch. "Oh, tomorrow's Sunday, so you'll have to come after one o'clock when we open."

I watched the light fade from Loba's eyes as the anesthetic kicked in. She slowly lowered her head onto both paws. Even doped up, she didn't take her eyes off me once. Just before they closed, Loba shot me a last pleading look, begging to stay by my side forever.

The phone call came the next morning at 11:53. I picked up the landline after one ring. "Hello."

I heard Mom pick up on the kitchen phone.

"Good morning. This is Dr. Pozniak."

Why's he calling? I thought they opened at one.

Something rough and heavy dropped in my stomach. I let Mom do the talking, since my throat was suddenly dry as dust.

"Good morning," she said. "What's up? Is Loba okay?"

"We kept her under observation all night," the vet said, "and she appeared to be sleeping comfortably."

"Is she okay?" I whispered.

"Well, this comes as much of a surprise to me as to you. After all, she only had a dislocated—"

"IS SHE OKAY?" I yelled.

"I'm sorry to tell you that your Loba died overnight."

An arrow skewered my heart. I was the dead jackrabbit on Nose Hill.

"WHAT?" Mom shrieked. "How? Why?"

"It may have been shock, or internal bleeding that we could not detect, or—"

"*You* killed her with all your drugs!" I yelled and slammed the phone down.

Whatever took her that night, I knew the real truth. I was the one who killed her. The one who walked blindly across that busy intersection, my nose glued to my phone, totally forgetting Loba, who was searching for me in the crush of cars.

And thanks to the marvels of cell phone technology, and

the darkness of Morris's jealous soul, my crime was posted on both of my blogs. Seconds after it happened, the world could watch one of the Internet's most famous dogs get creamed by a Coke truck.

REMAKE

Part of me knew I was insane. Maybe always would be. All the shrinks and doctors and rehabbers I'd seen the past few weeks told me I was getting better.

You'll get through this, they'd say. *You can do it.*

So why did I still feel like a crazy person? I'll tell you why. My best friend was dead. Worse, I killed her.

How could I be so stupid?

Her last look at the vet's. Begging to stay by my side.

I hated myself.

Then there were my other so-called friends. Where were they when I needed them?

They ignored me.

I'd dropped off their screens. Even Monica's.

Online or walking down the halls at school, it was the same vibe.

Who's Ian?

Who's Indio, for that matter?

No one knew the shit I was going through. No one cared.

If they weren't ignoring me, they were crucifying me. All I got was hate mail. I couldn't believe the names they called me. The most common was dog-killer. The only happy faces I got were from people paid to look after me.

My addiction rehab team.

Years ago, back in Xela, when I felt really lost or lonely, I could always find a loyal friend in my guitar. Always there for me, never judging, healing my wounds. Whether I played blues, Bach, or Berlioz, I always felt better after playing guitar.

That escape hatch wouldn't open for me now. Just looking at my guitar made me want to puke.

The choice was clear. Plan A: kill myself. Or Plan B: a total remake.

Plan A was pretty tempting, especially on those mornings when, even with my meds, just getting out of bed for a pee gave me panic attacks.

But this wasn't one of those mornings. Even though it was pissing rain and the sky was dark and gloomy, I was okay with another day alive.

That crazy raven was back, hanging out in the crabapple tree. He was making bizarre gurgling sounds that actually made me laugh. *Made me laugh!* First time in ages. That crazy raven stretched a wing out to me and pulled me out of bed.

So Plan B it was. For now, at least.

Time for a fresh selfie.

I decided to start with my hair. With the right app, I knew I could fake anything. Give myself shark teeth, a lion's mane, or maybe a ponytail and gorgeous black 'stache like Juan Carlos used to have. Before he shot that ...

Actually, no. Nix that. The Latin Indio was dead. Crucified.

I wanted to do this right, do it real. I had to get a haircut.

Maybe I'd shave my head like a monk in mourning. Or get that spiked Mohican cut I'd never had the balls for.

Whatever. I would know what to do once I was in the chair.

Time to redefine myself.

Again.

I glanced out the window as I pulled on my jeans and GOT2TEXT T-shirt.

No raven.

For a second, I had a prickly feeling it was never there.

"So where's Dad?" I asked Mom between mouthfuls of Lucky Charms.

Mom's smile was squarer than normal. Purple half-moons swung under her eyes. "Where else on a Saturday morning? At the track."

"Pissing away my inheritance."

She stopped cleaning dead things out of the fridge and looked at me. "You know he's been under a lot of stress lately."

"Oh, and I haven't?"

"We all deal with stress in different ways. You have your ... music," she said hopefully. "He has his—"

"Gambling."

"It's a *hobby*, Indio."

"Like your shopping's a hobby?"

She turned away, reaching deep into the fridge.

I stared at her back. "He steals Guatemalan gold, rapes their land. *Your* land! He leaves a trail of blood behind him, then blows all his loot on horse racing?"

"You know he's invested in schools down there. Remember, he bought those fancy computers for your high school in Xela."

"Which I hardly used because he made me practice so much."

"And he built that technical school in Siete Platos near the mine."

"Uh-huh. To help the villagers blow up more mountains and drive bigger trucks so Dad could steal their gold faster."

Mom huffed into the fridge. "What about all those guitars, Indio? You know he likes to invest in nice guitars."

"Which he never plays."

"Well ... he *is* busy these days."

"Yeah. Busy suing *your* people for stepping in front of *his* bulldozers."

Mom absentmindedly wiped her face with the yucky fridge rag. "Don't start that, Indio. They're *your* people, too, remember!" She suddenly looked away, then ducked back into the fridge.

It hit me that I was not the only alien around here. Mom had to be homesick for Guatemala.

"Nice to see you up so soon," came Mom's muffled voice. "You planning something?"

"I really need a haircut."

"Sure, Indio, but—"

"I need it bad, Mom. What car did Dad take?"

"The Porsche."

"So I can have the Range Rover?"

Mom popped out of the fridge. "It's in the body shop. Dad found a little ding on the passenger door. You know how he fusses with his toys."

"So then ..."

Mom checked the ceramic holder beside the fridge. A line of Mayan mamas held keys in their outstretched hands. Her fingers landed on a blue-and-white key ring stamped with the letters BMW. "Looks like it's the Beemer."

"Yess!"

Mom tossed me the keys. "You be extra careful, now. You know how Dad hates it when—"

"Don't worry. I won't let anyone breathe on it."

"And please, *please*, no texting and driving." She pushed the morning's paper across the table. Her finger tapped an article with the headline, *Hang up your phone or risk killing someone—like I did.* She shook her head. "So tragic. You really should read this, Indio."

I shoved the keys in my pocket. "Later, Mom. Anyway, you know I've reformed. After all you spent on rehab? Besides, who am I gonna text? All my friends abandoned me."

Mom pulled something green and furry out of the fridge. It might have been a tortilla. Or a pancake. She held it at arm's length like it might bite.

We both started laughing.

"You kinda missing Katrina?" I asked.

BEEMER TRIP

As I pulled out of the garage, it felt like I was backing into a carwash. The rain pounded on the fogged-up windshield. Even on full blast, the wipers couldn't keep up, and I had to guess where the driveway ended and the street began. The headlights clicked on automatically, tricked into thinking it was nighttime, not eleven in the morning.

Just before I hit the gas, I noticed a pretty pink rock tucked in beside the stick-shift. I held it to my face, studying it in the dim light—then chucked it in the back seat like it was a dried-up dog turd.

A glittering piece of gold ore stolen from Diadora's backyard.

I inched my way past Edgemont's mansions. Rainwater poured off their roofs in torn sheets. I turned on to Shaganappi and tucked in behind a red river of taillights.

I was relieved to see that Nose Hill was hidden under a bank of clouds. I didn't know if I could ever look at it again, let alone walk up there.

The traffic opened up. I floored it. My body jammed into the leather seat. Huge sheets of water rose up beside the car. I couldn't drive fast enough to shake the memories.

Loba rolling slo-mo beneath the Coke truck.

An orange Mustang filming the crime scene.

Loba's last pleading look at the vet's.

Dr. Pozniak's phone call.

I squeaked through an orange light and took an exit for downtown, aiming for a teen hair place that got high ratings online. I thought I'd memorized the address, but my fried brain was like a sieve. I fished in my pack for my iPhone.

"Siri, launch Calgary Yellow Pages."

I'm not texting, Mom. Just asking directions.

"Yellow Pages launched, Indio. How can I help you?"

"Address for Razor's Edge Salon, please, Siri."

I got an instant response, but couldn't make it out through the pounding rain. I thumbed up the volume. "Repeat, please, Siri."

"What was that, Indio?"

It sounded as if a giant mining truck was pouring gravel on the car. I glanced up through the moon roof. Hailstones the size of golf balls. My stomach clenched. Dad would really and truly kill me if his beloved Beemer got dented up.

I had to get out of there, but how? Tuck under a roof? Pull a U-ee and book it for home?

I spotted a gas station ahead with a big wide roof. As I put on my flicker, I saw it was already overflowing with cars taking cover.

The hail got worse. Everyone was getting antsy, actually

speeding up. I got caught in the flow, squinting ahead through the mess of water and ice for another gas station.

"Are you there, Indio?"

"Yes, Siri, hang on."

What's most important right now: a place to take cover or my haircut?

Then I thought, the hell with Dad's car. It was a Beemer, right? Tough as nails.

This haircut could not wait.

I figured I could get my cut and post a new selfie within a couple hours. I had to create a whole new profile. Put out a fresh blog. Repair my bombed-out bridges.

"Siri, what was that address?"

Again her response was garbled by machine-gun rattle on the roof, and I missed the last two numbers. I grabbed the iPhone off the seat and looked at the screen. I scrolled through the map. I zoomed in to look for parking spots.

"Easy as pie."

"Excuse me, Indio?"

I looked back to the road, smiling.

But not for long.

A sea of brake lights painted my windshield red.

Nothing was moving.

Except me.

I slammed both feet on the brake.

The tires grabbed pavement.

"*¡Gracias a Dios!*"

My shoulder strap bit into my collarbone.

I pushed harder on the brake.

The tires gulped water.

I was hydroplaning.

I pumped the brakes the way I'd learned in driver ed.

The car glided down the road like a hockey puck on ice.

I turned the wheel to the right.

Too fast. The car fishtailed. Now I was hydroplaning *backward*, facing the headlights of cars that a second ago were behind me, their high-beams flashing madly.

I cranked around in my seat and looked behind me—or was it in front of me? The sea of red lights was coming up fast.

"Jesucristo!"

"I'm sorry, Indio, but I didn't catch that."

"SHUT UP!" I screamed.

I pumped the brakes harder, faster. The tires finally bit. I yanked the wheel and aimed for a grassy boulevard. The car went into a spin.

Everything sped up ... and slowed down at the same time. The boulevard came at me at an impossible angle and I realized that half the car was in the air.

I'm sorry, Mom.

Something pink floated past my face. Instead of Dad's pet rock, it became a glass eye, winking at me before the air bag exploded and I blacked out.

GREEN MEN

A faraway light. I remember that. Way down there. I remember letting myself slip toward it, free-falling into a bottomless whirlpool.

I remember thinking about my granny, Mimita.

And Loba.

Am I about to see them?

The shouting broke my fall. Called me back.

I turned from the light. Slipped into my body.

Firemen, medics, shouting all around me.

A gurgling sound. I remember thinking, *My brain is spilling out on the ground.*

The sound of ripping metal, crunching plastic, popping glass.

Hanging upside down.

The smell of gasoline, burnt rubber.

Glass on my face.

Giant lobster claws eating Dad's BMW.

Rain on my face.

Big hands groping for me, easing me out of the car, wrapping me in a flannel cocoon.

Strong hands lifting me onto a stretcher and floating me like a feather into the ambulance.

I tried to say something to the men, so big and beefy in their lime-green uniforms. So gentle. This incredibly safe feeling, like I was a baby wrapped in a Mayan sling. I tried to move my mouth, my tongue.

Only grunts.

I remember crying.

Not from pain. That was yet to come.

I cried from the thanks I couldn't say. I knew I owed my life to these big green men, lifting me into the ambulance.

A door slammed. I was in another cocoon.

Hissing gas, beeping monitors, the heavy breathing of an angel cradling my head.

The ambulance lurched forward.

Furious pounding on the door.

The smell of coconut oil.

Mom's hand on my chest.

Her face suddenly hovered near mine, rutted with worry.

Soothing sounds came from her mouth.

I couldn't make out the words.

She looked out the door and shot an angry look at somebody. I managed to lift my head enough to see a lone figure in a yellow miner's raincoat. He stood in the shadows, his hunched form jumping in and out of view with every flash from the ambulance lights.

Dad.

His face twitched, like he was fighting something inside.

Fear. The guy looked petrified.

What's he afraid of?

Then, for the first time, I got really, really scared.

I started panting like a dog.

My head spun out of control.

My brain crackled like when the battery runs out on my acoustic guitar.

I scrunched my eyes.

My skull exploded.

The lights went out.

CHAMELEON EYES

I came to ten days later in the Alberta Children's Hospital, the one made from giant toy blocks.

For a long time, I had chameleon eyes. They roamed around on their own. This was strangely entertaining until I discovered it hurt like hell to focus.

It hurt to concentrate. Even to think.

All I could do was stare up at a light. It drifted in and out of focus with each breath.

I studied the ceiling tiles, trying to see straight. They were decorated with choo-choo trains and teddy bears.

Gradually I realized I was not alone. Someone was repeating a question close to my ear. A man's voice.

"... your right hand, Indio ... your hand ..."

I thought it was Magno, coaching me on my right-hand posture.

Guitar players live or die by their right hand.

"Can you feel your right hand, Indio?"

Not Magno.

Someone was squeezing my hand.

"Can you squeeze back?"

I squeezed back. The teddy bears went out of focus.

"Good, Indio. Now we're getting somewhere."

Rapid footsteps.

Mom's hands on my cheeks. "*¡Gracias a Dios!* Thank God you're okay, Indio!"

The bears, the trains, everything blurred in a flood of tears.

I blacked out.

BED OF ROSES

Brent, the nurse who emptied my bedpan the whole time I was in a coma, later told me my first words were, "I fucked up ... Sorry, Mom ..." and "Where's my phone?" Another time I woke up thrashing, calling a name over and over.

"Who's Loba?" he asked.

I opened my mouth but nothing came out. I felt like a total idiot.

"Save your breath," Brent said. "We got *lots* of time to get to know each other. Welcome to the Neurosurgery Clinic."

My stomach did a backflip. I slowly lifted both hands to my head. A slice of my scalp was shaved clean, crisscrossed by a dozen metal staples. Just below the staples, it felt like my brain was boiling. I could hear a bubbling sound.

My mouth fell open.

Brent gave me a tight smile. "You'll be fine, Indio."

My fingers retraced my bald patch and bounced over the staples.

They don't shave your head and install railroad tracks if you're fine.

"They did surgery to relieve the pressure on your brain. Everybody says you did really well."

All I could do was raise my eyebrows. *Everybody?*

"It was a long operation. Two neurosurgeons and a stellar cast of nurses. You kept us up all night, but that's gravy to us."

Brent pointed a flashlight at me. "Now, all you gotta do is follow the bouncing light. Okay?" He slowly swept it up and down and sideways.

While my brain burned, my eyes felt like they were stuck in cold molasses. I tried to follow his light, but it was like sight-reading a Bach sonata in double time.

A little frown darted across Brent's face and he scribbled something on a chart. "Okay, Indio. That's enough for today." He whipped out a needle and pointed it to the ceiling. "I'm going to give you something to help you sleep. Give your bruised brain a rest."

"No ... wait," I mumbled, amazed to learn I could speak.

But that's all I got out. Two words. He'd already jabbed the needle into my shoulder.

I was good and ready to hate this guy—till the sedative kicked in.

Next I was lying in a bed of roses. Brent became my angel of mercy.

I sank into a deep sleep drenched in Brazilian guitar études.

CONCUSSION

I felt much better when I woke up. Must've been the drugs. Until I realized I'd pissed myself in my sleep.

I wanted to fly out of bed but could barely lift my head. When I tried, my skull filled with red-hot lava. I lay there, grinding my teeth, until Brent finally came back.

"This will never do," he said, sniffing and grinning at me in a way that made me want to strangle him. His bulging biceps and bulldog neck told me I'd be no match at the best of times. I let him roll me around and mop me all over like some diaper brat. Talk about humiliating! He changed my sheets, then politely told me to get my shit together because some visitors were coming.

"Let's brighten things up a bit, shall we?" he said, yanking the window blinds open.

The sudden light filled my eyes with slivers of glass. "Aagh!"

"Oh, sorry about that."

Instead of closing the blinds, Brent dug in his pocket for

sunglasses. They had rainbow arms stamped with the word *Pride*. "Try these," he said, carefully slipping them on my head.

"So ... like ... where *is* my ph-ph-phone?" I asked, once I calmed down.

"RCMP took it."

"The cops ... s-s-stole my ... iPhone?" My mouth seemed light-years from my brain. My words stretched out like in a lousy Skype connection.

"Just part of their investigation."

"What inves-s-s ... tigation?" My brain was getting softer, like it was melting.

Brent put a hand on my shoulder.

I shrugged it off.

"Easy, Indio. You gotta keep a cool head." He glanced out the window. "It might help them figure out what happened out there."

Lava spread from my brain to my neck. "I can tell them ... whatever!"

The lava hit my stomach.

I didn't have a clue what happened out there.

Brent ducked out.

I checked to see if my fingers were working. I saw the sheet stirring where they must be. I struggled to bring both hands in front of my face. I could barely feel my fingers but they were moving, all ten of them.

My guitar fingers.

I fretted a soundless arpeggio. I plucked imaginary strings. This triggered a gush of cozy feelings about playing guitar. Joy, escape, friendship.

Then, memories of Dad breathing fire down my back, turning what I'd loved most into torture.

I tossed my invisible guitar across the room.

I checked to see if my brain was working.

I closed my eyes. Tried to think.

Who am I?

Indio McCracken. Aka Ian at school. Sixteen years old. Former caged guitarist, now teen blogger.

Good start. And my family?

My mother, Gabriela Canché, from the Mayan highlands of Guatemala. Shopaholic. Family peacemaker. My sister, Sofia, 12 years old. Family princess. Uncle Faustus. Pushing 90. My biggest fan.

So far, so good.

My father ...

Come on, Indio, you can do this ...

My father ... Edgar McCracken, born in Scotland, grew up in Canada. Gold miner. Guitar zero. Family dictator.

Great. Brain seemed to be firing. So, what *did* happen out there?

Humongous rainstorm ... hailstones ... hydroplaning ...

I heard the squeak of a wheelchair and opened my eyes. Uncle Faustus's smile blew me away. Amazing what a new pair of Canadian dentures could do for a dusty old *campesino* like him.

"*¿Qué tal, Indio?*"

"I'm g-g-good, Uncle. *M-m-muy bien, gracias.*"

He grabbed my hand in both of his.

Sofi plopped on a chair against the wall, like she'd get cooties if she got too close.

Mom held my other hand. "You're awake," she said, glancing at the top of my head, then into my eyes. I could tell she was struggling to keep her gaze there.

Sofi wrinkled her nose. "What's up with those metal things? And the rainbow shades?"

"Meet young Frankenstein," Brent said.

I struggled to focus on Mom's face. "Have you ... have you s-s-seen my phone?"

"Don't worry, Indio. The police have it."

Brent wasn't kidding.

"Yeah ... but for how long ...? I really need it."

"It doesn't matter. You're cut off from all that now. Until your brain heals."

"It d-d-does matter! What do you mean ... cut off?"

Uncle Faustus grinned and patted my hand. I noticed one of his eyes was totally clouded over, like a dead fish.

When did this happen? Wait ... What's he doing in a wheelchair? Where have I been to miss all this?

Mom gave me her posing-for-the-camera smile. Her eyes were bloodshot like she'd been up all night, crying or looking at online catalogs again. "You've had a major concussion, Indio. The doctors say you have to relax your brain, take it real easy. No texting, messaging, video games. No computers, movies, not even schoolwork."

"Lucky you!" Sofi said. "I could use a little concussion about now."

"You know I don't d-d-do video games."

"Yes, Indio, but all that other stuff you do. Forever post-ing, texting, chatting, blogging. Your little movie things, your—"

"I can ... I can control it."

Mom just looked at me.

She was right. I couldn't control it.

"But what about m-m-my homework? You know most of it's online and—"

"Sorry, Indio, but this concussion means no phones, no computers, no devices of any kind. The doctors say that any mental activities that need any concentration could delay your recovery ... or worse."

My eyes started wandering again, going out of focus. I was lying in sweat. "Worse?"

Mom squeezed my hand tighter. "Permanent brain dam-age, Indio. You might never talk straight again. Walk straight. Think straight. And what about your guitar career?"

"W-w-what about it?"

That's when I noticed Dad hanging back at the door.

"Uh ... hi, Indio. How ya doin'?"

"Just dandy. I g-g-guess that means a b-b-break from practicing, too ... eh, Dad?"

Something like a grin crossed his lips. "Whatever the doctors say."

I thought about Dad's beloved Beemer, steaming upside down in the rain. Almost as sacred to him as his Ramirez guitar. "S-s-sorry about your car."

"The car was totaled, Indio. You were lucky."

"I wasn't d-d-doing anything ... crazy. Just driving when—"

"When what?"

Mom brought her face close. "Were you texting, Indio?"

"What? No! At least … No. I wasn't. There was some rain and I—"

"*Some* rain?" Dad said. "It was a bloody—"

Mom looked at him over her shoulder. "Edgar, please."

"I don't know exactly w-w-what happened … I just … I … What is this? A police interrogation?"

Dad jammed his hands in his pockets. "Who in their right mind would be out in that kind of storm?"

I fiddled with the IV needle taped to my arm.

"Exactly *why* were you out there, Indio?"

"Haircut. I r-r-really needed a haircut."

Dad sucked a ton of air, then released it in a disgusted sigh. "Are you serious?"

Brent wove in front of Mom and placed a tray of yucky-looking hospital food on my lap. "That's enough chit-chat for one day, folks. Indio needs his strength."

The expression on Dad's face made another coma look good. "We'll talk about this later, Indio."

"About what."

"Everything."

"It wasn't my f-f-fault, Dad."

"We'll see," he said, and was gone.

Brent shooed everyone out the door. "Come along, folks. That's it for visiting hours."

Mom gave each of my cheeks a peck.

I couldn't feel her kisses. I couldn't smell her coconut scent.

Sofi stepped toward me and wiggled my big toe.

I tried to wiggle back but it was too far from my brain. "Stay out of trouble ... b-b-brat," I said, fighting off a wave of panic.

Uncle Faustus gave one last squeeze, then leaned forward in his wheelchair like he was sharing a secret. *"Prométeme. Nunca renunciar a la música."*

My head's split open, I can't feel my feet, and you want me to play guitar? To never give it up? "S-s-sure. *Le prometo, tío.* I promise you, uncle. *Nunca.* N-n-never."

Uncle Faustus gave me his big new smile. Sofi spun his wheelchair and headed for the door. Uncle Faustus craned around and winked at me with his frosty eye, my promise in his pocket.

Alone again.

I squinted out the window. Dad must have paid big bucks to get me this private room with a view over the Bow River.

Thanks, Dad, but I could really use some company.

I tried to figure how many days it had been since I last checked my messages or posted anything. The very thought got me sweating. That bubbling sound came back.

If only I had my phone, what a selfie I could take! I stretched out one arm, pretending to hold my phone, as I made a Frankenstein face and showed off the railroad tracks on my head. Add Brent's goofy shades and I'd get at least a thousand hits for sure.

I dropped my arm.

Surely the cops must be done with my phone.

Why do they want it? What are they looking for? It wasn't my fault.

My thumbs got all twitchy. At least I could move them.

I gotta get that phone back.

BRAIN DAMAGE

I don't remember much about my recovery. All I know is it got worse before it got better. A lot worse.

Mostly it's a blur. How I learned to walk all over again. How my speech got so bad I was blinking yes's and no's— two blinks yes, one blink no. How I got the shakes if I tried to do too much, like just watching TV, and my hospital bed would start bouncing off the floor.

Or how I'd wake up, screaming for my phone.

Which they refused to give me even after the cops were done with it.

They proved it, all right. That much I remember. The cops proved that I'd been thumbing my iPhone seconds before the car flipped.

The phone that killed my dog.

That almost killed me.

There were many days when I wish it had.

Mom kept pulling the brain damage card on me. Said if I went haywire online again, I'd become permanently depressed or crazy or just plain stupid.

Mom came by to see me every day. Sofi every weekend. Once she got over my Frankenstein stitches, Sofi started reading to me. Stuff she wrote for school or a book she was reading. She'd go on for over an hour or until my brain started bubbling. One day, she brought in an old *Prensa Libre* newspaper from our Guatemalan days and read me an article about Xela's Boy Wonder.

That almost sent me into convulsions.

Mom brought Uncle Faustus sometimes. Whenever he came, all he did was smile and keep repeating, "*Prométeme ... prométeme.*"

I knew exactly what he was talking about. That I never give up the music.

"*Le prometo, tío.*" I promise you, uncle.

What else could I say to the old guy?

It was only after a bunch of visits that Mom asked if I was aware that now, when I spoke, it was always Spanish. Even to the hospital staff. This came as a total surprise.

No wonder they give me such weird looks.

Brent later explained that this can be one of the side effects of a concussion. "If you know more than one language and your brain takes a hit," he said, "it'll default to the language you know best."

"*¿De verdad?*" I said.

Brent raised his eyebrows. "See?"

I tried to laugh. "I mean ... really?"

"Your battered brain's going to follow the path of least resistance. So it runs to the language closest to your ..." Brent shrugged, "... your *real* identity, I guess."

My real identity. Hmm.

The bubbling came back. I scrunched my eyes.

Brent stuck me with another sedative and I was blotto all over again.

Truth is, until I got my brain back, I wasn't talking much in any language. So nobody visited very long. As usual, I spent most of my time alone.

It was early February before my neurologist let me go home, more than three months after the crash. In all that time, I saw Dad once, the day I came out of my coma.

Mom insisted he came a few times when I was zonked out.

I didn't believe her.

BACK ONLINE

Another month went by before they let me go back on-line. It started with half an hour a day. Half an hour! Were they kidding me? It felt like Mom was being stricter about my online time than Dad ever was with my practice time.

If that's humanly possible.

Every day after supper, Mom came downstairs and un-locked my filing cabinet where she kept my laptop. She set it on my desk, waited for it to boot up, then started a timer on her cell phone. "Thirty minutes, Indio," she'd say, wag-ging a finger at me as I plowed into the keyboard. "Not a minute more. You don't want brain damage, do you?"

So it went every day.

Five minutes before my time was up, she was already marching downstairs. She hovered over my shoulder as I scrambled to finish whatever I was doing—checking my messages, posting a blog. The second her alarm went off, she'd slam the laptop shut, shove it in the filing cabinet, and lock it with a key she wore around her neck.

And I thought Dad was the family dictator! At least she didn't beat me over the shins.

God, it was frustrating.

As for my iPhone, I hadn't seen that since the crash. Luckily I still had my cheapie flip phone that I used at school every chance I could. I was back there part-time. Monica was talking to me again and Morris was out of the picture. They said he really did quit this time. Or got expelled. Or got shipped off to some addiction rehab center.

Who the hell cared? What mattered was that he was gone and I was back. At least until the headaches came or the dizzy spells knocked me over, or my eyes gave out even when I wore sunglasses in class.

Even on my best days, I was nowhere near the lightning texter I used to be. And blind texting under the desk was impossible. Instant headache. Grimsby, too, was always harping about brain damage, and ratted on me with a call home every time I got caught.

It was usually Mom who picked up the phone, since Dad was still away most of the time, fighting Guatemalan lawyers or kissing the butts of Colombian politicians.

Six months after the crash, I was back up to two hours online a day—officially, at least. I used a crowbar one night to wrench the back off my filing cabinet. Mom still thought she was in control, unlocking it and doing her timing thing. I acted super-cooperative when she came down to lock away my laptop. When everyone was in bed, I'd pull the cabinet away from the wall and slip my laptop out the back for endless hours of online fun.

I rebuilt my list of friends and followers. I created the coolest profiles ever. I hunted the far corners of the Web for the funniest pix and craziest videos. I fired out a couple of blogs every night. One from Ian, the champion of Canadian teens' rights and freedoms. The other from Indio, the Guatemalan guitar guru with tips and tricks to make you a star.

I merged back into the Internet, not caring for anything or anyone else. I felt powerful and alive like never before.

Until the next morning.

When I showed up for breakfast totally wiped, or couldn't get out of bed, I'd tell Mom the headaches were back and she'd let me stay home from school. She was so impressed with my supposed discipline on the computer that she put me on an honor system, letting me control my own time, up to the medically prescribed max of two hours a day.

Hah. Peanuts!

I managed to keep up my double life—the obedient son who stuck to his online ration, and the late-night Internet partier—until Sofi started stalking my blogs and realized I was cheating big time.

"You can't do this, Indio!" Sofi said, when she crept downstairs late one night and caught me on my laptop. "The doctor said—"

"Screw the doctor," I said, without looking up from the screen. "I'm okay."

"You're *not* okay and I'm telling."

"Don't you tell on me! Just let me finish this blog and I'll—"

But Sofi was already up the stairs and running for Mom.

They just didn't get it. How could something that felt so good be so bad? The Internet was *buena medicina* for me, right? It took my mind off the pain, off the loneliness. It fought my depression.

Made me a somebody.

They'd see.

There was no stopping me now.

ABDUCTION

*T*here. *That blog took a lot out of me, but it's always worth it. Can't let 10,891 followers down. Time to check out the rest of my world ... Scan my email .... Touch base with App Chat ... Visit the Guitar God forum ... Oh yeah, and see what my Israeli girlfriend Shoshana's up to. I need an oud fix. Haven't talked with her since last week and it's only —¡Jesucristo! How did it get to be 4:00 am? Oh well, more chance of catching her online with the time zone difference. I can sleep this weekend ... What about that math exam tomorrow? I'll have to fake sick again. This is important. Shoshana really seems interested in me in a new way. Like when I told her about my sore back, she wrote, "Visit me in Tel Aviv and I will give you a nice massage with my smooth fingers." Whoah! ... There was that profile glitch I have to fix, maybe add a new selfie ... And I better scan my blogs for any nasty comments. Gotta keep them squeaky clean ... I can squeeze all this in and get a couple hours sleep before Mom pounds on my door ... Gotta pee. Do I have time? ... God, my back hurts ... Just a little* *stretch then back to business ...*

I felt a muscled hand on my shoulder, rocking me out of a cyber sleep less than an hour old. Before I could open my eyes, someone lifted my face off the desk.

"Indio ... Indio," some guy was saying, cool as a cucumber. "Time to get up. We've got a busy day ahead. Let's go."

I struggled to open my eyes. A thirty-something stranger built like a football player stood over me. Another guy by the door flicked the overhead light on.

I buried my eyes in my arm. "Who the hell are you? What do you want?"

"My name's Erik," the first guy said. "And this is Larry. It's a big day for you, Indio. A new start. Everything's going to be all right, but we really have to go now."

Larry was turning on more lights, ripping the tinfoil off my windows, hefting a packed duffle bag out the door.

By now I was awake enough to wonder about my family.

"Where's my Mom?" I yelled.

"Your parents love you, Indio," Erik said. "They're sending you someplace where you can get it together again. Your stuff's all packed. We need to get going. Right now."

"What is this?" I yelled. "What have I done?" I started screaming for Mom, then *at* her, shrieking, cursing. When I stopped to catch my breath, I saw her by my door, sobbing.

"We love you, Indio!" she cried. "We love you!"

Then another shocker. The sound of cowboy boots coming down the stairs.

When did he get home?

My father, Edgar Stoneheart, stopped at my door, looking hunched and old in his bathrobe and dog-puke golf shirt. He had a lost look on his face I'd never seen before. He held some kind of form in one hand, a gold fountain pen in the other. "Good morning, Indio," he said without a trace of his fake cheer.

"Jesus, what are you doing to me now, Dad?"

Mom stepped in front of him.

Dad reached for her hand.

"You know, we tried everything, Indio," Mom said. "Limiting your online hours, rehab, therapy, group counseling. It's not working. Look at you. This thing is going to kill you."

"So we've found something that *will* work," Dad said as he stepped around Mom. He straightened up, like he was trying to arouse his crusty old self. "Something that *better* work." His darting eyes landed on me. "You'll like this place, nice and peaceful, away from all your ... your screen stuff. You need to unplug for a couple of months. Take a tech break. Discover another world out there." Dad's Blackberry went off and, amazingly, he ignored it. "Give it a chance, Indio. So we can get you back on that guitar, eh? Maybe ... maybe even do some jamming together? Like old times. What do you say?"

It felt like the longest conversation I'd ever had with my father. Except I wasn't talking. I just looked daggers at him. Let him stand there and bleed.

"*¡Nunca!* Never!"

His face darkened. I so knew that look. If he'd been holding a mining stake instead of a pen, he would've used it on me. "This is no joke, Indio. It's either this or next stop is lockdown at the psych hospital. Your choice."

"Hmm, imagine that," I said. "A lockdown. Your specialty."

I peeled myself out of my chair. For the first time I noticed I was as tall as my father, maybe taller. I caught my reflection in the mirror and saw little red squares on one cheek where it had lain squashed against the keyboard.

Dad thrust the form and pen at me. "Your choice, Indio," he said, his voice breaking into gravel.

I rubbed my eyes and stared at the paper. Camp Lifeboat—Intern Consent Form. Tons of fine print but not a word on where the place was. At the bottom was a big black x with my name printed beside it.

"Truly, Indio," Mom said, wiping her eyes, "it's like standing on the edge of a river, watching someone drown. We had no life preserver to throw you. This is the life preserver."

"Well?" Dad said.

I looked up at him with as much hatred as I could muster, given how wrecked I was.

His eyes tightened.

Did I see him flinch?

At that moment, the idea of getting out from under my father's roof seemed irresistible. But to unplug for a couple months? What about all my blog followers? My music fans? What about Shoshana and her smooth fingers?

I'd be as good as dead to all of them.

Erik nudged me forward. I flicked his hand off my shoulder like a bird had shit on me. "Go on, Indio, please sign it.

We really should be going."

Dad's mining stake face was back.

That settled it. I scrawled my name beside the x and threw the form and fountain pen at him. Black blood splashed over his dog-puke shirt. He looked down in disgust and snapped an order at his hired kidnappers. "Take him away!"

I reached for my iPhone, but Erik's hand was quicker and he carefully planted it in Dad's outstretched palm. "I'm sorry, Indio," Erik said.

I pushed past my father, not looking at him, not acknowledging his existence.

At the last moment, I looked back at Loba's sheepskin rug, wanting to give her at least a goodbye pat.

Then I remembered.

That's when I felt the fear break loose. This feeling, like my whole world was going down the toilet.

Part III

NORTHERN CANADA
ONE DAY LATER

I can no longer imagine being broken
without a wild place to fall apart in.

–Gary Ferguson, *Shouting at the Sky*

Something hidden, go and find it;
Go and look behind the ranges.
Something lost behind the ranges;
Lost and waiting for you—go!

–Rudyard Kipling, *The Explorer*

THE DROP

I was still repeating it under my breath when the van finally stopped. "Left from the airport, one sharp right, another sharp right, smell of cinnamon rolls, pavement ends, cow manure, a squeaky gate ... Left from the airport, one sharp right, another sharp right, smell of cinnamon rolls, pavement ends—"

Engine off. Blindfold off.

We were here. Wherever here was.

After we'd landed in Whitehorse, you'd think I would've gone ballistic when they told me to put a blindfold on for the van ride. But the nice goons who walked me to the plane in Calgary gave me a heads-up, so it was no surprise. "It's safer not to have a clue where they take you," Larry told me. "Less chance you'll run for the hills and fall off a mountain or get eaten by a grizzly." After all I'd been through, the blindfold had a strange calming effect, like I was a budgie with a blanket thrown over my cage.

The light stabbed my eyes. Seven months after my concussion, they were still super-sensitive. I dug around for my sunglasses, the rainbow ones Brent had given me in the hospital. Yup, the ones with *Pride* on the side. I didn't care if people thought I was gay. What mattered was what they thought of me online.

I hid behind my sunglasses, checking out who was in the van. I sat beside the driver, a Native guy with braided pigtails. He wore a black leather vest and a string tie with a hunk of turquoise slung under his neck. His hands hung limp over the steering wheel. He looked at me with a big grin, like I'd just won a lottery.

I snuck a look behind me. Three other delinquents, a tall skinny guy, a short round guy, and, somewhere in between, what I thought was a girl. It was hard to tell. Everyone's face was hidden by lowered ball caps or pulled-up hoodies.

But the vibe was clear. *What the fuck am I doing here?*

I looked out the van window at my latest cage. Some weird mutant between a summer camp and a prison. A two-story log building. A couple of yurts. A vegetable garden and volleyball court. A bunch of paths with signs pointing the way to *Meaning, Courage, Confidence,* and *Respect.*

Rehab-speak.

Make me puke.

Everything was laid out in a circle around a big tipi. Beside the tipi was a wooden sculpture of a guy and girl, leaning back-to-back, holding each other up. Carved on the base were the words, *Hope is a place.*

The whole compound was surrounded by a high chain-link fence. I checked the top for razor wire.

None.

There was hope for me, all right.

To get the hell out of here. To get back online.

Somebody booted the back of my seat really hard.

"I am *not* getting out of this van!"

So I was right. It was a girl.

A woman in the back of the van came forward and crouched beside her. The woman wore a blue tracksuit with a pink whistle around her neck. I could smell her fruity perfume. "Hey, hey, Alyssa," she said, her voice all chirpy. "It's going to be okay."

An even harder boot in my back.

"Like, I know you have no reason to believe anything I tell you," the woman said, "and I don't know what you've been through."

Alyssa crunched into a fetal position, hands over her ears, face crammed between her knees. "This is crazy!" she screamed to the floor. "I don't belong here!"

You and me both, I thought.

"Please, Alyssa, give it a try. I know the young people who come here usually aren't very happy. But I've seen the numbers. I follow the ones that finish this program. I can tell you it actually works. For most, at least. Just give it a try."

I spun around in my seat, fighting back tears.

WELCOME CIRCLE

We sat in the tipi on ratty cushions and soggy cardboard, the tall skinny guy and the short round guy. The Native guy with the pigtails sat beside me, silently rocking back and forth like he was grooving to a tune. I checked for earbuds but couldn't see any. Just the thought made me thwack my pants pocket. Empty.

What I'd give for my iPhone!

I noticed a beat-up steel-string guitar hanging from one of the tipi poles and felt a twitch in my fingers. A few bars of a Villa-Lobos étude crept into my head, then blew away when my father's voice crashed in.

It's not good enough, Indio!

The silence was insane, broken only by the flapping tipi door and vicious pounding and screaming from the van.

I stared at a blackened fire pit in the middle of the tipi floor, thinking about one thing. How to jump that fence and get back online.

We sat there for, like, half an hour. I ground my shoes into the gravel. My mind flopped around like a fish out of water.

Nobody talked.

Nothing happened.

Until I heard the van door slam.

Alyssa shuffled in, looking all screamed out. The cheer-leader had her arm around her.

I was working up a good scream myself, when an old guy ducked though the tipi door and marched into the center of the circle. He carried a curved stick with feathers hanging off one end and colored beads off the other. Looked like some kook from a homeless shelter.

He was pencil-thin with a hawk's nose, icy blue eyes, and a long grungy beard. His bare legs were covered in scars. He wore a faded blue T-shirt, showing a guy clawing up a cliff with a crocodile snapping at his heels, a tiger drooling above him, and the words, KNOW PAIN, KNOW GAIN.

He snapped his fingers and in popped a beautiful black and white Husky. He snapped again and the dog flopped down at his feet.

My bowels burned the instant this man opened his mouth and out came a faint Scottish accent. My father with a ratty beard and hiking boots. Everything about him reeked dictator.

"Welcome to Camp Lifeboat," he said, eyeing each of us. "Before I let you introduce yourselves, let me have a go at it. If I'm not mistaken, you are the kids from Hell. You lie and cheat and steal. You have a serious addiction problem. You're flunking out of school. You're in self-destruct mode, and what's left of your life is out of control."

He raised one bushy eyebrow. "Did I miss anything?"

I kicked a pebble into the fire pit. The Native guy looked at me with his goofy grin.

"In clinical terms, you're all in a state of global breakdown. All systems failing. Your health, your relationships, your confidence, your purpose. Your future, basically. You don't have one. And if you don't get serious about changing your ways, you'll never get your life back."

He studied the stick and stroked its feathers with his long bony fingers. "How am I doing?"

You could cut the air with a knife.

"The good news is your parents sent you here to get fixed. Whoever they are—doctors, lawyers, Indian chiefs, or drug addicts—right now, they're sitting in their living rooms, thinking you're going to come back home all nice and everything. Right? You'd think so, for all the money they spent to get you here."

"Four hundred bucks a day, eh, Woody?" the Native guy said.

The old guy nodded. "That's right, William. You certainly want to get your money's worth out of us. But I hate to break it to you, folks. Nobody here can fix you. Not me. Not anyone who works for me. Not anyone but *you*. The fixing part's your job. Setting all that up for you, that's ours. We're a team now, like it or not."

"How about not," I said.

"Go, team!" shouted the lady in the tracksuit.

"Thanks, Carrie. That's the magic word around here. *Team*. Just ask Togo, leader of my dog-team for ten years."

He snapped his fingers and the dog leapt up and licked his hand. "Togo's pulled me over many mountains in some of the world's toughest dog-sled races. One year, he led us to first place in the Yukon Quest, bringing home fifty thousand dollars, which I used as seed money to build this place."

Woody scratched the dog under its chin.

To me, this guy didn't deserve such a sweet dog.

"None of us would be here if it weren't for you, eh, Togo?" he said through puckered lips.

The tall guy pulled his hood even tighter. "Fuckin' thanks, mutt."

Woody looked at him. "Like you, every dog has different strengths and weaknesses. Whether you're pulling a sled or paddling a canoe, if you're not supporting the team, *you* are the weak link."

Woody said this like we'd already let him down. Did I ever know *that* feeling! Like when Dad would sit in Magno's chair, yelling at me for screwing up my music.

Never good enough.

Woody gripped Togo under his chin. "Keep a loose tug-line and we all lose the trail. Pull your weight, stick with the program, and I promise you'll get your life back."

Alyssa slapped her legs. "What if I don't *want* it back?"

"Don't worry, Alyssa," Woody said. "There's a new life waiting for you here. As long as you support the team."

Carrie stepped forward and Woody passed her the feathered stick. "Now, I'm not sure how much they told you about our program," she said.

"They?" I say.

"The men who delivered you to the airport."

"The kidnappers."

"Escorts," Woody snapped.

"Like, zero," I said.

"And you others?" Carrie asked.

"Fuck all," said the tall guy.

The round guy shrugged.

Alyssa turned to stone.

"Okay," Carrie said. "Our days in camp are simple. One-quarter recreation, one-quarter therapy—"

"Seen enough shrinks, thanks," I said.

"We call it rehab. I'm sure you—"

"Been there, done that."

"Ah, but this is *wilderness*-based rehab," Carrie said. "The idea is to turn challenges in the wild into growth experiences that help you have a healthier, happier life. We guide and protect you, while nature teaches you about yourself, heals you, and, yes, throws her curve balls at you. We're all trained in outdoor survival and fully licensed as wilderness therapists."

"The-*rapists*," said the tall guy.

William laughed. "Never heard that one!"

Carrie smiled sweetly.

I was trying real hard not to like her, but it wasn't easy.

"So that leaves half of each day for wilderness training," she said. "This includes camping, fire-starting, edible plants, first aid, climbing, and whitewater paddling. Twenty-one days in camp to get you ready for our fifty-day canoe trip!"

The tall guy yanked down his hood revealing long blonde hair and a stubby beard. "What the fuck? Nobody ever told me I'd have to ... You said *fifty* days?"

"I did, Wade. And if you can manage fifty days in the wilderness, learn to deal with whatever comes up, then no matter what waits for you at home, you'll be able to handle it."

"So, like, what if I can't handle it?" I said.

Woody snatched the feathered stick from Carrie. "It's basically your choice, Indio. Sink or swim."

"It's Ian," I said.

Woody nodded. "As you like ... Ian."

Wade pointed a finger at Woody, like he was holding a pistol. "You mean, you're gonna beat the shit out of us till we fly straight?'

"No, no. This is *not* a boot camp. This is life under a microscope, and nature is the laboratory. We give you skills to deal with difficult situations in the wild. You decide how to take them."

"And that big fence," I said, "what's up with that?"

"Merely a safety precaution. Keeps the bears out."

Yeah, right.

"We just finished electrifying it."

"It's a fuckin' jail!" shouted Wade.

"So we get fried if we touch it?" I asked.

"Good Lord, no," Woody said, like I was an idiot. "Simply triggers an alarm. When we first installed it, every perching bird would set it off. Drove us crazy. But we've since adjusted the voltage to keep you both safe and sane."

Long silence.

Wade dropped his head and scrunched his shoulders up around his ears. Alyssa scratched her arms till I thought they'd bleed. The round guy's eyes rolled behind his thick glasses.

I was shitting over what waited for us beyond the fence. Blood-thirsty bears, endless forests, raging rivers. "What's the deal with this canoe trip? Like, I grew up in … I mean, I got zero experience in the wilderness."

Woody looked down at his dog and rubbed its belly with his boot. "Yes, Ian, we know about your … unusual history. But I've seen this in hundreds of wounded kids."

Kids? Wounded?

"My belief," he said in a slow, preachy voice, "is that we grow most beyond our comfort zone. In risking the unknown, we learn our strengths, our true selves."

Alyssa looked up for the first time. She had the eyes of a Husky dog, one hazel, one blue. "That's bullshit!" she shouted.

Except for her eyes, she could've been William's cousin. Maybe even mine.

I noticed her bare legs were scarred up like Woody's but in a different way. His scars were probably from rocks and axes. Hers were straight and tidy from a blitz of razor blades and knives. She caught me staring at her legs and threw me the finger.

"We'll see about that, Alyssa," Woody said. "Always remember, it's *your* choice. Sink or swim." Woody stepped back, like he was winding up for another blast of hot air, and accidentally trampled on Togo's tail.

The dog jumped up with a yelp. He tripped over my legs and lifted his muzzle to my face.

What I saw made me want to puke.

Alyssa screamed and ran out of the tipi.

Where the Husky's bright eyes should have been were two empty sockets grown over with fur. I looked up at Woody, my jaw to the floor.

"We're all damaged goods here at Camp Lifeboat," he said, snapping his fingers at the dog. "But look at my lovely Togo, my champion, robbed of both eyes by a serious disease and *still* running with the team!"

I straightened up, trying to sound calm. "Excuse me, but there must be some mistake. I don't belong here."

Woody chuckled into his beard. "Funny how they all say that."

"No, really. Like, I'm not an addict. I don't do drugs."

Woody tightened his grip around the dog's neck. If Togo had eyes, they would have bulged out. The dog curled its lips, flashing yellow teeth at me. "I've studied your file, Indio ... or rather, Ian. What you do is PIDs."

"What? Is that like LSD? I'm telling you, I DON'T DO DRUGS!"

"PIDs," Woody said. "Personal isolation devices. Addiction to cell phones, smartphones, xboxes, iPhones, iPads, iThis's, iThat's. I, I, I! Or addiction to alcohol, crack, meth. Simply different poisons, same dead end. All robbing you of your full potential. We're here to help you deal with your junk, to help you get high off other things, like rushing rivers and howling wolves."

The guy was revving up like a TV evangelist. His cheeks flushed red above his rat's-nest beard.

"You signed up for this program and we'll do all we can to—"

"I never fuckin' signed up for this shit," Wade said.

"We have the forms, Wade, with your signature on them."

Wade jumped to his full height. He must've been six foot six. "No fuckin' way!" he yelled. "This was my dad's idea. He must've—"

Woody slowly raised a hand. "You're here for the long haul, Wade. I promise you'll hate it at first. You're going to be hot, cold, hungry, dirty, tired, sore most of the time, especially on our canoe trip. But once you get past all that, you're gold."

"Fuck your gold."

Well said, Wade. We might've got along if I was staying.

"Your body can do it," Woody said. "The challenge is mental."

"You're fuckin' mental," Wade said and he stomped toward the tipi door.

"Try and run and we'll come looking for you." Woody tapped his chest. Togo sprang up to him on two legs. "I tell you, Togo may be blind, but he has a miraculous nose." Woody started dancing with his dog. "Don't you, boy? We'll drag you back here till you've learned what the mountains can teach you."

I heard a frantic rattle coming from the gate. Alyssa started screaming again.

Jesucristo! Caged again.

MISTAKEN IDENTITY

My blogging days are over. My therapy has officially begun. It's my second day here and already they've started shrinking my head. Carrie's got us all journaling. She says it's a "safe" way to dig out my junk. We're supposed to find a quiet spot—in this zoo?? —and just start writing. Don't think things up, just write things down. Feelings, thoughts, memories, whatever. Even fake letters or conversations with anybody or anything. Maybe I'll sit down and have a conversation with Loba or write a letter to Segovia. Maybe interview my guitar. Or write a poem to my dad called: "You Asshole." I can see how this might get interesting. But it's still just homework. Carrie says we have to write at least three paragraphs a day or else no supper. Is she kidding? Writing with a pen and paper is really weird, like, I mean, Stone Age. There. One paragraph.

After Alyssa's third meltdown—or was it her tenth?—Carrie managed to haul her back into the tipi, cursing and kicking, and

213

it was our turn to talk. Enough of Woody's sermons. Not that anybody said much. The intros took, like, two minutes. I learned that
Alyssa is from up here someplace and has been in rehab forever.
Wade's never done it, wasn't about to start, and told Woody to
fuck off. All I learned about the round guy was his name. Obie.

After the intros and a weird ceremony when William burned
some stinky grass and waved it in our faces, they led us one by
one to the infirmary behind the kitchen. Berna, the camp nurse,
took too much blood and asked too many questions. Of course,
when it came to stuff about drugs and booze, I had nothing to
tell, and she seemed a little surprised I was even there. duh! Put
that in your report, Berna: a case of mistaken identity. Then came
the physical. With all her poking and prodding, it felt more like
a strip-search. Looking for knives, drugs, whatever. Embarrassing! Made me hand over my watch, empty my pockets (some gum,
twenty bucks, a couple guitar picks) and dump everything in a
plastic box with my name on it. Do you believe it? She knew all
about my concussion, but I still had to wrestle her for my sunglasses. So much for summer camp.

God, this is hard. I suck at writing on paper. Good only for
ass-wiping or starting fires. So different from keyboarding, like a
totally new language. I'd rather compose a guitar étude than this
shit. Wait. That's four paragraphs. So Carrie, if you're reading
this, do I get an extra dessert?

COLD TURKEY

LIFEBOAT JOURNAL, DAY 4

Today's assignment: withdrawal. What's it feel like physically? Emotionally? How will you cope? But don't you get it, Carrie? I'm not a druggie. Look at Wade. He's been following Berna all over the place and got caught twice trying to bust into her infirmary for drugs. He's got tracks up and down both arms. Talk to him about withdrawal. Or Alyssa. She's gone hoarse from shouting at the sky, and both her arms are bandaged from scratching herself. All I want from the nurse is some earplugs cause of Alyssa's nightly screaming binges. During the day she's like the walking dead. Werewolf by night, zombie by day. I don't know how Obie's doing. Never see him except in our evening sharing circle. He seems to be getting quieter, if that's possible.

So, okay, I'm missing my toys. I really felt it at the gate in the Calgary airport. I never used to chew my nails, especially my right ones. Pretty dumb idea when you're supposedly a guitar god. There was this diaper brat in a high chair across from me, watch-

ing Teletubbies on his mother's iPad. She had her nose so deep in her smartphone that I seriously thought of swiping the kid's device. Probably would have if it hadn't been for the goons—sorry, "escorts"—sitting on each side of me.

Another serious ache hit me on the plane to Whitehorse. Got all twitchy and my body started shaking like right after my concussion. Had to grip the armrests real hard. Somehow they'd put me beside an emergency exit, and I kept looking up at the red handle, wanting to pull it, to get sucked into the sky and fall and fall and never land. I actually caught my hand reaching up once. I might've done it, really done it, if the pilot hadn't come on with his blah-blah welcome aboard thing. Then it hit me that his cockpit must be stuffed with digital doodads connected to the Internet. I could check my email. Fire off a blog post from thirty-thousand feet up. Make a quick video of me flying the plane. I was rehearsing lines in my head to convince the pilot of my urgent need to reconnect with my online friends—I was sure he'd understand—when the plane started descending into Whitehorse.

In rehab-speak, I was totally "delusional." But it felt good just sitting there fantasizing. At least I stopped shaking.

SOLO

Since when did I talk to myself? Correction, talk to creeks? I'd been glaring at it since the sun came up, which was, like, 2:00 AM. Land of the midnight sun and all. Couldn't say exactly what time it rose, since they stole my watch.

I could hear Carrie's advice. I should be journaling out in the meadow or skinny dipping in the pond, or making a nice pancake and eggs breakfast over the fire. But my head was too screwed up to write and the water was too cold to swim. After blowing my only pack of matches, I couldn't get the damn fire going, anyway.

Worst of all, that creek was driving me nuts.

It had started soon after William dumped me there, "within screaming distance of camp," he'd said. I'd watched him disappear into the woods, feeling suddenly alone like never before.

It wasn't like being locked in my practice room in Xela, crying over my guitar. Or hiding in my Calgary dungeon. Or staring stupidly out the hospital window, waiting for my brain to rewire.

This was a new kind of loneliness.

I felt like my cyberworld had been spinning so fast, it spat me out and I'd landed here on yet another planet.

Just me and the creepy wilderness.

I stood there clutching my tent bag, feeling like my life had never happened. Never mattered to anyone.

Suddenly the dark cloud inside me lifted. I dropped the tent and laughed. *Laughed!*

In rehab-speak, for sure I was "manic." Pit of despair one minute, over the moon the next. Carrie warned us about this at our solo briefing.

I chucked my pack to the ground. *This is it, Indio!* I thought. *No Woody, no fence. Look out, Internet, I'm coming home!*

It seemed so easy. Hoof it to Whitehorse, get back online.

Until I started running.

One problem. I had no clue which way to go.

William had "trust-walked" me out here, aka, arm-in-arm with me in a blindfold again. Except for a little meadow downstream, the trees were thick all around me. The few mountaintops I could see all looked the same.

I crashed off in one direction and got tangled up in fallen trees. I tried another. Same story. I kept running every which way until I felt something warm and wet inside my shirtsleeve. I rolled it back to see I'd gouged my arm. Then I stepped on a fresh pile of bear shit and realized I'd left the pepper spray in my pack.

And get this. The whole time I'd been crashing through

the woods, I could hear Woody's psycho dog barking like he was right on my tail. *Weird!* His bark seemed to come from nowhere and everywhere at once.

Instead of getting hopelessly lost or eaten by a bear or mauled by a crazy blind dog, I limped back to my campsite and set up my tent.

It took forever but, once the tent was up, I felt a bit better. Nothing like a couple microns of nylon to protect you from bear claws. Or wolf fangs. Or mad trappers. Lying alone in that tent, I got this feeling I was a trespasser, that some power in that dark forest resented my very presence.

I dove deeper into my sleeping bag.

That's when I noticed the moaning.

It was hard enough to sleep when the sun was up past freakin' midnight. But that night my mind was in overdrive. The shakes had come back. I was lying there, trying to ride it out, when that moaning got louder. Like an old woman in pain.

It came from the creek.

The more I focused on the sound, the more it changed. Now some crazy person was outside my tent, gargling. Then singing in the shower. It kept changing: a locomotive, the bass line from a guitar piece I hated. A madly ticking metronome. *One-two-three, one-two-three, one-two-three ...*

"STOP!" I shouted.

I stared at a squirming mass of bugs dancing on the tent's ceiling. My head felt like an overblown balloon, ready to pop.

Then came the strangled cats, an army of monsters.

Everything got stirred together in a crazy soup of noise. I wondered if it was hallucinations from my concussion.

I wrapped my down vest around my head and pressed my hands tight over my ears.

Now it was voices, whispering at me.

Uncle Faustus: *Prométeme, prométeme.*

Brent at the hospital: *Who's Loba? Who's Loba?*

Woody: *Sink or swim. Sink or swim.*

My father: *Segovia, Segovia.*

I exploded out of the tent. I peered up and down the creek. That horrible feeling returned, that I didn't belong here, that something lurking close by wanted me dead.

I stared at whirlpools of water, frothy waves, logs bobbing in the current. I zeroed in on rock after rock, trying to find the villain, the source of those insane sounds.

There, that one!

I barged into the ice-cold water and attacked a turd-shaped boulder in the middle of the creek. I shoved my hands underneath it and pulled. I lost my grip and tumbled ass backwards into the water. I attacked it again, grunting, panting, crying over the rock until it finally broke free from the bottom. I hoisted it to my hips and heaved it to shore.

I stopped and listened.

Segovia, Segovia ...

I leapt on more boulders, clawing them loose, tossing them out of the creek.

One huge boulder rolled back on my foot and crushed a toe. "AAGH!"

I must have been at it for over an hour when I heard a new voice.

"So, what ya doin', eh?"

I looked up at William. That lottery-winning smile.

I felt like a complete idiot, up to my waist in the creek, my hands covered in slime. "I ... uh ... thought this was supposed to be a solo," I said.

"I'm your designated driver."

"What?"

"You get lost or go wandering off, I steer you back."

"You mean my prison guard."

William pulled out a pack of tobacco and rolling paper. "Just doin' my job."

"So, what are *you* doing?"

William rolled a quick cigarette in one hand then gave it a happy sniff. "Hey, don't worry. The tobacco's organic. And the company's a hundred percent Native-owned."

I stood up and wiped snails and gunk off my hands. "But, like, nicotine? Drugs? Aren't we in rehab here?"

"That's your job. Already did my time." William lit up, gazing at the mountains. "Mountain climbing's a drug. Shootin' rapids is a drug. Moving rocks, too, I guess, eh?" He laughed.

I looked at the jumble of rocks I'd chucked all over the place, like someone had thrown a grenade in the creek. I'd changed the sound of the water, all right. All I could hear now was laughing. "I was just—"

"Rearranging the furniture?"

"Well ... there were these weird sounds and ... yeah."

My neck hairs bristled at the sound of a long drawn-out wolf howl.

William thwacked his beaded vest, then pulled out a yellow iPhone *just like mine.*

I froze, forgetting how to breathe. There in William's hand, so close I could leap up and grab it, was a portal to another world.

My world.

He glanced at the call display, frowned, then stuffed the iPhone back in his vest.

"Who was it?" I asked, barely able to form the words.

"Huh? Oh, nobody."

"Do you ... uh ... suppose I could borrow that thing sometime? You know, like, call my mom, maybe."

"Umm. Don't think so. Lousy signal out here. Camp phone's best." William looked at me funny. "Ya gonna stand in that creek all day?"

William built a huge campfire while I ripped off my soaked jeans and hoody and hung them in a tree. Wearing nothing but blue boxers, I sat across from William on a log by the fire.

I was surprised how comfortable I already felt with William, even though, technically, he was one of my jailers. I still twitched inside whenever I looked at the bulge in his vest where he kept his iPhone. But the warmth of the fire on my wet legs took my mind off it.

William broke off a hunk of baker's chocolate and offered it to me.

"You steal this from the kitchen?" I asked.

"Who, me?"

"Another drug, right?"

"Pick your poison."

We sat in silence sucking our chocolate. The creek just sounded like a creek. I heard the rush of wings above us and a duck came bombing through the trees.

William turned to watch it land in the pond. "Didn't Carrie tell you to try going buck-naked if you're gonna swim out here?"

"To enjoy the psychotherapeutic benefits of being one with the elements, you mean?"

"Yeah, that."

"She did. I guess I got caught up moving rocks."

"Hmm. Maybe the trick isn't to fix the rocks."

"They were driving me nuts."

"That's what I mean. Fix how you *hear* 'em."

I didn't feel like arguing.

"It's Indio, right?" William said after a long pause.

"It's Ian, actually."

"Right, but all your forms say—"

"Must be a typo."

"Hmm," he said with a big question in his eyes.

"Look, I changed it, okay?"

"Sure. Ian it is."

William folded his arms, still looking at me funny. "Just curious," he said. "So, what kinda name is that?"

My stomach tightened. "Which?"

"Indio."

"Nothing special."

"So where'd ya grow up, anyways?"

"Guatemala."

"Guata-who?"

"Let's say Latin America."

William nodded, puckering his lips. "I knew I heard an accent. So you speak Latin, eh?"

I couldn't tell if he was bullshitting me. "Uh ... no. Spanish. Just think Mexico, only one stop further south."

William looked up at a passing raven and stroked his chin.

"You ... you do know where Mexico is," I said.

He shrugged. "Guatever. I know this place best."

"This?"

William twirled a finger at the mountains all around us. They looked dead and dark under a blanket of clouds rolling toward us. I heard thunder way back behind the peaks. "You're taking us in *there*?" I asked.

"Yup. Hand in hand with a marching band."

"And Woody?"

"Yup. Carrie, too. We're all ... How did she put it? Licensed wilderness therapists."

"The rapists."

William laughed. "That would be us." He looked up at the mountains. "There's nothing to fear out there, except for ..."

He took a deep drag on his cigarette.

"Except for *what*?"

William slowly turned and looked at me, eyes wide. He shot smoke out of one corner of his mouth. "Except for ... You sure you're ready for this?"

"Like, never. C'mon!"

"There's nothing to fear except for … the *beast* you see in the mirror."

"Jesus!"

William's face lit up and he slapped me on the back. "No. Not Jesus. You!"

HAS-BEEN

LIFEBOAT JOURNAL, DAY 10, THIRD AND LAST DAY OF SOLO

I'm kicking round this campfire
Won't ever let it out
Kicking round this campfire
All this silence makes me shout.

There's voices in the creekbed
Voices in my head
Screaming, Indio, where are you?
They say that you are dead.

I don't know where I'm going
I wish that I could blog
I feel like such a has-been
Just sitting on this log.

DEBRIEF

It was Carrie who came to pull me off solo. I'd never seen her out of her tracksuit, but that morning she was all bush woman with her plaid shirt, braided hair, and a bandana around her neck. I noticed her fruity scent was mixed with a heavy dose of bug dope.

"That's quite the campfire ring," she said as she sat down beside me on a log. I'd constructed an elaborate windscreen of piled rocks that included a stone slab to keep stuff warm and a woven willow clothesline to dry my socks. Building this rig, journaling, cooking, and William's daily check-ins, kept me sane for my three-day solo. He'd slipped me an extra box of matches on his last visit, "so you won't starve to death," he said.

Next to my nightly panic attacks, the journaling was the toughest part. It was weird how I could bang off a thousand-word blog post in ten minutes, yet it took me hours to write a few paragraphs in my journal. I had to wrestle with each word and didn't like some of the shit that rose to the surface.

In the end, I filled about twenty pages of rants and ramblings, spun a couple of poems, even made a few crude sketches—the bombed-out creek, the porcupine that chewed my hiking boot, the grizzly bear I never saw, the face of that Mayan mother murdered in front of our Xela home.

When I was feeling especially crappy, I'd jot down a few bars from a favorite guitar étude. I was surprised how much that helped.

Maybe someday I'd pull some juicy bits out of that journal for my blog. I could see it: *The Making of a Mountain Man.*

I offered Carrie a cup of Labrador tea, which William had shown me how to make. "A fistful of leaves per cup," he told me. "Not too strong or it'll kill you. Good for hangovers." I'd made about ten pots of the stuff before I got it right.

I held my breath as I watched Carrie take a long sniff, a cautious sip, and then ... a big smile.

After tea, it was the usual barrage of questions. Rehab time.

"So, what would you like to tell me about your solo?"

I tossed Carrie my charcoal-smeared journal. "You can read all about it in my latest blog."

"Uh-huh," she said, as she glanced through it then quickly handed it back to me. "Nice."

That's it? Nice?

I clutched my journal with both hands as steam rose to my ears. I slowly squished it into an accordion. After I'd wracked my brain, squeezed out all those words, dug up all that shit, it wasn't worth reading?

"Well, screw it then!" I said and tossed my journal in the fire.

"Hey!" Carrie said, "What are you doing?" She jumped up, grabbed it out of the flames, and whacked the burning cover on her jeans. "You know you don't have to share a word of this with anyone."

"But ... I thought I was writing it for—"

"For *you*, Ian. Only you. If there are some things you want to share, great. But it's really a tool for you to explore your stuff, to help you deal with it."

"What stuff?"

Carrie always took these heavy pauses when she was in her therapy mode. Even closed her eyes.

Drove me nuts.

"Well, in camp you've already shared a bit about your father, your trouble adjusting to school in Canada, your car accident ..."

All things I wrote about.

"... and the lady who passed away in front of your—"

"Passed away? She was shot in cold blood! One of my dad's trigger-happy guards."

Carrie nodded slowly, opened her eyes. "Who was she, Ian?"

"Nobody."

"Could she be related to you?"

Jesus! I'd never thought of that. "No way," I said.

"So ... why do you find her death so disturbing?"

"What's disturbing is all your questions."

"Okay, okay."

I opened the journal at the Mayan woman's face. I'd squashed some berries and flowers onto the page to make the reds, blues, and yellows of her traditional blouse. Her long hair was black as charcoal, because that's what I used. Her skin was brown from the inner bark of a tree. My sketch was burned in one corner but her face was intact, full of fight against my father's gold mine.

In my picture, she couldn't see the bullet zinging for her head.

Carrie pointed a twig at a black hump behind the woman's shoulder. "Is that a baby on her back?"

I nodded slowly. "Yup."

"That's terrible."

"Tell my dad that."

"You're quite the artist."

I slapped the journal shut. "No, I'm not."

Long pause. "What was the best part of your solo?"

"Sleeping. Once the birds shut up and I figured out a blindfold. It's *insane*, this midnight sun!"

Carrie laughed. "Last night was the solstice."

"The what?"

"The summer solstice. June 21st. Longest day of the year. You won't see stars again till August."

"August?"

"For sure. We'll be well down the Keele River by then and you can—"

"Forget it. I'll be long gone. I'll be cured in a week."

Carrie smiled. "We'll see."

We'll see, all right, I thought. *I'll be gone once I have an escape plan. Soon I'll be back online!*

Carrie closed her eyes again. "And so, Ian ..."

"Yes."

"What was the toughest part of your solo?"

"Writing. I just don't get it."

"How so?"

"I'm such a good blogger. I can do it in my sleep. Really, I can *text* in my sleep."

"Interesting."

I could tell she didn't believe me. "They call it sleep-texting."

"Uh-huh." Carrie poured me another cup of Labrador tea, took some for herself. "Why do you think writing is so hard for you, Ian—on paper, I mean?"

"Missing a keyboard, I guess. It feels so weird, scratching away on paper."

"Hmm. Makes sense. They really are different species."

"What do you mean?"

"A blog is very public. You're basically sharing ideas and opinions, mostly *head* stuff. You're reaching out to anyone on earth who's plugged into the Internet, most of them anonymous. Right?"

"Yeah, but I have a *lot* of online friends! They eat up my blogs. They expect at least one post a day."

"Uh-huh. Now, on the other hand, a journal entry is very private, very personal. Mostly *heart* stuff. Totally unplugged from the electronic universe you're so comfortable in."

231

I stood up, suddenly suffocating in Carrie's therapy bubble.

She looked up at me with her cheerleader eyes. "Will you grant me one last question?"

I hit the fire with a long stick, sending up a tower of sparks. "Including that one?"

Carrie laughed. "What do you think you learned during your solo?"

"Well ... I learned how to make Labrador tea. Is it any good?"

"It's perfect, Ian. I drink this stuff every morning with my granola and yogurt. Lots of vitamin C. But I mean, what did you learn about yourself?"

"Not much."

"Nothing?"

I stared at the dancing flames, remembering how I'd crashed through the woods, chucked boulders out of the creek, that horrible feeling of something out to get me, William sharing his chocolate by the fire. And last night, lying in my tent, listening to the wind ripping through the pines, feeling super alone but ... somehow not so lonely.

"I don't know. There's a lot of stuff out here that can mess you up, even kill you. But it's not a big power thing like when there's people around."

"Like who?"

"Like my dad. Like Woody. Total power trippers. Control freaks."

"Uh-huh."

"I spent a lot of time alone as a kid, just me and my guitar, locked in my room. But it's different out here on solo. There's no locks. Nobody trying to control me. Sun, wind, clouds, birds." I looked down at my chewed boot. "Porcupines. Everything just ... *is*."

"I see. So who *is* in control?"

A raven swished overhead and it was like I could hear my own breath in its wings. "Dunno."

"Who decides what kind of day you're going to have?"

"Me, I guess."

"So there you go. *You* are in control."

"Yeah, sure," I said, feeling the throb of my gouged arm and crushed toe. Wounds inflicted on myself while running around like a crazy person.

You call that being in control?

Maybe it was my beasty side that William had warned me about. What Uncle Faustus would call *el demonio dentro*—the demon inside.

Little did I know that the real beast was waiting for me back in camp.

CIRCLE-UP

Woody slapped me on the back as Carrie and I stooped through the tipi door. Togo greeted me with a deranged show of teeth. "It's his way of smiling," Woody assured me.

We circled-up for a feelings check. The idea was you passed the talking stick around as everyone tossed out a one-liner on what kind of mood they were in after their solos. *I feel anxious. I feel sad.* Like that.

"I'm feeling lucky," Wade said, boasting about his attempted escape. Halfway into his solo, he'd jumped his campsite and found the road. Trouble was, he ran the wrong way, toward camp, and Togo sniffed him out of the ditch before he could turn around. "You won't fucking catch me next time," he said as he winged the talking stick at Togo's head.

Woody crouched over Togo, checking for wounds. The dog snarled at Wade. "Careful, Wade," he said. "You don't want to get on Togo's wrong side."

Woody picked up the talking stick and passed it to Obie, who managed four words, "I'm feeling really shitty."

When it was Alyssa's turn, she looked up, all bleary-eyed, like she hadn't slept for days. "Why didn't you just leave me there to *die*?"

Berna went over to her, whispered something, then they disappeared out the tipi door. Off to the infirmary to up her meds.

"Just give her time," Woody said. "We send you out alone for three days to see if you enjoy the company. Sometimes it takes a while to get on friendly terms with yourself."

Obie accidently jabbed my wounded arm while passing me the talking stick.

"Jesus!" I shouted.

Obie shrank away into himself.

"You found Jesus out there?" Woody asked with a fake smile.

"Uh ... sure."

Woody was about to ask me something else when I heard the gate squeak and the van pull in. "Ah, at last," he said, combing his ratty beard with his fingers. "The new intern."

New intern? I was just getting used to these freaks.

Woody sprang through the door and we all piled out after him.

I squinted through the late afternoon sun and saw William, all smiles, taking the blindfold off a big guy beside him. The guy had William laughing even before it was off. The van windows were closed so I couldn't hear his voice, but there was something about his form that made me grab the fence beside me. Of course, this triggered the alarm, and the whole camp was flooded in a shrill howl, like we were about to be bombed.

The passenger turned to see what was up and flashed me a movie star smile that instantly froze the blood in my veins.

Morris Kritch.

TRAIL BLAZING

I'd never seen a lock so big. You'd need a bazooka to blow it off the gate. Woody paused before he opened it. "As far as I know, none of you has a history as an axe murderer. Am I right?"

Silence. As usual, no one was in the mood for Woody's sick humor.

What was funny was seeing everyone decked out in steel-toed boots, yellow safety vests, and orange hard hats. I felt like a well-outfitted slave.

William pulled up beside us with a wheelbarrow full of axes, bush saws, and machetes. I stared at the machetes, feeling a strange twinge of homesickness. I thought of how so many Guatemalans used machetes to prune banana trees, clear coffee plantations, or hack trails through the jungle. Some also liked to wave them in front of the people they were robbing, or worse.

Seeing Morris brush his thumb over a freshly sharpened machete blade did not make my day any brighter. I still couldn't believe he was here. Woody even put us on the same work team, like we were old buds.

"When it comes to shaking out your junk, this kind of grunt work is way more fun than beating a tennis racquet on a pillow," Woody told us. "And a lot more useful. Today you are going to clear a new trail out to a pretty little lake where we can all go for a swim." He held up a painted sign with the word *Connection*. "The focus of this trail experience will be *connecting*. Connecting with the land, with each other, with your truest, bravest self."

"Sounds good, sir."

There goes Morris, already sucking up to Woody like he was one of the staff.

William was about to hand me an axe, then suddenly yanked it away. "Are you *sure* you're not an axe murderer?"

I looked sideways at Morris who was looking sideways at me. "Not yet, at least."

There was no smile on Morris's face. No kidding around.

William gave a bush saw to Alyssa. He kept the chainsaw for himself. Once everyone had a tool, Woody pulled out a key from one of the fifty pockets in his bush pants and clicked the lock open. He gave one good push on the gate and we were free.

Sort of.

Between Woody, William, and Carrie, there were walk-ie-talkies popping off all around us as we cleared the trail. Togo circled us the whole time, occasionally nipping our heels if we strayed too far, like we were runaway cattle. And if we went into the woods to take a dump or something, we were ordered to count out loud or whistle or sing, so our jailers knew exactly where we were every moment. Embarrassing or what!

Halfway through the morning, Morris and I were working shoulder to shoulder on the trail, attacking a stubborn willow with machetes. William and Woody were bringing down some big shrubs with the chainsaw. Carrie was working with Alyssa, dumping brush in the woods. I was suddenly feeling unsupervised in a way I didn't like. I mean, working with Morris, so close I could smell his BO, and the same sickly scent of hair gel hair that had made me cringe at school. Still did.

I straightened up to wave to William, and felt a sharp *thunk* against my steel-toed boot. I looked down at a two-inch gash. A sliver of steel shone through the rubber like exposed bone. "Jesus! Watch where you swing that thing!"

Morris gave me a blank face. That face I loved to hate. "Oops, sorry, Pedro," he said without a trace of apology. "You keep out of my face or the next time it won't be an accident."

By lunchtime, I'd already grown and popped three blisters on my hands. It was hot, sweaty, scratchy work, and the bugs were getting thicker by the hour. We were less than halfway down the so-called trail.

Woody had led us to a grassy hill that stuck out of the forest to supposedly catch some breeze. But there wasn't a breath of wind, and a cloud of bugs hovered above our small circle of addicts. Among the many life skills I was learning was how to eat a PB&J sandwich without smearing it all over the bug hat that covered my face.

"Remember, team," Woody said, "Know pain, know gain! This is the *pain* part. But imagine how that swim's going to feel once we cut our way to the lake. That's the *gain* part." He said all this while pacing around our circle, stopping now and then to gaze up at the mountains. In two weeks, I hadn't seen the guy sit down once.

Like most of our meals, I wanted more at the end of lunch. One measly sandwich, one droopy carrot, and a couple of dried apricots. At Camp Lifeboat, they served up just enough food to stop our stomachs from grumbling and not a crumb more.

I think Woody used starvation as just another form of therapy. He told us as much in one of his sermons, declaring that "hunger is a good tool to build character." No wonder the guy's body was so skinny and his ego so fat.

"So, Ian, feeling *connected*?" William asked as he offered me some moose jerky.

"Thanks," I said, grabbing a piece. He made the stuff himself. Shot the moose. Cured and dried the meat. Made it sweet and salty. Mouth-watering, especially after such a skimpy lunch. "Connected? Hah, really. What I'd give for an Internet connection."

"Lousy bandwidth. Besides, you'd miss all this."

"All what?"

"This."

"You mean the blood? The sweat?"

"And don't forget the tears, eh?"

I lifted my bug hat a crack and fired the jerky in my mouth.

William laughed. "You're getting good at that." He plucked a piece of sweet-smelling sage and twirled it under his nose. I noticed he wasn't wearing a bug hat.

"How do you do that?"

"Do what?"

"There's no bugs around you."

"Hmm. I'm a bug whisperer."

"No shit."

William waved a stick of jerky at me. "Actually, the trick is only bathing once a year."

I chewed in silence, staring at my gashed work boot.

William followed my gaze. "Those machetes can be dangerous, eh?"

"Depends who's swinging it," I said, looking across at Morris, who sneered back.

William watched this exchange without a word. "Look," he said, pointing down the valley.

"What?"

"That little meadow. See it? With the creek."

"So?"

"Don't recognize it?"

At first it was just another barren patch of wilderness. Then I got it. "My solo camp," I said, and it suddenly came alive with memories.

I saw myself down there, a speck in that huge wild valley, crashing through the woods, going insane in the creek bed, sitting on a log, staring at the fire, scratching in my journal. It was like I'd left a piece of myself down there. Another piece in camp. More pieces along this trail. Like I was falling apart. Soon there'd be nothing left.

"Feel connected to that place?" William said, watching me closely.

"I remember baker's chocolate. Got any more?"

William leaned toward me, holding one finger to his lips. "Don't give me away," he whispered. "I'm supposed to be reformed."

I looked up and noticed Morris staring at me like I was a dog eating out of his bowl.

The gain part never came. After another few hours of slashing through the bush, Woody lost the trail of orange flagging tape we'd been following. We never did find the promised lake.

Or so he made it seem.

I decided he was faking it, that there never was a lake, and he'd set us up like that just to break us down. To "shake out our junk," as he always said.

I plodded into camp feeling like a cow going to slaughter. My legs and arms were scratched all over and pockmarked with bug bites. My whole body ached. My throat and tongue were as dry as toast. The very thought of doing another circle-up with Morris, let alone eating with him or sleeping in the same dorm, made me retch.

I stopped cold, staring at Woody pulling on the giant chain-link gate. His bare hands were all over it as it creaked open.

No alarm.

Togo put his nose up against it.

No alarm.

I remembered on Day 1, when Alyssa went screaming out of the tipi and started shaking the gate like crazy.

No alarm.

On the way in, I gave the fence beside it a light smack to test my theory. It chirped like a car alarm.

Woody spun around and glared at me. "What's the big idea?"

"Sorry. I tripped."

At last I'd found a way out. And none too soon.

FLIGHT

The whole camp woke the next morning to find Togo brutally murdered.

Alyssa had stumbled on him behind the kitchen before breakfast. Somebody had slit Togo's throat and stuck a machete through his ribs. We were all pretty used to Alyssa's fits, but there was something in this scream that brought everyone running.

Everyone but me.

I'd been awake all night, thinking about that gate, going over the day's routine in my head, trying to figure out the best time to break out. I ran barefoot out of the dorm when the screaming started, but held back when I saw everyone hunched over Togo's body. It reminded me of Loba lying crumpled on the road, and I felt a stab of pain for the blind sled dog that had so freaked me out.

That place was a loony bin, run by an egomaniac slave driver. Random screaming in the night. Starving all the time. Morris threatening me with his machete.

And now this. A murderer in camp.

Who's next in line for a machete through the ribs?

Woody's back was to me but I could read vengeance all over it.

Another good reason to get the hell out of there.

How would he find the killer? Was it Morris? Wade? Obie? Maybe a disgruntled kitchen worker? Who?

God help you when you're caught.

I truly felt for Woody, but his amazing dog couldn't track me now.

I glanced back at the gate and saw it was hidden by the dining hall and dorms.

This is it, I thought.

The gate was taller than I'd thought, and I ripped my pajama bottoms wide open going over the top. Right in the ass. Both feet slipped off the chain-links as I started down the other side. I stopped my fall by grabbing a handful of pointy bits up top. I let out a yelp as something like a nail drove into my left palm.

I'm too young to be crucified!

Luckily Alyssa's latest scream-fest drowned out my agony. Nobody came after me as I scrambled down the gate and hit the road running.

I ran as fast as I could down the middle of the road, feeling a mix of deathly fear and heavenly bliss.

Soon I'll be back online!

I kept running until I heard the crunch of gravel from an approaching vehicle.

I lunged for the ditch.

Too late, they'd seen me!

A sixty-something couple driving an old Ford pickup. At the last second, I decided to play it cool and pretend I was just out for an early morning jog. I moved to the side of the road and trotted along, smooth and steady, like the jock I never was. I even waved and smiled as they passed.

They did the same.

Then it hit me that I was running barefoot in my plaid pajama bottoms with my ass hanging out for all to enjoy.

I looked back and saw their brake lights go on.

¡Jesucristo! It's over.

Then off they went into the dust.

I ducked down a sandy side road into the woods. I needed to think.

I sat down behind a big pine tree and closed my eyes, like I was blindfolded all over again. I tried to remember the sequence of turns and textures on the road from Whitehorse. *Left from the airport, one sharp right, another sharp right, smell of cinnamon rolls, pavement ends ...*

I became aware of a stabbing pain in my left hand. I opened my eyes and saw it was gouged and gory, covered with blood. "*Vale la pena,*" I said out loud—worth the pain—and tipped my head to the sky, laughing.

I was back on the road again, diving into the ditch whenever a vehicle kicked up a dust cloud. The pine forest thinned out and I ran past little hay farms, complete with cows, horses, chickens, the whole bit. I remembered smelling cow manure on the way in. I knew I'd hit pavement soon.

I kept running.

My feet were already fringed with blood but I didn't care. I was free. And getting closer to my World Wide friends.

Somebody had planted a little vegetable patch and stuck a classic scarecrow in the middle. I made a quick detour. Minutes later, I came out wearing a tattered flannel shirt, a pair of ripped jeans, a Blue Jays ball cap, and a beat-up pair of size thirteen rubber boots.

The boots saved my feet but slowed me way down. I decided to shadow the road, taking cover in the fields and forests.

The road squeezed between two high ridges, went past a big beautiful lake—Annie Lake, according to the sign—and crossed a river where I dropped down to clean my wound and drink gallons of water.

Good thing, too.

Just as I lifted my lips from the river, I heard the familiar rattle of the Camp Lifeboat van, cruising slowly down the road. I flew into the woods and hunkered down into thick moss.

It cruised by.

I didn't move.

Minutes later, a low-flying helicopter zoomed straight for me, its flight path following every curve of the Annie Lake road.

I didn't breathe, hoping my red scarecrow shirt wouldn't give me away.

It flew on.

I sat tight.

Then a police siren.

An RCMP cruiser whipped by, headed for camp, siren blasting, lights blazing.

Everybody was out looking for guess who.

And they were not going to find me.

Poor Togo. Amazing Togo. I was so glad he wasn't on my tail.

Left from the airport, one sharp right, another sharp right … I was thinking the whole route through in reverse when I got to the cinnamon roll part.

Not in my head. In my nose.

I'd been shadowing the paved part of the road, when I saw an intersection up ahead and caught a whiff that got my stomach rumbling big time. I had no clue how long I'd been running. All I knew was I was "fungry," as Wade would say, fucking hungry, and these smells were killing me.

I crossed an old railway line and snuck closer to the intersection. The delicious smells were leaking out of a log cafe that had a bunch of motorcycles and tourist RV's parked out front. Ritchie's Roadhouse.

I reached into my pockets. Both hands pushed through to my knees. *Cheap scarecrow*, I thought. But what would I have done with money, anyhow? The cops must have left a description of me at the cafe, like they would for any criminal on the loose.

Be on the lookout for a scrawny teenage Latino male, five foot six, black hair, brown eyes. Distinguishing features may include abnormally long fingernails on right hand and scars on both shins from repeated beatings. Suspect has a known history of addiction, lying, cheating, stealing.

Look out, world, I thought. *Here I come. One of Woody's kids from Hell!*

I was about to sneak closer to the cafe, when I heard the RCMP cruiser coming back. I dove into the ditch, almost smashing my face on a rock. I rolled behind a tree just in time.

"Jesus, look who's going to jail!" I whispered. As the cruiser whipped by, I saw a tall guy in the back seat, pounding his handcuffed wrists against the window.

I guess that's one way to get kicked out of camp. Kill the director's dog.

I shook my head. "You bastard, Wade."

As much as those cinnamon rolls were calling me, I decided to give Ritchie's Roadhouse a pass. Too much going on. I turned, not left toward Whitehorse—that's the first place they'd look for me—but right, toward ... I didn't know what.

There was a lot more traffic on the connecting road, so I doubled back and started hoofing down the old railway tracks. I was glad to see small trees popping up between the railway ties. I wouldn't be bothered by a train anytime soon. Probably hadn't been one down that line in twenty years.

I could openly walk in the sunshine, a free man, just me and the bears and the wolves, until I keeled over from starvation and they started picking my bones.

THE CABIN

I hadn't planned to celebrate my freedom in an abandoned log cabin. I hadn't planned anything other than to get the hell out of that concentration camp. But after no sleep the night before, and a brutal day of clumping along the railway tracks in my scarecrow boots, I felt like the walking dead.

Where to sleep? At one point, I lay down on a thick bed of moss, unbelievably comfy, and almost passed out. But when I heard something screeching in the woods, the thought of sleeping in the open lost its charm. I dragged myself off the moss and kept walking, till I found an old cabin beside the tracks.

It looked a hundred years old, everything carved out of the wilderness—the door, the bed, the lone table and chair. Replace the log walls with adobe and I could have been back in Guatemala, visiting Diadora and her goats.

I cracked open the cupboard and discovered a couple of broken candles, a box of matches, and an empty bottle labeled "Gibson's Finest Whiskey." I sniffed the bottle, then slammed it down as memories of my father invaded the stillness.

I jumped when something metallic crashed to the floor. An old dented gold pan. I rubbed my fingers over its flat bottom, imagining it covered in gold dust. I thought about the prospector who had lived here by the river. Was he lonely? Did he ever find his Eldorado?

Someone had left a note on the table, scribbled on a piece of cardboard. I brushed the dust off and held it near the window.

Hello person/people of the Yukon! I am Lisa Kemble, a 17-year-old drifter from Calgary, Alberta. If you are reading this, please email me when you are back in civilization. I would like to get to know other drifters whose path led them to this special place. Enjoy your stay in this awesome cabin! (lisak@hotmail.com)

"Hah! Calgary!" I said out loud. "How cool to connect with her once I'm back online!"

I noticed a rolled-up sleeping bag hanging from the ceiling, probably to keep mice and stuff from wrecking it. I pulled it down and unrolled it on the bed. I crawled inside, catching a faint rosy scent that might've been Lisa's. "Thanks, Lisa," I said. I'd like to think she left this bag for fellow drifters like me.

I lay there for hours. Couldn't sleep. I saw myself from the cabin ceiling, from the top of the big pine tree beside it, from the mountain ridge above that, from a cloud hanging over the valley. My mind zoomed out like Google Earth, until I was a tiny speck of nothing swallowed by the wilderness.

That loneliness ambushed me again, like I'd never felt anywhere but in these mountains. It was like the silence sucked it out of me and held it under my nose.

You're a nothing! shouted the silence, *and a nobody!*

My mind wandered to a story William had told me about a local prospector who went crazy from loneliness and threw himself in front of a train. My eyes popped open when I realized this had to be his cabin!

I buried my head in Lisa's sleeping bag. I breathed in her scent. I squeezed all the comfort I could from the friendship of a girl I'd never met, who lived a million miles away.

It seemed to work. I calmed down.

I was good at this. After all, didn't I do it all the time online?

I was woken hours later by a pain in my stomach, a notch or two above fungry.

I checked the cupboard for any food I might have missed in my zombie state the night before. Not a crumb. I made a mental note of Lisa's email address, then scrambled down to the river to dunk my head. When the snails and green scum on the rocks began to look appetizing, I realized my drifting days might soon be over if I didn't find food.

CARCROSS

W hat is it with baked goodies in the Yukon? I was still clomping south down the tracks when my nose started jumping again. Not cinnamon rolls this time. Pie! The abandoned rail line had swung closer to the road and I could hear traffic, even voices. Following my nose, I snuck a peek across the road at another pit stop. Spirit Lake Lodge. An old couple sat on the outside deck, eating ice cream cones.

A big kid came pounding down the stairs, holding a lemon meringue pie. I bit my lip. He carefully set the pie on the hood of a car then ran inside, like he forgot to ask for the keys. A raven started circling above the pie.

"Oh, no you don't," I said to the raven. I blasted across the road, grabbed the pie, and ran.

I heard a screen door slam behind me just as I ducked into the woods.

"Hey! Where ya goin' with my pie?"

The kid had a thick American accent. I'd just caused an

international incident. I hit the tracks and kept running, so fast there were hunks of meringue flying up in my face.

Once I'd dealt with that hunger, another one surfaced, even fiercer than the first.

To get an Internet fix.

The tracks led straight to a little village that a rusty sign told me was Carcross. It was a pretty little place, parked at the sandy junction of two big mountain lakes. But what I found most appealing about it was all the satellite dishes. One on every house. Even though I was miles from nowhere, I knew that where there was satellite, there'd be Internet. And where there was Internet, I could be a somebody again.

I tucked in my tattered shirt, jerked down my Blue Jays cap, and slunk along the edge of town. I toyed with looking for a library that could plug me in, but Woody had probably given them a heads-up about me. What I really needed was—

There!

A little house backing onto some sand dunes. It had a big beautiful satellite dish hanging off the back deck. No cars in the driveway. No dog tied up. No sign of life.

I staked out in the bushes behind the house and watched.

I inched a little closer, hiding behind a toolshed.

I crept right up to it and tried the back door.

Didn't budge.

"Jesus!" I whispered, not quite believing what I was doing.

Maybe Woody was right. We are the kids from Hell. I'm already stealing stuff. What's next?

I jumped away from the house. I started easing back toward the dunes, ready to get the hell out of Carcross, to follow those tracks wherever they led ... when I glimpsed little green lights inviting me to come inside.

I moved up to the window and cupped my hands against it. There on a desk was a WiFi-router, flashing brightly with every tickle of the World Wide Web. Right beside it, an open laptop with tropical fish swimming across the screen.

"Yess!"

I pulled the door again, now with two hands. I ripped the screen off the window and clawed all around it. I pulled the back door with all my strength, this time bracing both feet beside it.

Bolted solid.

I searched the backyard for something heavy, found a big piece of pipe, and rammed it through the stained glass beside the door frame.

I'm in!

The minutes passed. Hours maybe. I was oblivious to time. To the cottage I'd busted into. There was only the friendly glow of the screen and the rush of emails, messages, and posts to catch up on. I was lost in the world I loved, updating my blogs, tweaking my profiles, sanitizing any comments. I was in the middle of an email to my new drifter friend, Lisa, when I heard a bark at the back door.

I froze. For the first time, I noticed blood pooling over the keyboard. It had leaked from the wound I got jumping Woody's fence.

Heavy knocking.

"Ian?"

I turned toward the voice. Through the smashed glass, I saw a telltale yellow stripe on the pant leg of an RCMP officer. One hand rested on his holstered gun, while the other kept knocking.

"Ian. We know you're in there. Please come out."

I got up and walked to the door as if to the gallows. I slowly opened it. The sunlight killed my eyes and I staggered backward into the room.

I heard a familiar laugh. "Ho-leee, you look like a friggin' scarecrow!"

I uncovered my eyes and saw William standing beside the cop. A little white dog circled his heels, growling at me.

"You sure love these solos, eh?" William said.

"How ... how the hell did you find me?"

William pulled out his iPhone and waved it at me. "You might want to turn off your location function next time you're banging away on a computer," he said. "Between that and my partner here, you were a sittin' duck."

"Your what?"

William clapped his hands and the dog jumped into his arms. "You thought Togo was amazing. Meet Butch."

I squinted at the dog. Locked in his jaws was a piece of plaid pajamas torn from my ass.

A SECOND CHANCE

I wanted the cop to blare his siren like he did for Wade. Give me the flashing lights, handcuffs, the whole bit. Tell the world, "Look out, dangerous criminal on board! One of Woody's kids from Hell!"

The shoe fit well after what I'd just done. That must be who I am.

But I didn't even get the siren. "Hard on Butch's ears," William told me, as he kissed his dog in the back of an RCMP cruiser bombing north up the Carcross road.

I didn't say much, didn't ask what would happen to me. Until we turned left at Ritchie's Roadhouse, I figured I was going straight to the jail in Whitehorse. Or straight to the airport and back to my dungeon in Calgary. That is, if my father didn't kill me before I stepped through the door.

But the cop was taking us straight back to Camp Lifeboat.

It wasn't a prison guard I had to face, or my father. It was Woody.

We arrived in the middle of supper. Spaghetti again. The

dining hall went silent when we walked in. Woody hardly looked up from his plate when the cop handed me over. "Have a seat, Ian," Woody said.

I just stood there. The smell of meat sauce got my nostrils flaring. William and the cop whispered behind my back. Alyssa and Obie stared at me like I was standing before a firing squad. Morris made a gurgly noise as he ran a thumb across his neck.

Woody pushed an empty plate toward me and motioned for me to sit. "Please, Ian. You must be hungry." He looked tired, beaten down, somehow.

Then I remembered about his dog. About Wade.

"Too bad about Togo," I said, surprising myself.

Woody's lips tightened. "Yes ... Thank you."

I scooped some spaghetti out of the pot, just enough to cover my plate.

Woody watched my every move, like I'd already taken too much.

I started putting some back.

"No, no," he said. "Take as much as you like. You've had a long day."

I heaped some sauce on top.

"Bison meatballs," Woody said, leaning back and folding his arms.

I got the weird feeling that there really was a firing squad waiting for me, and this was my last meal. *Why would Woody be so nice at a time like this?*

"Sorry I screwed up," I mumbled after a couple of mouthfuls.

Woody waved at the cop. "Thanks, Roger. We'll take it from here."

I looked up at Woody. "What happens now?"

Woody sighed. "Addiction can make you do crazy things."

"Why did he do it?" I said.

"I'm talking about *you*, not Wade."

"Yeah, but I'm not ..."

Woody raised his eyebrows. "No?"

Carrie came running out of the kitchen with soapsuds on her hands. "Ian! We were *so* worried about you. Welcome home."

I almost choked on a meatball. "Home?"

"It's either here or a young offenders center in Edmonton," Woody said.

"Where you sent Wade?"

"Correct. Wade gave me no choice. In your case, I'm leaving that choice up to you."

"Me?"

"A second chance," Carrie said, pulling up a chair beside me.

I was almost knocked over by her cheerleader freshness, and suddenly realized how I must stink.

"You've had a little setback, Ian," Carrie said. "You fell out of the driver's seat and your addiction took the wheel."

"But I—"

Carrie hushed me with a finger over her lips. "Let's agree you've hit bottom, okay?"

I shrugged. "I dunno ... Did I?"

"I certainly hope so," Woody said firmly.

"Stick around and we'll help you take back the wheel," Carrie said. She gently lifted my wounded hand. Fresh blood was leaking through the bandage William had put on in Carcross. "Oh, my. We better get Berna to have a look at this."

The next day, while William and I were pulling weeds in the vegetable garden, he told me that Wade was kicked out to avoid another murder. "His *own*," William said. "Never seen Woody so messed up. Or so friggin' mad. Togo was like a ... whatchacallit ... a soulmate."

Sweet Loba. Could I ever relate.

William also told me that I could be jailed "a long, long time" for breaking and entering a private home. "I know what I'm talking about," he said, like he'd been there, done that.

Luckily the people who owned the house I'd busted into never laid charges against me. I later found out from Mom that it was because Dad not only paid for the window I'd smashed, but also gave them a fat check plus several shares in his gold company—a mineral near and dear to Yukoners' hearts.

For good measure, he even sent Woody a well-timed donation to help keep me out of jail.

Thanks for that, Dad.

If my father was good at anything, it was protecting the McCracken name from the crimes we'd committed.

Most of the time, anyway.

CANOE LESSON

"Hey, look, there's my scarecrow," I said to Carrie as she drove our crew of delinquents to Annie Lake. The scarecrow stood in the same little vegetable patch I had dived into during my great escape. Now it wore an old wetsuit, snorkel, and mask. It toted a beat-up speargun. Plastic flowers poked out the top of its snorkel.

"Wow!" Carrie said. "A total remake. That's what our canoe trip could do for you, Ian."

"Yeah, right."

"But first, you need to learn how to paddle."

Woody had gone ahead with the canoes and had them lined up on shore by the time we pulled in, bright red canoes with a lifeboat logo stuck on the side.

Fifty days in one of those things? I thought. I'd been trying real hard to be Canadian, but canoes were as familiar to me as flying saucers.

Much to my disgust, Woody assigned Morris and me to the same canoe. He put me up front, the bow, I was told, and

Morris in back—the stern. I'd never touched a paddle in my life. I got the feeling Morris hadn't either but, of course, he faked it in front of Woody. While I struggled just to get my life jacket on, Morris was acting like he was Joe Outdoorsman, lining the paddle up against one eye and sniffing it.

"Birch, right?" he said to Woody.

"Good guess," Woody said. "Try maple. Now get in and try paddling out to me."

In one smooth movement, Woody gripped the gunwales of his canoe, swung his body into it, and kicked off from the gravel shore. He paddled effortlessly out into the crystal lake with a kind of poetry of motion I hadn't seen since watching Magno play his guitar.

Woody had taught us basic "canoe etiquette" in camp. But nothing could've prepared me for the feel of that canoe. It came alive as soon as I touched it.

Morris had already taken his throne in the stern, with the canoe still half on land.

"Like, I'm supposed to drag you in, or what?" I asked him.

"You want me to get my feet wet?" he said. "Of course you drag me in. It's a lot of work back here, you know, steering and everything."

While Morris made a big show of grunting and pushing his paddle in the gravel, I tugged and twisted the canoe until we finally got it afloat.

"Next time, you might want to launch it first," Woody shouted, "*then* get in."

I turned to Morris. "See?"

He threw me a quick finger.

I stepped into the bow. The canoe rolled like a frisky dog.

"What the fuck are you doing?" Morris said, white-knuck-ling the gunwales.

"Center!" Woody shouted. "Always step in the center!"

I tried to climb in again. The canoe bucked like a horse.

"Stay low!" Woody shouted.

I shifted my weight too fast. One gunwale bit the surface and buckets of water poured in.

"Hey!" Morris yelled as water swirled around his design-er hiking boots. He jumped up, flipping the boat complete-ly, which, in turn, knocked me flat on my ass.

As I lay belly up in the shallow water, I could hear clap-ping from the shore.

"Go, team!" Carrie shouted between fits of laughter.

WHITEWATER

I can still feel the sting of rope burns around my neck. As much as Morris might have liked to kill me, I don't think this was how he'd planned it.

Woody's approach to wilderness training seemed to be: give us a few crumbs of technical skills, then throw us to the wolves. It was all about "turning challenges into growth experiences," he kept telling us.

Great, Woody. That is, if I live through them.

I remember standing at the edge of the Wheaton River, staring at a jumble of waves and spray and rocks, feeling the vibration of crashing water come up through my feet. I'm thinking, *There's no way I'm getting in a canoe and paddling through that stuff!*

But after watching Obie and Carrie somehow make it through alive, accompanied by massive cheers from the rest of us, I figured, what the hell. Besides, William and Morris were set up downstream with safety ropes, right?

I lost some nerve when Woody put Alyssa and me

together. She was still pretty much a zombie around camp. But when I steadied the canoe for her, watching her creep toward the bow, I could tell by the way she moved that she had some experience in a canoe.

At least, more than me.

I managed to slip into the stern without dumping us. I knelt low, spreading my knees to grip the sides like Woody showed us. My stomach was tight as a drum as I pushed off from shore with a cautious poke of my paddle. We drifted into a calm eddy just above the rapids.

"Focus!" Woody shouted from his canoe upstream of us. "Aim for the v!"

The so-called safe route we'd scouted from shore was invisible from the water. I didn't recognize one wave, one rock.

I felt the river suddenly grip our canoe. There was no turning back.

"Okay, Alyssa," I hollered over the rushing water. "This is it! Yell if you see trouble."

I think I saw her nod.

We quickly gained speed. I lined us up and we hit the top of the v dead on. We tobogganed down it and sliced through a big standing wave. "All right!" I shouted as the spray hit my grinning face.

We flew through the curling, twisting water, skimming past big rocks and rollers that could've eaten our canoe.

What a rush!

Must have been beginner's luck.

The second time, we flipped at the top of the rapids.

The shock of hitting the cold water took my breath away, and I cried out like someone had slapped me hard. As we bobbed through the rapids, I remembered to stick my feet downstream, like we'd been told, and I shouted to Alyssa to do the same. My butt still took a serious beating from bashing into rocks.

The current finally loosened its grip on us. But we got stuck in an eddy in the center of the river, and a huge roller blocked us from shore.

"Rope!" I heard William shout, and his throwbag zinged out of the woods, trailing the rescue rope behind it. I let myself drift downstream toward it but, before I could grab it, I heard Morris's voice—"Rope!" —and another throwbag flew past me on my upstream side.

"You go for that one!" I shouted to Alyssa.

But the wonky currents had other ideas. They took the ropes in opposite directions and, before I could grab either, they'd crossed and closed around my neck.

I hadn't really felt the strength of that river until I tried ripping those ropes off my neck while fighting for air. Till my dying day—and I truly thought that was it—I'll know I never could have done it alone.

It wasn't really anybody's fault. The tangled ropes, I mean. But I know who saved me.

Alyssa.

And it wouldn't be the last time.

HOT SPRINGS

It had been five weeks since I'd last sat on a real toilet seat. What a wonderful invention. This one was in a roofless outhouse parked beside the Redstone hot springs. Civilization was pretty thin on the Keele River, and we took what comforts we could get. Of course I was whistling, so my jailers knew I hadn't run off into the mountains again.

I was sitting there on that real toilet seat, enjoying a form of Canadian culture that was new to me. A dog-eared journal hung by a string on the outhouse wall. On the cover were the words, SHIT LIT.

Paddled 8 hours to make it here last night. Got caught in a freak blizzard, snow filling our canoes, wind up our asses, shivered all day in wet gear. Worth every paddle-stroke once we jumped in the hot springs! So surreal! So beautiful! Thank you, Mother Earth!

Man, I wish I could shit here every day!

From southern Chile to northern Canada. Worth the trip! Please take care of God's country!—Alejandro

Got charged by a mother grizzly and her cubs as we did a "float-n-bloat" down the river. Mama bear kicked up quite a spray along the shore, then stood up and shook her fist at us. I shit you not! Never paddled faster!!

Knock on the door. "Is that you in there, Ian?"

I don't think Obie had shit in the woods once since the camp van had dropped us way back at the Canol Road, at the headwaters of the Keele. Obie was deathly afraid of bears. "How'd you like to die with your pants down?" he had asked me one day when we were paddling together. His solution was to eat like a bird, in spite of Carrie's lectures on anorexia. The guy had lost about twenty pounds. But he'd gained lots of muscle, like the rest of us.

"Yeah, yeah. Just give me a minute," I said.

"You've only been in there for like—"

"Just hold tight, Obie. You're the sphincter expert."

I grabbed a pencil jammed between the logs and scribbled the first thing that came to my head.

Believe in the music! Love, Indio.

I stared at the words, wondering who wrote them.

Knock, knock.

I slapped the journal shut. "It's all yours, Obie."

"Hurry! I can't hold it!"

"Is this the *gain* part?" I asked Woody, as I slipped back into the steaming pool dug into the riverside rocks. The swirling hot water penetrated my bones. My head was giddy with the sulfur fumes.

Carrie nudged a floating barrel lid over to me, loaded high with fancy cheeses, crackers, and chocolates she'd kept hidden for weeks. There were even some Oreo cookies and a jar of Nutella.

"No harm in rewarding the pain it took to get this far," Woody said. "But your team is still pretty rough around the edges."

Obie returned from the outhouse, still whistling. He rolled into the water almost drowning the barrel lid. "Ahhhhh."

Morris pretended to cough, horked up something gross, and spit in the water in front of Obie.

"Would you kindly fuck off, Morris?" Obie said.

"See what I mean?" Woody said. "Rough around the edges."

"You seem to be in a good mood, eh, Obie?" William said.

"That was the best shit *ever*," he said, leaning his head on a boulder and closing his eyes.

"I've been wondering, Obie," William said. "Where'd ya get that name?"

"I'm special. It's short for Oberon, King of the Fairies."

Morris choked on a chocolate.

"You okay?" Alyssa said, thumping Morris on the back.

"Thanks, yeah," he said, his eyes watering.

"It's also one of the moons of Uranus," Obie added.

"Whose anus?" Morris asked.

"Up yours," Obie said.

Carrie joined in, trying to de-escalate as usual. "So ... uh ... Morris, what does your name mean?"

"Conqueror of fairies."

"You're full of it," Obie said, reaching for a handful of crackers.

However rough the team might have been in Woody's eyes, Obie was definitely going places. He was talking twenty times more than when he arrived. He was standing up to Morris. More than that, he seemed to know who he was. Took pride in his name.

I couldn't help feeling a twinge of envy.

"How far did we paddle today?" I asked Woody.

"Best day yet," he said. "Nearly forty miles. At this rate, we'll be at the Flats in a couple of days."

"Almost home," Alyssa said.

"*Your* home, maybe," I said.

"Where's yours?" she asked.

"Dunno," I said honestly.

"What's the Flats?" Obie said.

"You'll see," was all Woody said, like he'd already told us too much. After all these weeks on the river, he was still zipper-lipped on location details.

As if I was about to run off into these bear-infested mountains!

"We're getting to be a pretty well-oiled machine, eh, Woody?" Obie said, now working his way through the chocolates and Oreos. "Oh, my God ... mmm ... oh ... I think I'm having a mouthgasm."

Woody studied him for a moment, then pulled the barrel lid away. "Beware, Obie. Get too cocky and shit happens, especially on the home stretch."

William reached for the barrel lid and built himself a triple-decker of crackers, Nutella, and chocolates. "This may be the world's only job where, when things start going really well, you know you're doing something wrong."

"What kind of shit?" Obie asked Woody.

"This river isn't done with us yet. As the valley opens up, changes in wind or water levels can play hell with your canoe. Riverbanks are more apt to come unhinged and drop on you. More moose down here, too."

"Moose? Obie said. "What's the big—"

"No matter how many of Carrie's chocolates you eat, Obie, you'll be no match for the fifteen-hundred-pound moose you surprise on a portage."

William cupped his hands around his mouth and grunted at Obie like a horny moose.

Obie slid closer to Carrie.

Woody continued his sermon. We'd almost made it through the day without one. "Then of course, no matter where you are, you can always do something stupid, like get cocky in the rapids, or forget to tie up your canoe, or let your guard down and hit a rock, and then ..." Woody twirled a hand in the air, then plunged it into the pool. "... shit happens."

I looked at William for a reality check. "The Beast, right?"

William made a Halloween face and popped his claws out of the water.

"The beast?" Obie said.

I pointed at his hairless chest. "You."

Obie held up both hands. "Me?"

"Well, I don't mean *you*, exactly."

"You do mean you," William said.

"What is this shit?" Alyssa said.

William squinted at her. "You, too. Beast alert!"

Carrie nailed William with a slap of steamy water. "He's saying that, out here, you are your own worst enemy."

"Back home, too," Woody said. "*Especially* back home."

"So ... what are we supposed to do?" Obie asked.

"You're doing it," Woody said. "Shaking out your junk and flushing it down the river."

William put on his best noble savage face. "Obie, just stay calm, be brave, and watch for the signs." Then he dropped his head below the surface under a storm of bubbles.

The howling started while he was underwater.

I kicked William's leg, harder than I meant to.

He exploded to the surface. "What's the pro—" His eyes went big.

So, I didn't imagine it.

A long shrill howl gushed out of the mountains, filling the whole valley.

The hair on the back of my neck wanted to fly off.

"What the fuck?" Morris said. His movie-star mask cracked open, revealing the chicken face of a ten-year-old.

All heads turned upstream where the sound spilled from.

Carrie looked spooked but tried to keep it together. "Sounds like when I was in labor with my first child," she said. "Refused to come out no matter how I screamed."

Obie slid closer to Carrie, and I saw her reach underwater for his hand.

Woody was as unreadable as ever. Any emotions that might've leaked out were trapped in his beard, which, in the hot springs, looked like a nest of snakes.

"We're lucky," Alyssa said calmly.

I sculled toward her and noticed her breasts bobbing like ripe mangoes beneath her T-shirt. "What do you mean, lucky?"

She wouldn't look back at me.

The howling went on and on, for maybe five minutes. It rose, fell, seemed to circle around us, then whooshed downriver. It ended as fast as it started.

"It was the wind," Carrie assured us. "Yes, some kind of wind-tunnel effect. Did you hear the way it ..." She glanced back at the spruce trees lining the river. Not a branch stirred. She looked at the fingers of steam rising unruffled all around us. "Hmm, maybe not the wind."

"It was an elk," Obie said matter-of-factly. "I've heard them just like that down in Banff."

Woody shook his head. "Nearest elk is a thousand miles away. It was definitely a wolf. Caught in a trap by the sound of it."

Long silence broken only by the gurgling river.

"Trolls!" said Obie. "That's it. Had to be trolls."

Nervous laughter all around.

Butch came blasting out of the willows and did a running leap into the pool. William grabbed his collar and pulled him close. The dog shook in his arms.

Then, moving as one well-oiled team, everyone sank deeper into the pool, hiding behind a wall of steam.

Listening.

"Is this one of your *signs*?" I whispered to William.

He shrugged. "Dunno. Maybe somebody's just working out their karma, eh?"

THE AMERICANS

At breakfast, nobody talked about the howling. Like it didn't happen. But there was a new edge in the air that infected even William. He kept glancing upstream where the sound came from. Or he'd squint up at the mountains like he was peering at something we couldn't see.

I couldn't shake this feeling that things were disintegrating.

Half a day's paddle away, we rounded a bend and saw two figures sitting on the edge of a bald gravel bar in the middle of the river. Woody suddenly waved his paddle and signaled for us to land. He and Carrie booted over to it.

I was sterning that day, with Morris in the bow and Alyssa in the middle as "mojo." Woody had called this crew configuration an "experiment" when we'd set off that morning. "To help rub off those rough edges," he'd said. Right now, it felt like the experiment was not working. "Come on!" I yelled. "Paddle, you lily-dippers!" Morris put more effort into flipping water in my face than paddling. Alyssa's back went limp and she almost dropped her paddle in the river. "Don't give up on me, Alyssa! Gimme all ya got!" The current was stronger after a night of rain, and we had to paddle our asses off to avoid sailing past the gravel bar.

I lost control as we hit a calm eddy near the shore and we T-boned Woody's canoe at full steam.

"Please!" Woody said as he and Carrie dragged their canoe onto the gravel.

I looked upstream for William and Obie's canoe and saw them cruising with the current, right on target, facing the wrong way. As William tried to spin them around, they ran broadside into a big standing wave that almost swamped their boat.

"Ran into a bit of a speed bump," William said as they crunched ashore.

The two figures on the gravel bar watched the whole show like statues. Butch jumped out, soaking wet, and ran circles around them. No reaction, not even when Butch shook water all over them. As we walked closer, I saw it was an old guy and his girlfriend. Burned-out hippies. They were sitting on river boulders, both dressed head-to-toe in buckskin and looking like they'd been in the bush far too long.

Woody went up to them with his hand extended. The man shook it limply without standing.

"Who are you?" the man asked suspiciously.

American, I thought. *Deep South. Living their dream. Or their nightmare.*

"We're a bunch of drug addicts and thieves," Morris told

him, his signature smile glued back on. "Better watch your stuff."

The woman stood abruptly. The man took a long drag on his cigarette and looked up at Woody.

"Camp Lifeboat," Woody said. "Heard of it?"

The man shook his head. I noticed a carton's worth of butts at his feet.

"Wilderness therapy program," Woody said proudly.

"I could *sure* use some of that ol' therapy right now," the man said. "Did you hear somethin' strange last night?"

We all looked at each other.

It traveled this far?

"A sound?" Carrie said.

"A bloody wailing sound. Did you hear that? What the hell was it?"

"I'm not sure what you mean," Woody said.

The guy stood up, a cold light in his eyes. "Oh, yes, you do. You heard it, all right. What the hell was it?"

Obie stepped forward. "We think it was trolls, sir."

The man laughed crazily. "Hah! Trolls. Ya hear that, Wendy? Bloody trolls!"

"Enough, Ben," she said. "Let's go."

The man sprang off his boulder.

Butch growled at him.

"Yes!" he said, as he shoved Butch aside with his moccasined foot. "Let's go. Let's get the hell outta here!"

The man flicked his half-smoked cigarette into the river. William watched it drift away like he might go after it.

The Americans broke into a run straight for their canoe, a

cheap plastic model, hand-painted to look like birch bark. We watched in silence as they randomly fired their stuff into their boat, dragged it to the river, and took off, paddling like devils.

"Impressive team," said William. "Zero to sixty in a minute flat."

THE FLATS

Except for pee and snack breaks, we'd been paddling all afternoon. With our heads on swivel, we'd drifted past some incredible mountain scenery. We'd shot some decent rapids that would've scared the shit out of us weeks ago, when we were still bumbling beginners. I discovered that I could tolerate paddling with Morris as long as there was lots of whitewater to keep him busy. His strength actually allowed us to tackle some kick-ass rapids that the other interns couldn't touch.

But most of the rapids were now behind us. As Woody predicted, the valley started to open up and spit us out. The mountains were retreating from us on both sides, as the Keele River split into a million channels.

"Welcome to the Flats," Woody said during a float-n-bloat of gummy bears and brownies.

The change came suddenly, like somebody had swapped a screensaver or flipped a Web page on me when I wasn't looking.

Back in the mountains, I'd sometimes felt claustrophobic, like they were just another set of walls hemming me in. But at least the mountains were solid, and it seemed things had been that way forever. In the mountains, I felt I knew where I stood and had something to hold onto. No matter how crazy the current, the river always obeyed the lay of the land.

Down here in the Flats, it was the opposite. We'd entered a shifty world of willows, wind, and water where the river seemed to do whatever the hell it wanted. As we drifted along with our canoes lashed together by our dangling legs, the water poured around us, tearing at the sandy banks, spilling away in all directions, disappearing in a chaos of islands.

From here to Guatemala, it was the loneliest, most exposed place I'd ever seen. Everything seemed to be falling apart, and I got the strange feeling that I might be next. "How do you know which way is out?" I asked Woody.

"All channels lead out eventually, if by *out* you mean the Mackenzie River and civilization."

"Whatever."

"The better question is, how *long* do you want to spend getting out of here?"

"I'm ready to get out now," Morris said. "By that I mean I'm fixed. Therapy's over. Beam me up."

Carrie snatched the bag of gummy bears from him. "Not so fast, Morris," she said. "There's still the final exam."

"When's that?" I asked.

"Usually when you least expect it," Woody said. "You'll be

evaluated on how well you can hold it together when the river pushes all your buttons. How well you can contribute to—"

"The greater glory of the team," I said. "Right. We get it, Woody. But you still haven't told us which way is out."

"Some channels will float you through to the Mackenzie easy as a conveyor belt. Others shrink to a trickle around the next bend, and you'll be dragging your canoe out of here. For *days*, actually."

"Been there, done that," Obie said. "Enough dragging."

"Good, then," Woody said, lifting his leg out of our canoe. "It's therefore critical that we stick close together, that we always keep within shouting distance of each other."

"Go, team!" Carrie said, and our flotilla broke apart into three crews, bobbing within a paddle-whack of each other.

I stared at Carrie as she paddled so strong and steady in the bow of Woody's canoe. I was remembering the first time I heard her say that. *Go, team!* That day, centuries ago, when I rolled into Camp Lifeboat blindfolded to the world.

Who was that kid? I wondered.

Then, even more baffling: *Who am I now?*

FLIPPED

After another night of heavy rain, the Keele was extra muddy. The day before, it had looked like creamy tea. This morning it was chocolate milk. The water was so thick with silt, we could hear it hissing under our canoe, like it was scratching to get in and sink us. The water had risen so much overnight that we had to wolf down a cold breakfast and clear off the island where we'd camped before it disappeared underwater. The river seemed more muscular this morning, more menacing. It was choked with logs that had washed down from the mountains while we slept.

Woody had stuck three of us together, "for some final polishing work," he said. This time he put Morris in the stern, Alyssa up front and me as "mojo"—the useless middle guy who can't steer, can't navigate, can't do anything but paddle. I normally hated being mojo where, as Carrie says, "all you can control is your attitude." But, between Obie snoring and the random crash of slumping banks, I'd had a crappy sleep. So I was glad to zone out and leave the driving to Morris. In this current, we barely needed to paddle, let alone steer. I even closed my eyes, falling into the mellow groove of my paddle-strokes. *One-two-three, one-two-three ...*

I could've gone on like that for hours. As long as Morris kept us slotted in behind Woody, riding one of his conveyor belts to the Mackenzie, what could go wrong?

A lot, actually.

It started with machine-gun fire. Above the hissing current, I heard a sudden *rat-a-tat-tat* sound on the water right beside us. I opened my eyes to see a trickle of small stones ripping through the surface. I looked up. My breath stopped. We were paddling under a crumbling cliff of sand that could go any second.

I spotted the two other canoes way across the channel. I spun around and saw Morris lying back on the stern deck, his paddle dangling in the water. "Jesus Christ, Morris, wake up! That thing's gonna go!"

"What thing?" he said, looking around like the stoner that he was.

I pointed my paddle at the cliff above us. "That!" I yelled, and a big hunk splooshed right beside us, almost beaning Alyssa.

She screamed like it was the end of the world.

"Don't scream!" I said, in a screaming whisper. "You'll bring the whole friggin' thing down on us. Just paddle!"

Morris kicked up a rooster tail behind the boat. Alyssa paddled like I'd never seen her. I dug and dug at the water until every muscle in my body was on fire. More hunks of sand crashed around us like we were under mortar attack. One biggie nailed me square on the back, almost knocking the wind out of me. "PADDLE!" I yelled.

"What the fuck do you think I'm doing?" Morris shouted.

Woody madly waved his paddle, signaling *Left! Left!*

"*¡Jesucristo!*"

"What?" Alyssa said.

"They're turning!"

I heard shouting from the other boats but didn't catch a word of it. I whimpered like a kid when I saw they were already committed to a new channel where most of the current was going.

And we were not.

So many channels. We'd never find them if we got separated.

Woody's warning about the Flats stormed into my head. *It's critical that we stick close together ... Always keep within shouting distance of each other ...*

I looked back at the cliff as a car-sized hunk of dirt peeled off and slammed into the water a paddle-length from Morris. The wave swallowed our stern and flooded the boat with chocolate milk.

Alyssa jerked her paddle up as ice-water drowned her feet. The paddle slipped from her fingers into the river. She lunged for it, almost dumping us. I slapped a high brace on the opposite side, barely stopping the canoe from dumping.

"Jesus, Alyssa! Don't do that!"

I went to grab her paddle but the current had already torn it away.

I yanked out the spare and shoved it at her. "Paddle!" I yelled.

The extra weight of water turned our canoe into a floating brick. "Left! Left!" I shouted.

"I can't ..." Morris yelled. "I can't turn! Help me turn, damn it!"

"We gotta catch them before—"

There was another crash behind us as half the cliff gave way. The second wave hit us broadside and flipped us over like a bathtub toy.

I smashed my head on a floating log when I came to the surface. Our flipped canoe was already headed downstream and I couldn't see either Alyssa or Morris. I thrashed my way over to it, my muscles turning to ice.

I managed to catch the canoe and flop my body over it. Just downstream I saw the bobbing heads of my crewmates.

Last thing I saw of the other canoes was Woody's paddle waving high in the air before disappearing behind a wall of willows.

IN THE POCKET

I can't say how far we drifted. Or for how long.

Hang on for three days and three nights.

That's what Woody said to do if our canoe flipped. In this frigid water, we'd all be dead long before that. But we got Woody's point and hung on, starfish style, with our arms linked over the canoe's red belly. After much cursing and spluttering, we concluded that our canoe was impossible to steer. All we had to do was stay alive until we crashed into something solid or got close enough to shore to make a dash for it.

Alyssa's teeth got rattling so bad I could hear them over the rushing water. Morris and I tried to boost her onto the canoe so she could lie in the sun and warm up.

Bad plan.

The canoe couldn't hold her and we got totally soaked all over again.

I felt Alyssa's grip loosening by the minute. I glanced across the hull at Morris and could tell he felt it, too. It took all our strength to hang on so she wouldn't get torn away by the current like her paddle.

I began to space out, getting hypothermic myself, when my feet scraped the gravel bottom. The current had carried us toward a little island. But not close enough. On this course, we'd drift right past it.

I got an idea. "Let's flip it!"

"You crazy?" Morris said. "I'm gonna swim for it."

"And kiss the boat goodbye?"

"Just pull it behind you."

"Upside down? You know that's nuts."

But Morris was already flailing for the island.

"So much for teamwork!" I yelled after him.

Morris didn't look like much of a swimmer to me but, at that moment, I had other things to worry about. Alyssa was on the downstream side of the canoe. With Morris gone, I could barely hold her. Her lips were blue. Her skin all pasty.

"You okay, Alyssa?"

"Just let me go," she said. "I'll be all right. I'm almost ..."

"What, Alyssa? What?" I realized I needed to keep her talking.

"I'm almost ... almost home," she said, barely audible above the surging water.

My feet scraped bottom again. "Try to stand up, Alyssa! You gotta try!"

She tried. She stood. The canoe bowled her over. She disappeared.

Never get downstream of a dumped canoe. Woody's voice in my head again.

"Alyssa! Alyssa!"

Water gurgling around the canoe.

"Alyssa!"

A raven swooped over the canoe, looking for dead things to eat.

"ALYSSA!"

"Help!" came a muffled voice.

I still couldn't see her.

"Ian! Under here!"

"Where?"

"The canoe! I can't breathe!"

She's in the air pocket!

I groped under the canoe. I found her thighs, her arm, her hand. She clamped onto mine.

"Just take a deep breath!" I shouted. "I'll pull you out!"

"I can't breathe!"

"You can! Don't let go of me!"

"Get me out of here!"

"Ready, one, two, three ... Big breath!"

I heard knocking from inside. Either that signaled she was ready or she was drowning. I reached under with both arms, wrapped them around her waist, and pulled her toward me. She popped up and out of the river like a breaching whale.

"Thanks," she said as her body went limp in my arms.

The canoe was taking off again. The river wanted it. Wanted me. Wanted everything in this valley.

Getting shallower.

I tried to prop Alyssa on her feet. This motion triggered

a sudden flashback of helping Sofi learn to walk when she was still a diaper brat.

My family. Will I ever see them again?

"Can you stand up? Alyssa, can you walk to the island?"

She shook her head and gave me a weak smile.

Of all the places to see Alyssa's first smile!

The canoe was drifting out of reach.

Alyssa was drifting out of consciousness.

"Morris! Morris, you shit, where are you? MORRIS!"

I felt a hand on my back. Not Alyssa's.

"Give her to me," Morris said. "Get the fucking boat."

Morris hoisted Alyssa up on his brawny shoulders, locked her into a perfect fireman's carry, and stumbled to shore.

THE ISLAND

It wasn't much of an island. A shoal was more like it, and it wouldn't be around for long. The river wanted to claim this, too. Nothing but a strip of river rocks and sand, a few scrawny willow bushes, and a fringe of battered driftwood. But it was dry, the sand was hot, and the sun was blazing.

Once our canoe was safely pulled up, Morris and I did a quick inventory of stuff that survived the dumping. The good news: we still had one paddle and all the gear we'd strapped into our boat that morning, including the hatchet. The bad news: the canoe with a mojo paddler always carried the least stuff. So no food barrel, no tent.

I looked up at Morris. "No food or shelter. But hey, we've got each other."

"To eat, you mean?"

I bit my tongue. After all the shit this guy had put me through at school, online, back at camp, I refused to laugh. "May the toughest cannibal win."

"Deal."

Alyssa, who'd gone off for a pee, appeared over the side of the canoe, clutching a mini barrel. "Finders keepers, eh?"

I noticed her lips were still bluish but her speech was much clearer. Her Husky eyes, hazel and blue, were brighter than I'd ever seen them. "Where the hell did you find that?"

Alyssa pointed her chin at a pile of driftwood. "In those logs."

"Cool," I said. "Must've floated downriver after we dumped."

Morris grabbed it and shook it. "What's in it?"

"Carrie's secret stash of goodies," I said.

Alyssa grabbed it back. "Like in the hot springs?"

I nodded, suddenly feeling a hit of hunger.

"Well?" said Morris. "Let's eat."

We talked about an escape plan all through lunch. Two plans, actually.

Plan A: stay put and wait for a rescue. We'd already spread out our orange tarp and piled rocks around it. Between that and our bright red canoe, a pilot would have to be blind drunk to miss us.

Plan B: paddle out. Just carve a second paddle from some driftwood, then slot back into the main current. Though Woody had told us dick about the route, we knew it wasn't far to the Mackenzie River. Alyssa's home turf. She could steer us back to civilization.

Plan A looked pretty good to us that sunny afternoon. Lie around on the hot sand, waiting for a rescue boat or chopper to pick us up.

Surely by now, Woody would have called for help on the

satellite phone.

So, after inhaling a bunch of dates, Nutella-smeared crackers, and Oreo cookies, I stripped down to my gonch, flung my wet clothes at a willow bush, and flopped onto the sand.

The three of us became lizards, basking on the sand, alone in our thoughts.

Alyssa crouched in her default fetal pose that used to scare me in camp but, out here, looked chill.

Morris flicked sand at a spider that kept popping out of a piece of driftwood.

I mostly watched the river, wondering how it could be out to kill you one minute, then singing to the sunshine the next.

I settled deeper into the sand and focused on the water. I realized that after weeks of dragging, drifting, shooting, and paddling this river, I'd never really *looked* at it. The boiling patterns on the surface. The silent bubbles drifting by. The twisted reflections of clouds, trees, and mountains. And through it all, the river just kept running, changing every second but always there, always the same.

I'd never really *listened* to it either, the way Magno would if he'd been sitting there beside me on the sand. I missed Magno. I missed my music, the way we used to listen to it. Like I was listening now to this river. Magno called it "deep listening."

I discovered voices in the river, whispering, laughing, humming, shouting. Not like that crazy creek on my solo. This was different. This was real. I discovered music, too.

Catchy rhythms, pulsing grooves, hints of a melody I once loved.

The river became a screen, reflecting nature's non-stop stream of life.

Live streaming—for real!

I had to laugh out loud.

"You okay?" Alyssa asked.

"Huh? Yeah. Just bushed, I guess."

I looked back at the river, as if I'd interrupted an important conversation, a lesson.

The river latched onto me, looked back at me.

Something inside cracked open, like Diadora's adobe hut, like my father's walls after the earthquake, like that cliff of sand that almost killed us.

Grietas en el alma. Cracks in my soul.

I heard echoes of exploding mountains, Diadora's sobs, marching army boots. I heard chanting students, Monica's bubbly laugh, hailstones on a car roof. I heard Togo's echoing bark, the camp alarm, and that eerie wail whooshing down the valley.

I shuddered as three worlds collided inside of me. Guatemala, Calgary, and here, now.

I closed my eyes and took a couple of huge yoga breaths, like Magno taught me.

One, two ... one, two ...

I calmed down. I wiggled my bare toes in the hot sand. Morris's spider crawled up my arm. I lightly brushed it off.

Part of me could stay by this river forever.

Alyssa was first to break the silence. There was that smile

again. Incredible! "That was touch and go out there, eh, boys?"

Morris and I looked at each other and shrugged at the exact same moment. Then, as much as I fought it, we burst into laughter.

"No, really," Alyssa said. "You kinda saved my life."

"It was worth it," Morris said.

"Go, team!" I said in my best Carrie voice.

RED DOG

The shift to Plan B—paddle out—happened fast. After kicking around that dinky island for another day, watching the wind pick up and the ceiling come down, we had no choice.

"There's no friggin' way they'd fly in this stuff," Alyssa said, looking up at a thick blanket of clouds that almost touched the treetops.

"So why not just wait for a boat?" I said.

Alyssa shook her head. "In this wind? Forget it."

Morris pointed to the whitecaps marching up the river. "It's not so bad out there. We've paddled in worse shit."

"Here, maybe," Alyssa said. "But on the Mackenzie? No way. Huge waves. Swamp even a jetboat."

"So then ... we wait it out," Morris said. "They'll come when—"

"There's one more little thing," I said. "Our island's shrinking fast."

Without a tent the night before, we'd crammed ourselves

under the canoe to sleep. I'd actually felt pretty snug in there—until I woke up and heard how much closer the river sounded. The shore that had saved us the day before had been flushed downstream.

"That's bullshit," Morris said.

I stood up and brushed the sand off my legs. "No, Morris. You didn't notice?"

"Prove it."

I showed him the gouged-out shoreline by the canoe. We took a quick walk around the island and discovered that more big hunks had disappeared, even since we'd got up.

"Holy shit," is all Morris said when he saw the destruction.

So Plan B it was.

Our carving project did not go well.

"I say we go with the one paddle," Morris announced.

Morris sat back on his hands, surrounded by wood chips, glaring at our second attempt. We'd discovered that the driftwood was packed with sand, which dulled the hatchet blade with every blow. Just when he had something that began to look like a paddle, the handle broke.

"There could be more rapids ahead," I said. "One person steering a loaded boat couldn't—"

"Fuck the rapids," Morris said. "We can line 'em if we have to. Portage 'em. Whatever. Let's go."

"There's no more rapids," Alyssa said. "Not now, anyway."

Morris and I both turned to her. "How do you know?" I said.

"I've been here before."

"This shitty little island?" Morris said.

"No. But around here. My granddad took us moose hunting as far as Red Dog once."

"Red Dog?" I said.

Alyssa pointed to an unimpressive hill half-shrouded by low clouds. "Red Dog Mountain."

"What's so special about it?" I asked.

"Supposed to be a big scary dog up there."

I thought of the Mayan stories my mother used to tell me about giant animals in the Guatemalan highlands. "You mean like a *spirit* animal?"

Alyssa shrugged. "Used to give people a rough time."

"Like, *eat* them?" I said.

"Maybe. Or drown them. Used to be a big whirlpool that would open up if people didn't show respect. Didn't make some kind of offering."

"Like paying the water with tobacco," I said, "the way William showed us?"

"Yeah, I guess. Some people leave matches, maybe shoot off a few bullets as they go by."

Morris chucked the half-carved paddle in the river. "Enough bullshit. Let's get out of here."

I stood up and studied an even darker bank of clouds, creeping toward us from upriver. I licked my finger and checked the wind. It had swung around, now coming from the north. I noticed that the willow leaves were all "ass up," as William would say. Not good. The river seemed higher, faster, greedier. We'd lost about a quarter of the island since we'd landed.

I could feel William by my side as I inspected the elements, seeing things that would have been invisible to me before I met him.

I imagined Obie looking up through his thick glasses and rhyming off the names of clouds. Oberon, King of the Fairies.

I thought about Woody, wondering what he'd do if he was marooned on this island.

And Carrie. Boy, how I could've used some of her TLC right then.

I sure hope those guys are okay.

"I still think we'd be better off with two paddles," I said. "And look at that sky. You want to launch in *this*?"

Morris winged the hatchet at a log near my bare feet. It stuck in perfectly, like he did this all the time. I stared at the hatchet, wondering if he used such talents on the street while pushing drugs.

"Your turn, then," Morris said. "Three strikes and we're outta here." He stomped over to the canoe, pulled out Carrie's snack barrel, and started rifling through it for choice goodies. I opened my mouth to say something about food rationing but, given his present mood—like an overwound guitar string—I decided against it.

Alyssa withdrew back into her fetal cave and took her smile with her.

Our team was fraying at the edges.

FIRE

The storm cloud moved over us like a giant black spaceship. I'd been hacking away at another paddle for hours. Morris paced the island like a caged bear. Alyssa had curled up under the canoe.

I don't know if it was that cloud or that thing they call night—something I hadn't seen since coming north—but it was getting too dark to work safely. I decided to dedicate a couple of our precious matches to a bonfire. Might cheer things up a bit, too.

The wind had other ideas and, a dozen matches later, I called Morris over to give me some cover.

"You cold or something?" Morris said.

"Did you maybe notice it was getting dark?"

Morris looked up at the ominous sky. "Weird, eh? You forget."

"So much for the midnight sun," I said.

"Yeah."

"If we can just get this fire going, I can finish this thing and—"

"We're outta here!"

Morris huddled closer, sheltering me from the wind with his great bulk.

The wood crackled. We had a fire. The flames jumped from log to log. They jumped into me.

"Why did you do it?" I asked.

"Do what?"

"That pedophile thing."

Morris leapt back like I'd thrust a flaming stick in his face. "It was ... just a joke. Can't you take a little *joke*?"

"It almost killed me, Morris." I was suddenly yelling. "Almost fucking *killed* me!"

"It's not my fault you took it so damn serious." Morris picked up a piece of driftwood the size of a baseball bat.

"And that video."

"What video?"

"You know fucking well what video. My dog getting creamed by a Coke truck!"

"Hey, I just happened to ... I thought maybe the police or somebody might—"

"BULLSHIT! You just had to post that, didn't you! DIDN'T YOU? On MY blog! Was that a fucking joke, too? WAS IT?"

Morris gripped the driftwood tighter.

Then I was crying. Bawling. Face in my hands. "I'm sorry, Loba ... I'm sorry, girl ... I'm so sorry."

A bolt of lightning suddenly turned the whole valley to ice. Half a second later, an ear-splitting CRACK of thunder.

I jerked my head up. *Where's Morris? Vaporized by the lightning?*

For a second, I wondered if God took him. *Straight to Hell, I hope!*

The fire sizzled in time with the first raindrops. Then buckets fell and killed it.

I dove for the canoe. A flash of lightning showed two pairs of legs sticking out of it. "Lemme in!" I yelled as another thunderclap ripped the sky open.

STORM

I'd heard the river's many tongues, whispering, humming, laughing. The wind that night seemed to have only one voice. Screaming at the top of its lungs.

During the odd lull, when it seemed the sky was inhaling for another blast, I could hear the splash and gurgle of collapsing banks all around us, as the rising flood bit off big hunks of sand and carried them away. The shrieking wind and pounding rain made it impossible to sleep, to talk, to do anything but lie there under the canoe and wait for the end.

The end of the storm or the end of our island. Whichever came first.

Alyssa was curled into a tight ball under the middle of the canoe. We'd found only one sleeping bag in our gear and she was buried under it. Morris and I were crammed in at either end of the canoe. I think we instinctively placed ourselves that way as if on suicide watch. Alyssa seemed more uptight after spilling that red dog story, and there was no telling what she might do. Whenever the wind threw an extra big fist at us, she'd moan or squeal or shout something crazy like, "Not now!" or "I'm not ready!" or "Soon! Soon!"

I'm no therapist, but that kind of talk did not sound healthy.

After a few hours of this, I was ready for a little therapy myself.

I felt like parts of me were being whittled away by the raw power of the storm. I couldn't shake this gnawing feeling that there was something more at play here, more than wind and rain and river. Something pressing down on us, listening, watching, waiting for our next move.

I pulled in my arms, covered my face, hugged my knees to my chest. I adopted Alyssa's favorite escape pose but it didn't help. Inside, I was trembling from the truth that my life had no more meaning or purpose than the grains of wet sand I was lying on. And, like the sand, my life could be swept away just as easily.

"Hey, Ian!"

Morris's shout hit me like a slap in the face.

"What?" I yelled.

"You got any of that tobacco?"

I stuck my head out in the rain to see his face. A distant flash of lightning showed me he was scared, too. "I didn't know you smoked."

"No, ya dumb shit. To ... you know."

"Right," I yelled. "To make an offering. Pay the water."

"Yeah. That."

"William's got the tobacco pouch."

"Too bad."

More fists of wind.

"Hey, but Morris," I yelled.

"What?"

"I don't think a carton of Players would help."

"Yeah, maybe not."

More thunder. I started pulling my head under the canoe when I heard another shout.

"Ian!"

"What now?"

"I'm sorry."

I stuck my head out again and turned my face to the rain, letting it wash away a sudden gush of tears.

"Ian?"

"Yeah, I'm here. Thanks, Morris."

THE OFFERING

I'm in my practice room below the domed skylight, hugging my zebrawood guitar. I move my hands to ready position and take a deep breath. I strum an open D minor, the chordal home of "Capricho Arabe." My guitar shivers with delight. So do I. I get the beat going in my head and lightly pluck the first harmonic at the seventh fret.

A few bars in, I hear a noise behind the door. Along the crack of light below it, I see the shadow of shoes tapping in time with my music.

I freeze.

Just let me play, Dad! Just let me play how I want!

I see a third shadow on the polished marble floor. The tip of Uncle Faustus's cane.

"*Venga, tío, venga.* Come in, Uncle!"

Uncle Faustus slowly opens the door and limps over to me, his face beaming. He grips my shoulder with one hand and flicks the strings of my guitar with the other.

"Prométeme," he says—promise me. *"Nunca renunciar a la música!"*

Never give up the music.

I reach out to him, to seal my promise with a handshake, when Loba jumps up from her sheepskin rug. She puts her front paws on my lap, throws her head back, and starts howling up a storm. It's her singing howl, the happy one I taught her. She's inviting me to keep playing. Keep playing. Her howl goes on and on, filling my practice room, gliding out the window, harmonizing with the wind ... the wind ...

I bend over to nuzzle Loba's neck but recoil when I feel it's all wet and cold ...

I woke to find my face buried in a soaked sleeping bag.

With no one in it.

"Alyssa!"

I leapt to my feet, knocking the canoe over and pinning one of Morris's arms.

"What the fuck?" he shouted. He stood up, ready to slug me.

"Alyssa's gone!"

My jaw dropped when I saw how much of the island got swept away overnight. The river had eaten more than half of it and now the wind, which seemed stronger than ever, wanted to blow away the rest. It had already stolen our orange rescue tarp. And our canoe, which we'd carefully placed in the center of the island, was now almost in the river.

My eyes scoured what was left of the driftwood piles, the willows.

"Where is she?" Morris yelled.

I ran past him toward the other end of the island. I found her sandals, Teen Wolf T-shirt, and jean shorts. Then her bra and panties.

I ran faster.

There! Off the downstream tip of the island, up to her waist in the galloping river.

I stopped for a second, thinking she might just be enjoying an early morning skinny dip, like we did sometimes in the mountains on the hottest mornings. But there was a bloody gale trying to knock her over, and her body language said this was no skinny dip.

"Alyssa!"

She didn't look back.

"ALYSSA!"

I heard Morris panting beside me. "What the fuck is she up to now?"

"Come on!" I yelled, running straight into the icy water.

"Leave me!" she shouted and waded in deeper. "It's okay."

A couple more steps and the river will take her.

"It's not okay!" I yelled. "What are you doing?"

"Did you hear it last night?"

"What?"

"The howling."

"Yeah ... I mean, no ... I don't know! Grab my hand!"

"Red dog," she said, wading further. "Needs it ... An offering ... It's okay."

The current tore around her, tried to lift her. She was almost afloat.

"Not *you*, Alyssa! We can offer something else."

She turned to me defiantly, so beautiful in her nakedness, so proud. "Like what?"

"I don't know ... chocolates ... whatever. Don't do this, Alyssa!"

I lunged for her arm, losing one of my legs to the current, and almost fell in. It took all my strength to get back on two feet. I looked at Morris, who stood on the shore, paralyzed by fear. "For Christ's sake, give me a hand, Morris!"

Alyssa inched further into the current.

"NO!" I yelled and I lunged again, this time clamping onto her hand.

The combined resistance of our bodies against the current was too much for me. "MORRIS!"

"It's really okay," Alyssa said, struggling to untangle her hand from mine.

I felt a sudden drag on my arm. She had lifted both feet off the bottom and was now drifting free.

Alyssa was about to drag me downriver with her.

Then I felt Morris's hand clutch my other arm and he hauled us both to shore.

Alyssa slumped to the sand, sobbing.

"Watch her!" I shouted and sprinted back toward the canoe for the sleeping bag.

Above the howling wind I heard a hollow thump and a splash.

¡Jesucristo! It's gone!

I got to our campsite just in time to see our red canoe bobbing merrily down the Keele River, right side up, on its final journey to the Mackenzie.

TEAM CAPTAIN

"Now we're truly fucked," Morris said.

I threw another chunk of driftwood on the fire. "Hey, at least we've got—"

"Each other!" Morris said, spitting out the words.

"Guess we won't need that extra paddle now," I said.

Alyssa stuck her face out from the sleeping bag. Her hair was still caked with sand. "If you'd only let me ..."

Her eyes locked on something upstream.

I followed her gaze to a mob of ravens, hovering over a knot of logs that had piled up against the island during the storm. "What, Alyssa?"

"Ravens."

"Got it," Morris said. "Ravens. So what? You gonna eat 'em?"

"There's something there," she said.

"Watch her," Morris said as he jumped up to investigate.

He climbed over the logs then raised his hands. "Holy shit! Breakfast!"

We both got up to have a look. I let Alyssa go ahead of me so she couldn't try any funny business.

It was two bull moose, their antlers locked together, their impossibly long legs wedged between the logs. "*¡Dios mío!*" I said. "Must've drowned in the flood last night. But *two* of them?"

"It happens," Alyssa said softly. "Never seen it, but it happens."

"What happens?" I asked.

"The bulls get all horny once night comes back. Fight each other for a mate. Bash heads. Sometimes they get stuck together."

"Holy shit," Morris said again.

Alyssa stared at the two dead moose. She looked like a little kid beside them. I couldn't believe how big they were.

What strange creatures.

"We're good now," she said.

"What do you mean?" Morris said.

"Our offering."

"Two dead moose?"

Alyssa dropped to her knees and pulled her sleeping bag tight. "Yeah. And, like, what we can do with them."

"Like *eat* them?" Morris said.

"Do you think the meat's safe?" I said, looking at Alyssa like she was now team captain.

"Yeah, probably. Only been dead a few hours. But that's not what I mean."

Morris kneeled beside her. "Well, then, what the hell *do* you mean?"

"We can go home now."

My stomach clenched. "Now don't start that kind of talk again."

"No ... I'm okay." Alyssa looked back at what was left of our gear, the stuff I couldn't lash to the canoe last night in all the wind and rain. "Do we still have the hatchet?"

"Yup," Morris said.

"The clothesline, sewing kit, your buck knife, Ian?"

I slapped my pants pocket where I kept my knife, where I used to keep my iPhone. "Carrie's barrel went with the canoe," I said. "But, yeah, we've got all that."

Alyssa gazed up at Red Dog Mountain then down at the moose. Her face softened. A faint but knowing smile stole across it.

That smile.

TULITA

It wasn't until we were partway down the Mackenzie River that the clouds finally lifted and the chopper found us. It circled over us again and again while we waved our hand-carved paddles. As it hovered nearer, checking us out, I saw a flash of white in the rear passenger window.

Butch.

William stuck his hand out and gave us a thumbs-up. We all thumbed him back.

No need for a rescue now.

As soon as we rounded the last point upstream of Tulita, we heard a blast of sirens.

For a few seconds, that sound took me back to the mining riots in Xela, and my whole body shrank. It was still there, some of that inner junk that I guess I still had to work on. Then I saw several big pickups at the boat launch, flashing red, blue, and orange lights at us.

"What, are they going to arrest us?" Morris asked.

"Not unless you try pushing drugs on them," I said.

"It's the cops," Alyssa said. "And the wildlife guys. Basically, anyone who's got a siren to blow. It's how we welcome bigshots."

"That would be *us*?" Morris said.

"Oh, yeah. This is big."

I got an idea of just how big our arrival was to the community of Tulita when I saw hundreds of people and their dogs lining the beach. Others couldn't wait for us to land, and were already headed our way in a parade of motorboats and canoes. In a village this small, it looked like pretty much everybody wanted to welcome us. And to marvel at the bizarre boat we had built together.

The sound of moose skin grinding into gravel had made my flesh crawl ever since we'd pushed off from our fast-shrinking island. Today it was the sound of victory.

I admit I was doubtful from the start.

A moose-skin boat? Ridiculous!

But it held up. It got us there safely, as had others like it for generations of Alyssa's people, bobbing down the Keele River with a winter's worth of fresh meat. Most moose-skin boats were much bigger than ours, built from the hides of at least half a dozen moose, not two.

We'd called it Plan C. Building that crazy boat. With the island disappearing beneath our feet and the canoe long gone, we knew it was basically build the thing or drown.

But look who I had to work with: a heavyweight drug dealer who'd almost bullied me to death. An obsessive cutter with a history of multiple suicide attempts.

After depending on over ten thousand online friends to keep me happy, I was down to two fellow addicts to keep me alive.

Leading our team, guiding construction every step of the way, was Alyssa.

For sure, Morris was the muscle behind the work. Without his strength, we'd never have been able to shift those moose around and peel off their skins.

But Alyssa was the brains. She showed us how to skin the moose and scrape their hides. She showed us how to shape and split the driftwood to make gunwales, ribs, and a keel. When we'd used up our clothesline to tie the boat frame together from all the pieces, she showed us how to pound sinew out of stringy connective tissue to make extra thread. "Moose thread," she called it.

We worked hard and fast. There was no time for any bullshit or meltdowns. The water kept rising and our teeny island was disappearing before our eyes. We worked carefully. From start to finish, we knew that one slip of the hatchet or buck knife and we were sunk, literally.

Sink or swim, eh, Woody?

At one point, we stopped to cook some moose meat over the fire, and a big male grizzly showed up on the bank right across from us. The bear stood up on two legs, looking just like a big hairy human, shaking his head around, sniffing the air like crazy.

I was freaking inside.

Alyssa motioned for us to sit down and keep still.

My heart pounded at the sight of this magnificent, terrible animal.

Morris kept waving the hatchet at it like he was lining up a headshot. He probably could've done it, too, even at that distance.

The bear dropped to all fours and made a few bold charges at us. Luckily, the current was too strong for it to swim across. It took off in a huff, as if to say, "Well, piss on ya!"

Our work continued into the night by the light of a roaring bonfire. By sundown the next day, we'd stitched the hides together, stretched them over the frame, and lashed them on, all thanks to Alyssa.

And *still* no sign of a rescue.

Had the wind stopped the rescue boats? The clouds stopped the search planes? Had the rest of our team all drowned and nobody even knew we were in trouble?

We had no time to debate such questions. Our island was going fast.

That night around the fire, we carved three decent paddles in record time.

Funny how a life or death situation improved our carving skills!

The next morning's weather: no change. High winds, low clouds.

We greased every seam with moose fat, tested our boat for leaks, and declared it seaworthy.

I figured we were ready for takeoff.

I was wrong.

"Wait," Alyssa said firmly, as Morris and I started nudging our homemade boat into the river.

"Wait?" Morris said. "For *what*?"

Alyssa just stared at the water, humming a private tune.

The Keele River swirled around my bare feet, still waiting, watching.

The clouds seemed to move closer, holding their breath.

Our island had been reduced to a few scrawny willows, clinging to a sliver of sand. Soon everything would be ripped away, including us.

It was still super-windy but at least we'd have a tailwind. Hopefully manageable.

Whatever. We had to take our chances. To wait any longer would be guaranteed suicide.

"It's now or never, Alyssa!" I said.

"No," Morris said, grabbing my arm while looking at Alyssa. "I get it. We gotta pay the water, right?"

"Yes," Alyssa said. She reached into the boat and pulled out a hunk of smoked moose meat, our only food source until we reached safety—again, it was Alyssa who'd taught us how to make it. She tore off a strip for each of us. "This'll do," she said, pausing for a moment before she gave hers to the river.

Morris and I did the same. As I watched my offering drift downstream, I suddenly jerked my head up.

What was that new sound coming from the river?

I swear it was applause.

Once we got the thing launched, we discovered that, for such a weird-looking boat, it handled surprisingly well.

With the wind at our backs, we mostly just drifted downstream, occasionally tweaking our course and eating smoked moose meat.

By the time we hit the Mackenzie, the wind had died enough for us to cross it, a river so wide I thought at first we'd taken a wrong turn and spilled into some giant lake.

A few hours later, the clouds lifted and blew away.

On that home stretch to Tulita, we had nothing much to do but bask in the sun.

Three lizards in a moose-skin teacup.

An old man with a walnut face like my Uncle Faustus stepped out of the crowd and gave Alyssa a big bear hug. Jonas, her grandfather. I could hear in his voice, though the words were strange to me, that he was overjoyed to see her and the work of her hands. He was the elder who had taught Alyssa and her classmates how to build a moose-skin boat, that time, years ago, when he led them up the Keele River to the foot of Red Dog Mountain.

I made a point to shake his hand and thank him, using words that Alyssa had taught me on the river. "*Mahsi cho*, Jonas. *Mahsi cho*." A big thanks. His hand was rough but warm in mine. I got this strange feeling that I was shaking a chain of human hands that reached way back into the mountains.

After all we'd been through, the biggest threat to our moose-skin boat came blasting out of the crowd, gave my ankle a few quick humps, then started chewing on the bow like it was a giant rawhide bone.

"Butch! Come here, you little brat!" William scooped him up with one arm and wrapped the other around all three of us. "Don't scare me like that, you guys," he said with a tremor in his voice. "You wouldn't believe all the chocolate I ate, worrying about you!"

"So what the hell happened?" I asked William, wiping my eyes.

"Well, when you guys decided to go for a little joy ride, Woody tried to pull a quick U-ee and dumped."

"*Woody* dumped?"

William shrugged. "Hey, the guy's human."

"So why didn't you phone for help?"

"No sat phone."

"But I thought—"

"Uh-uh. See, Carrie happened to have the phone out when they dumped, wishing her dad a happy birthday or something, and the river ate it."

"Whoah," Morris said.

"Then, when we got to the Mackenzie, the wind pinned us to the wrong shore, and we had to sit there chewin' our nails till it swung around and we booted it over here."

"When?" I asked.

"Like, this morning." William pumped a fist. "But we beat ya anyways!"

Butch let out a yelp as Carrie dove in for a group hug. "Look at me," she said. "I'm bawling!"

"You should see a shrink," Morris said, and we were all laughing till it hurt.

"Fixed yet?" came a voice with a faint Scottish accent.

"Hey, Woody," I said. "We're gettin' there."

Carrie ran her hand along our boat's driftwood gunwale. "I'd say they all passed the final exam, wouldn't you agree, Woody?"

"We'll have our debrief later," he said. "The jury's still out until you get back home."

I caught an awkward flash in Woody's eyes, like he might even be proud of us, would maybe even miss us. I figured that was some of the junk *he* needed to work on. How to say what you feel.

Woody gave us all a token pat on the back, then disappeared into the crowd.

I spotted a short round guy standing on the dock, wildly flapping a homemade banner with the words, GO, TEAM!

"Hey, Obie!" I yelled.

"Thanks for leaving me with the wolves!" he yelled back.

After all the handshaking and backslapping and drumming on the beach, after the final tobacco offering to the river, we were walking up the hill for the community feast. I looked up at a row of small houses lining Tulita's riverside road.

My legs froze.

A satellite dish hung from every one.

"You okay?" Alyssa asked.

I turned and looked back at the shining river, wondering how much junk I'd actually shaken into it.

I kept walking up the hill. "Yeah, I'm good, Alyssa. Thanks."

HOMECOMING

My fist froze a micron from the solid oak door. I closed my eyes, took a deep breath, then gave it all I had. I heard footsteps behind the door.

Cowboy boots.

Dad opened the door, looked me up and down, then quietly closed it.

After locking me in all those years, now you're locking me out?

I pounded the door. "Hey! Aren't you just a *little* glad to see me? Don't you like surprises? Where's Mom? Where's Sofi?"

Dad opened the door again. He looked pale, worn out, even scared. Mom told me on the phone that he'd lost his lawsuit. The villagers had turned around and were suing him. Diadora's family was leading the charge.

"Hi Indio. Uh ... the girls are out shopping."

"Again, eh?"

"Yeah."

"Shoes or something, eh?"

Dad shrugged. "Yeah, probably."

Dad was staring at my arm. At the new tattoo I got in Yellowknife after we flew down from Tulita. He mouthed the words in barely a whisper. *"Le prometo tío."*

The color surged back into his cheeks, from deathly pale to cherry red. I instinctively backed away from him, like how William taught me if you suddenly meet a grizzly on the trail. With the scraggly beard he'd grown over the summer, he kind of looked like a bear.

"What's all *this* about?" Dad demanded. "Did you go out and get your body pierced, too? I mean, where does all this end?"

"No, Dad," I said as calmly as I could. "No piercing. Not yet, anyway."

Dad raised his eyebrows. His breathing was choppy.

I covered the tattoo with my hand, like my father's gaze might defile it. "It's for Uncle," I said. "I promised him."

"Faustus?"

"Yeah."

"You heard he—"

"Yeah, I did. We were in the mountains. Kind of off grid."

"What did you promise him?"

"After the crash. Don't you remember?"

"No ... I ... I don't."

"I promised I'd never give up the music. *Nunca renunciar a la música.*"

A little light went on in Dad's tired eyes, the one I'd see when he used to listen to me play. When he'd just sit and listen, as one guitar player to another.

Before all the bullshit and pain.

"Now that *is* good news," he said, extending his hand, as much to shake mine as to draw me back home.

SKY DEVICE

I heard the sliding glass doors open but didn't look down. There was a raven I wanted to keep my eye on. Almost in the clouds.

"You out here, Ian? Ian? Your mom said—"

"Yeah, I'm here."

"Like ... *where*?"

I rolled over and saw the top of Monica's head right below me, her blonde hair swirling as she twisted from side to side. I slowly plucked a ripe, red crabapple, took aim, and let it fall. It bounced off her guitar case.

Monica looked up, laughing—that bubbly laugh I'd heard in the river. "Hey! What are you doing up there?"

"Just hangin' out."

"Hey, sorry I'm late for my lesson. Did you get my text?"

"Yeah, I got it."

"I've been crazy busy planning the Halloween dance and—"

"Don't worry. But if it happens again, I'll have to email

you a bunch more scales to practice."

"Please, have mercy, *Maestro*."

"How else do you expect to get any better?"

Her smile got bigger. "Room for one more up there?"

"For sure. Just hoist yourself up those two big branches and I'll grab you."

"No sweat," she said. Still clutching her guitar case, she wrapped one arm around the lowest branch as her legs flailed for the next.

I laughed into my hands. "Uh ... maybe *without* the guitar."

"Right."

I pulled her up to me, enjoying her vanilla scent and the touch of her warm, sweaty hand. "Welcome, Madame President."

"Nice tree fort," she said, surveying my simple wooden platform, just long enough to stretch out on.

I rolled onto my back and checked for the raven. Swallowed by the clouds. "No. Not a tree fort."

"Your practice studio, then?"

"Nope. My sky device."

Monica lay down beside me, looking up at the sky. "Uh-huh."

"No, really," I said, shifting closer. I hadn't designed this thing for anyone but me and space was tight. Deliciously so.

She waved an arm above us. "So, like, I'm now looking at the screen, right?"

"You got it."

"And does your sky device have many apps?"

"Oh, yeah. Lots. It has sun, clouds, moon, stars."

"You *sleep* out here?"

"Sometimes, yup."

"Hmm."

I spotted the raven dive-bombing out of a cloud. "And look, another app. Birds."

"Cool. So ... do you ever have to recharge your sky device?"

"Nope. Never. It recharges *me*."

Monica let out a long, lazy sigh. "It's nice, Ian. Plug me in."

Long pause.

"You know what?" I said, watching the sun break out from behind a cloud. "I'd really like it if you called me Indio."

"How come?"

"It's my name."

"I like it. Okay, Indio it is."

ACKNOWLEDGMENTS

This is a work of pure fiction. I made the whole thing up and had a lot of fun doing it. The truth is though, there's a lot of real world stuff in this book, from Xela, Guatemala to Carcross, Yukon, and beyond. A lot of real people inspired unreal characters but I'm not telling who you are. This is fiction, remember, so you can't sue me. But I will say who helped me tell this story, in so many important ways.

For starters, I have to thank Jack Panayi (again) for giving me brutally honest feedback on the title—as only a fourteen-year old can—and ultimately picking it. And Jim Savage, for his insightful advice on the cover.

Thank you, Mari Urizar, for taking such good care of us in your Xela home, meal after meal, day after day. *¡Muchísimas gracias!* Another big *gracias* to all the staff at Xela's PLQE Spanish school for organizing such amazing field trips that took us into the Mayan heartland of Guatemala.

Thank you, Bob Hans and Bruce Ontko, for making us feel so at home in Quito, Ecuador and for sharing your reflections on living the expat life and raising a family away from your native Alberta.

Thank you, Indio Saravanja, Argentinian-born, Yellowknife-reborn, guitarist and songster who shed a dazzling light on what it means to be named "Indio," and to be parachuted onto Canadian soil at a tender young age. And thanks to Andres Benitez, for sharing stories about the teen challenges you faced when uprooting from your native Colombia and moving north.

I thank Bill Hans for the tour of Indio's stomping grounds in Calgary including one heck of a rainstorm up on Nose Hill.

I thank my nephew, Braden Greenlaw, who shared his journey into and out of a car crash that left him with a major concussion and an unplugged life.

I thank my daughters, Jaya and Nimisha, and my almost daughter, Bella Cole Huberman, for sharing your journals and stories about your own fifty-day canoe trips through the great wild North. And thank you Bill Stirling, Laurie Nowakowski, and John Stephenson for sharing your Keele River stories with me, and to Darren Keith and Marie-Claude Lebeau for joining us down that river to discover stories of our own.

Tobin Leckie, you were the first real live wilderness therapy guide I'd ever met. I thank you for your colorful anecdotes from the forested frontlines, and for the trail of contacts you opened up for me, including fellow guide, Jen Redvers, Meghan McIntosh of Ontario's Pine River Institute, and Carolyn Godfrey of Alberta's Enviros Wilderness

School Association.

I thank my indefatigable editor, Peter Carver for, as usual, helping me find the fire behind the smoke of my early drafts.

Many thanks to Sharon Fitzhenry, Richard Dionne, and all the skilled crew at Red Deer Press and Fitzhenry & Whiteside for supporting this book from start to finish. And to the Canada Council for the Arts whose generous financial support made this book possible.

Finally I offer a sky-high thanks to my wife Brenda for your fine-tooth combing of the manuscript and your unflagging support of my writing habit.

Selfie taken near the summit of Cuba's highest mountain, Pico Turquino.

INTERVIEW WITH JAMIE BASTEDO

Why did you want to tell this story? Where did it come from, in your mind?

All of my novels are fueled by my love of adventure. But behind each book is some Big Theme that I've been chewing on and want to explore through the power of story.

The Big Theme behind *Cut Off* is teen cyberaddiction—young people getting so hooked to the online world that normal relations with the "real" world suffer—friends, family, school, health, basically everything.

As much as I depend on digital devices to do my work as a writer and stay connected with friends and family, I believe most of us who use these tools succumb now and then to using them compulsively. Gotta check my email for the tenth time today, I better send that text right now, etc. etc. In that sense, many of us sit somewhere on the cyberaddiction spectrum. What's it like to slide to the darkest end of that spectrum? What kind of forces could drive a person into cyberaddiction? How does one escape it? These are some of the questions I wanted to explore in this story.

Your own experiences in Latin America and in the Canadian North obviously inform the story. To what extent did you see the Guatemalan part of the story—the description of the Canadian gold mine for example—as containing a political message?

Soon after I started this book, my wife and I took several months off to live and travel in Central and South America. We spent two of these months studying Spanish at a school in Indio's hometown of Xela (aka Quetzaltenango) in the western highlands of Guatemala. The school taught much more than Spanish verb tenses and vocabulary. It also offered amazing field trips aimed at exposing foreign students like us to the social, economic, and political realities of Guatemala.

Besides visiting farms run by war refugees and the mountain camps of ex-guerrillas, we took a tour of a Canadian gold mine. And, just like Indio's tour, the focus was on the perspective of neighboring villagers, not the miners themselves. What happens in the "Eldorado Mine" chapter of the book is basically a fictionalized version of what I saw and heard during our own field trip—including Diadora's sorry tale.

During our travels we also visited the homes of wealthy Canadian "expats" who managed other resource development projects across Latin America. Like Indio's father, they lived in grand, heavily guarded homes, married local women from the host country, and were raising children of mixed Canadian and Latino blood.

Were these dimensions of my story added as a political statement about Canada's role in foreign resource development? Not exactly. But, as a writer, I know a good story when I *feel* it. That unforgettable field trip to the gold mine, and my experience of the cushioned lives of expats moved me deeply and raised many questions about what I had witnessed. Writing helps me process these experiences without necessarily seeking answers.

Indio's addiction to the Internet is partly a consequence of stresses in his earlier life. Do you think most addictions have that characteristic—of springing from pre-existing tensions in the life of an addict?

My original idea for this story was to follow a "screenager's" plunge into cyberaddiction and his ultimate rise out of it through a wilderness adventure therapy program—basically a story about addiction and redemption. That seemed to me to be a solid stage on which to build my tale. But a casual conversation with an addictions counselor told me that I was missing a key plank in my story platform. He told me, "Behind every addiction is a childhood trauma." As the character of Indio grew, I realized that understanding the *roots* of his cyberaddiction was extremely important to the story.

So I asked myself, "What trauma did Indio suffer as a

child?" After much scribbling and brainstorming I discovered that Indio was a gifted guitarist oppressed by an overbearing stage dad, kind of like Michael Jackson and many child prodigies before him. My own love of classical guitar and many rich experiences in Latin America allowed me to add color to this part of his story. This central trauma became the third plank of my story platform, as reflected in the three parts of the novel—*oppression* in Guatemala, *addiction* in Calgary, and *redemption* in the northern wilderness.

The experience Indio has in the wilderness is based on actual real-life addiction rehab programs. What can you tell us about these programs?

Mainstream approaches to treating teen addicts might include a mix of counseling, psychotherapy, medication, or live-in rehab programs. Wilderness therapy is another very powerful option, often chosen in cases like Indio's, where more common approaches seem to have failed.

Camp Lifeboat is based on real-life wilderness therapy programs that I researched for this book. One of the most important sources for me was *Shouting at the Sky—Troubled teens and the promise of the wild*, by nature writer Gary Ferguson. He describes how teen alcoholics, drug users, cutters, drop-outs, and runaways are thrust together with a team of therapists and guides in the red rock wilds of southern Utah for up to two months to "shake out their junk," as Woody would say. Some of the characters Indio meets at

Camp Lifeboat were directly inspired by the troubled teens portrayed in Ferguson's book. Others sprang from young addicts I talked with during a visit to the Pine River Institute, a wilderness therapy program in southern Ontario. Another inspiration was Alberta's Enviros Base Camp which runs a three-month adventure-based treatment program in the Kananaskis region.

You can drive down the Annie Lake Road off the Carcross highway and look for Camp Lifeboat. But you won't find it—it doesn't exist. What you will find, as Indio did, is a wild mountain landscape full of mysterious beauty that will tug at your soul. This story gave me a chance to write about one of my favorite places on Earth, the Carcross valley in the southern Yukon, where the North first cast its spell on me when I was a biology graduate student many years ago. Being a city boy from Ontario, that wild country and the challenges it threw at me had a huge and lasting impact on my life. This kind of personal transformation is at the root of any well-run wilderness therapy program—one cannot leave the experience unchanged in some positive way.

In this novel you suggest that an individual can best discover the essence of her or his character in a wilderness situation. Yet isn't it true that most young people today don't have the kind of access to the wilderness that Indio ultimately experiences?

I totally agree. In our heavily urbanized and digitized world it's tougher than ever to connect with real live nature.

That's a big motivation for me as a nature writer. Besides, it's an important part of any writer's job to connect readers to amazing places, real or imagined, that they will never see. Living in Canada's far North, I feel very lucky to be surrounded by wild landscapes like the ones described in Part III of the book—big beautiful lakes, wild rivers, virgin forests, and endless mountains.

The whole premise behind wilderness adventure therapy is that nature can, as Carrie says, "teach you about yourself, heal you, and yes, throw her curve balls at you." It's how we deal with nature's curve balls—the challenges, surprises, and tough lessons it presents to us—that offers a fertile field for personal growth and self-discovery. My feeling is that you don't have to be immersed in untamed wilderness for weeks and weeks, like Indio was, for nature to teach you about yourself.

Though the last part of the story takes place in one of the wildest parts of the planet, I purposely introduced several moments in earlier scenes where nature unexpectedly crashes into Indio's world. For example, when Indio hears "thunder ricocheting off the mountains that protect Xela," when he visits his father's gold mine and beholds a "bare naked mountain" stripped of all life, when he gets a "prickly feeling" looking for an elusive raven behind his Calgary home, or when he's up on Nose Hill and finds the dead jackrabbit "skewered clean through by some kid's arrow." Such glimpses into the natural world lift a temporary veil on Indio's small, lonesome life, and trigger a flash of connection to a much greater and more mysterious world.

Indio's process of awakening to the "recharging" power of nature finds its most poignant expression while he's lying on his simple "sky device" in the backyard of his Calgary home. I steered the story back to this non-exotic setting to show what a normal teenager Indio really is and to help "bring home" the possibility of readers making similar connections, literally in their own backyards!

You're interested in the effect on Indio of being a celebrity—whether as a musical prodigy or as a prolific blogger. But isn't it true that in the end that celebrity status doesn't really have benefits for him?

Some wise Indian guru once said that all the pitfalls of human nature boil down to blindly chasing one or more of the "4 P's" —Power, Profit, Pleasure, or Prestige. If we lump fame in the "Prestige" basket, it makes sense that Indio's celebrity status doesn't bring an end to his troubles.

At best, Indio's fame is a double-edged sword. For instance, after viewing the flood of glowing feedback from the video his father posted after the Xela Christmas concert, Indio feels that, for the first time ever, a new door has opened for him. But soon after, his father "pulls the Segovia card" and Indio's life only gets lonelier.

His life is a crazy ride from elation to depression, with little stability in between. Indio's hunger for applause and public attention temporarily buoys him up, while masking the deeper love he feels for the music itself. That love is ultimately suffocated by his father's heavy-handed control.

It's the same story with Indio's blogging fame. This fame brings Indio great gifts with one hand, and it stabs him in the back with the other. In the end, it is Indio's online fame that almost kills him after his *Loba's Lullaby* video goes viral and he has to keep dealing with the flood of online attention. I modeled Indio's breakdown following the astounding success of his video after the experience of Californian children's rights activist, Jason Russell, whose video *Kony 2012*, captured millions of views almost overnight and triggered a psychological collapse. Medical reports attributed Russell's breakdown to "extreme exhaustion, stress, and dehydration as a result of the popularity of his video."

Thank you, Jamie.